THE DAUGHTER

The Daughter

A NOVEL BASED ON THE
LIFE OF ELEANOR MARX
— BY —

JUDITH CHERNAIK

1817

HARPER & ROW, PUBLISHERS

New York, Hagerstown, San Francisco, London

FIRST EDITION

Library of Congress Cataloging in Publication Data

Chernaik, Judith.
    The daughter.
    1. Aveling, Eleanor Marx, 1855–1898—Fiction.
I. Title.
PZ4.C519Dau 1979   [PS3553.H354]   813'.5'4
    ISBN   0–06–010757–X   78–69618

79 80 81 82 10 9 8 7 6 5 4 3 2 1

In memory of Luba Shefkowitz, Rose Lapidus,
Augusta Parker, and Henrietta Lowenstein

A note to the reader . . .

The published writings of the historical persons who appear in these pages—Eleanor Marx and Edward Aveling, Olive Schreiner, Havelock Ellis, the Radfords, Shaw, May Morris, and others more or less well-known—would fill a respectable library. Poets, novelists, dramatists, journalists, propagandists, they wrote comprehensively on subjects literary, political, social, historical, psychological, and sexual. What follows is in no way intended as a literal reconstruction of real events.

1

We are to imagine a crowded courtroom in the Town Hall of Sydenham, a small village five miles southeast of London. It is April, 1898; rain is driving against the mullioned windowpanes, and though it is still early afternoon, the porter has switched on the newly installed electric lamps. Behind a plain deal table sits the town coroner, a thin man in his middle fifties, long familiarity with human misery marking his features with a perpetual irritable grimace; he is not a man to waste time crying over broken eggs. To his right on a low dais sit the all-male jury, soberly dressed artisans, tradesmen, and clerks. Three witnesses who have already submitted statements to the coroner wait in the front row to be called to testify: a young woman in a brown cloth cape and bonnet, an older woman in black crepe, a bald middle-aged gentleman, with steel spectacles, who appears extremely distraught, from time to time wiping his forehead and shining pate with a large checked handkerchief. The first witness is seated in the witness chair: a slight, stoop-shouldered man of about fifty, with protuberant eyes, a prominent aquiline nose, a thin mouth.

"Will you state your name, occupation, and residence?"

"Edward Aveling, author. The Den, Jews' Walk."

The witness's voice is resonant, the voice of an actor or orator. Now and at each subsequent utterance a faint ripple disturbs the spectators; they never quite become used to the basso profundo of so small and ill a man.

"You are commonly known as Dr. Aveling, I believe."

"I am."

"But you are not, in fact, a qualified medical practitioner?"

(pause) "That is correct."

"Was the deceased your wife?"

"Legally, do you mean?"

"Were you married to the deceased?"

(pause) "Not legally."

"Did the deceased live with you as your wife?"

"Yes."

The coroner snorts, visibly impatient.

"Will you describe in your own words the events of Thursday last?"

"You have my testimony."

"Please be so kind as to repeat it for the benefit of the jury."

"Very well. I left home at a quarter past ten in the morning to perform errands in town, returning at five in the evening. Several persons will attest to the time. On my return I was informed that Mrs. Aveling had taken poison."

"Had you any idea that she would destroy herself?"

"She threatened to commit suicide on several occasions."

"Did she make such a threat before you left the house?"

"She did."

"Did you not feel it your duty to see that she did not carry out her threat?"

"I regarded her words as idle."

"Did you order from the chemist, Mr. Dale, on that Thursday morning, two ounces of chloroform and one drachm of prussic acid, ostensibly for a dog?"

"That is true."

"Is it also true that you were present when a chemist's parcel containing chloroform and prussic acid was received and signed for by the deceased?"

"I was present."

"Am I to understand that you ordered prussic acid at the request of the deceased, who stated her intention of taking her life; and that shortly after receipt of the poison you left the house?"

(pause) "You have my sworn testimony."

(angrily) "You are a most difficult man to deal with. Are you— were you at that time of the opinion that the deceased was of sound mind?"

2

"I was and am of that opinion."

"Was there to your knowledge a particular reason why she should have desired to take her life?"

"To a person of morbid disposition, there will always be particular reasons."

There are stirrings among the spectators, murmurs of anger and disbelief.

"Had you any disagreement with Mrs. Aveling before you left the house?"

"None whatever."

"You say you were not married to the deceased. Will you tell the jury her proper name?"

"Her name was Eleanor Marx."

"That will do for the moment."

Aveling, walking with pain, takes a seat in the front row and stares ahead impassively.

The next witness is Gertrude Gentry, the young woman in brown. She testifies in a soft, shaken voice, barely audible, her manner suggesting strongly that horror has taken hold of her and will not lessen its grip. She gives her occupation as "servant to Mrs. Aveling," her residence as The Den.

"Will you describe in your own words the events of last Thursday?"

"Just before ten o'clock it was, Dr. and Mrs. Aveling was in the sitting room. . . ."

"Will you speak up, young woman, so the reporter can take down your words?"

"Yes. Well, Mrs. Aveling, she rung for me, she and Dr. Aveling was in the sitting room, and she asked me to take a note to the chemist. I took the note and Mr. Dale, he give me a parcel with the book to sign. I give the parcel and the book to Mrs. Aveling, and Mrs. Aveling . . . [pause] she took the book into the back room, where she keeps her writing things, and then she give the book back to me to take to Mr. Dale."

"Did she sign the chemist's book?"

"Yes, sir."

"Was Mr. Aveling present when she signed it?"

"He was with her when I give her the book, then she took it in the other room."

"Then he was not present when she signed it."

"Yes, sir. I mean no, sir."

"Go on, please."

(hesitates) "Well, Dr. Aveling, he left the house a few minutes later." (She looks fearfully at Aveling.) "There was a bit of a row."

"You mean between Mr. and Mrs. Aveling?"

"She didn't want him to go." (glances quickly at Aveling) "On account of he'd been so sick."

"Did you have any conversation with Mrs. Aveling?"

"She told me she was going upstairs and she didn't want to be disturbed. I took the book back to Mr. Dale, and then I went back to the house. I had a funny feeling, or maybe it was the smell—I thought I'd just have a look upstairs. So I went up quiet, and opened the door a crack. Mrs. Aveling was lying on the bed in her night clothes. I tiptoed closer to see was she all right, and she was breathing hard and quick, and I asked her was she all right but she didn't answer. So I ran next door to Mrs. Kell and she told me to go find Dr. Shackleton."

"At what time did you enter Mrs. Aveling's bedroom?"

"Just gone twenty to eleven, it was." She bursts into tears.

"That will do. Thank you very much."

Mrs. Kell, the older woman in black, testifies that upon her arrival she had found Mrs. Aveling to be quite dead. A note lay on the dressing table, which she had given to Dr. Shackleton, and she understood it was in the court's possession.

Mr. Dale, the chemist, is the last witness. This is the bald gentleman with the steel spectacles, which he has removed and wiped clean three times at least during the preceding testimony.

"I must warn you that your testimony may be used against you, should proceedings be taken. I am not sure you have not exceeded the act of Parliament."

(Angry mutterings from the back.)

"If there is further disruption I shall be obliged to clear this room. Our business is to ascertain the cause of death, and to recommend further proceedings if the laws of the land have been abused. Now then, you can please yourself whether you answer any of the questions I may put. Were you acquainted with the deceased?"

"Slightly. As a customer."

"And with her husband?"

4

"Yes, as a customer."

"Did you receive a communication from Mr. Aveling Thursday morning?"

(wrings his hands) "Yes."

"Did the communication read as follows: [unfolds sheet of paper] 'Please give bearer chloroform and small quantity of prussic acid for dog, initialed E. A.' "

"Yes."

"What was your response?"

"I hesitated whether to send the poison. But, as I believed Dr. Aveling was a qualified practitioner, I thought it was allowable to send it."

"Had you any idea that Dr. Aveling was not a qualified man?"

(perspiring) "I believed he was qualified. I had no reason to believe he was not on the register. I always addressed him as 'doctor.' "

"Had you supplied Mr. Aveling before?"

"I had supplied him with laudanum."

"Frequently?"

"From time to time. I would have to check my book. It is all in the book."

"Did you not notice that the signature in the book differed from the initials on the original request?"

"I am afraid I didn't notice it at the time."

"It was quite improper for you to supply Mr. Aveling. It will be my duty to report your conduct to the public prosecutor. It is no use having acts of Parliament if they are to be disregarded in this perfunctory manner. You may return to your seat, Mr. Dale. I have a deposition here from Dr. Shackleton to the effect that he conducted a post-mortem on the deceased and ascertained that death was caused by cyanide poisoning. This will be turned over with other written materials to the jury. We will take a fifteen-minute recess."

Three friends of Eleanor Marx wait for the jury to return a verdict. Their whispered conversation is audible to the row in front.

Dollie Radford: "Murderer!"

Clementina Black: "We must insist on an investigation."

Olive Schreiner: "She's better off dead."

5

A quarter of an hour later the jury files in. The foreman, perspiring with the weight of his responsibility, rises to pronounce the verdict.

"Mr. Coroner, we find the cause of death to be suicide while in a state of temporary insanity."

"Thank you, Mr. Foreman." (whispers to a clerk) "Mr. Aveling has asked permission to speak."

Aveling rises in place.

"I wish to request the return of written materials now in the custody of the jury."

"You seem, sir, to have conducted your affairs with total indifference to the requirements of propriety. In the absence of criminal offense, however, I can find no reason to withhold personal documents from you. They will be returned forthwith."

Aveling nods his head slightly in acknowledgment. He betrays no flicker of emotion, no relief, no regret, only a weariness which may be attributed to his ill health.

The angry, restive spectators disperse, and Aveling leaves quickly by a side door, his papers in his vest pocket; no doubt he is anxious to avoid a confrontation with the friends of the dead woman. He stops briefly at a public house, not the nearest but a workingman's tavern further down the road, and orders a double brandy, drinking at the bar. As he swallows the brandy, and the rough common talk ebbs and flows around him, the hard lines of his forehead and mouth relax fractionally. His left side aches, a dull, steady throbbing; he should get home and to bed.

The rain has become heavier. He hails a cab for the short ride to Jews' Walk and gives the cabbie a shilling. He lets himself into the dark house, removes his hat and cape, and goes upstairs to the front bedroom. The gas fire is lit and the bedside lamp on.

"Gertie? Gertie, is that you?"

Gertie appears in the doorway.

"I thought you might like a fire."

"That was considerate of you, Gertie."

(hesitates) "Shall I lay out some supper?"

"I wouldn't object to a cup of tea."

She leaves the room, and Aveling, as he has done each day

since last Thursday, rifles through the drawers of the dressing table, tapping the wood as if for hidden cubbyholes.

Gertie reappears with a tray containing tea, sugar and milk, and a cold pork pie.

"Bring a cup for yourself, Gertie."

"It's very good of you, sir, but I've already had my tea."

"I see you've put fresh sheets on."

"Oh yes. And I fixed a hot–water bottle."

"Thank you, Gertie. I appreciate your thoughtfulness. I seem to have no bodily warmth. . . . Could you warm an old sack of bones like me, girl?"

"I don't know, sir."

(irritably) "Well, don't just stand there like a stick. Come to the fire. I won't hurt you."

He settles her on his lap, and plays with the fine hair at the back of her neck. During the ensuing conversation his fingers continue to play along her neck and throat, as if he gains an absent-minded reassurance from the contact with young flesh.

"Tell me, Gertie, do you think Mrs. Aveling had a secret place where she kept her things?"

"Oh no, sir, I can't imagine that she did. It wouldn't have been like her at all."

"No, I suppose it wouldn't. But she might have had a secret drawer, a hiding place under the bed or behind the cupboard. . . ."

"Why, whatever would she have put in it?"

"Well, that's what I don't know. Money, perhaps, or papers."

"I'm sure she didn't have any money hidden away, because she was talking only the other day about not having the money to pay the doctor."

"Yes, I suppose you're right, she wouldn't have had any money hidden away. . . . Oh, Gertie, I don't feel at all well."

"Why don't you go to bed, sir? I'll heat a brick for the foot of the bed."

"You're very kind. I shall miss you, Gertie."

"I didn't know as I'd be going just yet."

"You can stay on for the week if you like. But I'll be clearing out tomorrow. I'll be going far away, Gertie. A hundred miles away from this accursed house and all it contains . . . If it weren't for this damnable pain . . ."

7

"Wouldn't you be better off in bed, sir?"

"Stay with me. . . . I won't touch you. I'm a sick man. Lie with me for a few minutes."

Gertie pulls free.

"Oh no, sir. Not in her bed. I couldn't."

(angrily) "Go along, then. I thought you were a sensible girl."

"I can see that you're unwell, sir."

"Yes, and you can leave me to shiver here, sick as I am. . . ."

"I'll sit by you."

"Do you think I want your conversation, you foolish girl? Go to your room."

"I'll stay, if you like."

"Then take your things off and get into bed. Go on . . . you're not going to be shy with me, are you?"

"I'll just leave my shift on."

"Leave on anything you like. Do you think you're any different underneath from a hundred others? I told you I won't touch you."

Aveling changes into his night clothes, urinates with pain, and washes his hands and face. Gertie awaits him in bed, lying rigidly to one side. He turns the gas fire low, gets in beside her, and switches off the bedside light.

"Now then, don't be afraid. Come a bit closer so I can feel your warmth, that's a good girl. Don't think about anything. Thinking is bad for women; it spoils their complexion and sours their disposition. . . . I'm not hurting you, am I?"

"No, sir."

"You're a dear girl, and some good spirit will reward you for your goodness to me. . . . Why, what's the matter? Why are you sniveling?"

"It's just what she said to me. Those very words. Oh, sir, do you know why she did it?"

(deliberately) "I think I do, Gertie. I think she was weary of life and wanted to have done with it. I understand how she felt. I respect her for her decision."

"I think it was the letter upset her."

"Perhaps."

"I didn't say anything about the letter coming that morning and upsetting her."

"You did the right thing."

8

"I can't stop thinking about it. How she looked with her eyes staring like that and not seeing anything . . ."

"It's not a pleasant death. Quick and sure, but nasty as the devil. She was a brave woman. I couldn't have done it."

"Nor could I, I'm sure."

"I'm afraid to die, Gertie. I'm not a good man, and I probably deserve to die, but I don't want to, not yet. I want to feel the warm body of a young girl next to mine. There, you've stopped crying and I've stopped shivering. Do my hands feel cold to you? What do you have under here? My word, it's a complicated business being a woman. Now will you tell me, my dear girl, why you bind up your tits so thoroughly, and from the waist down you go about as Mother Nature made you? You've a lovely bottom, Gertie, soft as a baby. . . ."

(demure) "You did promise . . ."

"Yes, I promised. I'm a dreadfully ill man. Sick as a dog. But I feel stronger when I hold you close, when I feel your young strong heart pounding next to mine, when I stroke your lovely fat buttocks. . . ."

"Oh, yer a naughty one!"

"Stop wriggling, my girl, or I'll give ye the flat of me hand. Would ye like a whipping, now? You've surely heard about the men who flog little girls with hot pokers, ay, and stick them front and back too. Best to lie quietly and behave yourself."

"Ow! yer hurting me!"

"Why, you're as tight as a new glove. Thee wants stretching. . . . that's better, much better. You'll make a fine juicy dish for the right man. . . . Do you mind if I stroke you? No, I don't think this little girl minds at all. I think she rather likes having me down there, in and among her private parts. Don't you, my dear? We're getting on nicely, you and I. . . ."

"Devil!"

"So, that's the way it is, it bites and squirms. . . . Ay, a little excitement . . . Oh, these hot younguns, what they won't do to a man for their pleasure! Poor little girl, I can't do anything more for you. I'm a sick man; it would be quite dangerous. But I'll do the best I can. You don't feel terribly unfinished, do you, my dear? I'm afraid we need a great healthy numbskull of a lad to bring you off properly. Ay, he'll tickle you, he'll board you, he'll ram you . . . There, that's enough."

9

"Oh, how can you . . ."

"Lord, it wants more!"

"I want to know what Mrs. Aveling wrote in that note Mrs. Kell found and give to Dr. Shackleton."

"Why, that's my private business, isn't it? Now stop that sniveling and go to sleep."

The day after the inquest, Aveling removed his clothing, books, and papers from The Den to a three-roomed flat in Southampton Buildings, Holborn, which he had rented ten months earlier under his pen name, Alec Nelson. There he was greeted anxiously by his twenty-two-year-old wife, a singer of German parentage named Eva Frye. The door shut behind them, and that, as far as Aveling was concerned, was to be the end of a messy business.

Not everyone was happy with the result of the inquest, however. The socialist journal *Neue Zeit* published German translations of a dozen letters from Eleanor Marx to her half brother, Freddy Demuth, which hinted at blackmail and worse, and angry letters in the international socialist press demanded an investigation.

At the same time Dollie Radford, who had known Eleanor Marx since girlhood, decided to write a novel in which she would recreate her friend's tragedy, as she understood it—the tragedy of a socialist, an artist, and, above all, a woman. Eleanor, or Tussy, as she was known to her family and intimate friends, was to be the heroine; Dollie herself the friend who failed her in her need.

From Dollie Radford's file.

1. Laura Lafargue to D. R.

I warn you I will have nothing to do with any further inquiry. Tussy and I had our differences; she disapproved of the way I live, and I disapproved of the man with whom she chose to unite her life. But we were sisters; our blood was stronger than any temporary disagreements we may have had. On any important issue we thought and breathed with the same impulse.

You will find that we three—my two sisters and I—made our own beds. We were not in the habit of listening to advice, still less of taking it. I cannot see that other people are to blame for the evils that have befallen us.

Yours fraternally, etc.

2. From Bernard Shaw.

. . . No, I certainly would not choose to write a play about her. Aveling, on the other hand, interests me. He is by way of being a disciple of mine, with a difference; he happens to have a natural genius for exposing as hypocrites men and women of impeccable socialist principles. Property, they insist, is theft. Why then are they outraged when he fails to return the five quid he borrowed two months back? They claim to believe in free love, and congratulate themselves on their broad-mindedness in welcoming the Avelings to their homes as man and wife. But when he "adopts" an actress, their moral hackles rise and they call with one voice, "Traducer!" They all say he betrayed Eleanor. I'm not so sure. It may be that they were both victims, she of his weakness for women, he of her awful integrity.

Obviously you are not alone in suspecting that Aveling was responsible for Eleanor's death. But she wished to die. At her request he procured for her the most efficient means of inducing death, then left her to it. There is no evidence to suggest that anyone other than Eleanor herself actually administered the poison.

It remains possible that something occurred that morning which made life suddenly and definitively intolerable to her. It is also possible that she was a hysteric, who used suicide to revenge herself on the man whom, living, she no longer had the power to influence.

I prefer to think of her as she was when I knew her—a free, brave, and generous human being, who exercised her freedom to terminate an existence which had ceased to have meaning and purpose for her and to give pleasure to others.

I suspect that if and when all the facts are known, it will be found that money had as much to do with her death as love.

3. From Clementina Black.

You and I know what she had to live for; her work in the movement. Evidently it was not enough.

11

I often thought that she craved happiness the way others crave drink or drugs. Her work with us should have given her happiness, but she was cursed with the power of sympathy; she was unable to rejoice at our victories because they were purchased at such a cost.

My sister Constance and I had the good fortune to fall early into vocations which were appropriate and practicable. We were blessed in being naturally self-confident, and also in having modest ambitions. Tussy was neither modest, nor, unfortunately, self-confident. She drove herself remorselessly, but she was never very far from the abyss. On reflection I can see that there was a self-destructive side to everything she did—her work for us, her literary enthusiasms, and of course her private life.

I felt very strongly at first that Aveling should be brought to justice. But I understand that he is very ill. Despite everything, Tussy believed in forgiveness. Should we not follow her wishes in the matter?

4. From May Morris.

I must disabuse you of the notion that I have been intimate with Eleanor Marx in recent years.

My father, as of course you know, was closely associated with the Avelings through the Socialist League. Until his death two years ago he supported Dr. Aveling against persistent rumor and innuendo both within and without the League. My father took the position that Dr. Aveling's peccadilloes were of no consequence to anyone else if Mrs. Aveling chose to overlook them. It is easy to apportion blame when one knows only the outward appearances. My father's own domestic misery made him tolerant of irregularities in other people's lives, and reluctant to pass judgment.

Certainly it was her great misfortune to choose for her life companion a man who was totally antipathetic to her in character. Beyond this, which of us can say why some marriages are a lasting source of strength and comfort, while others are productive of unending misery and shame? It is a lottery in which some few, a very few, alas, are fortunate.

As you may know, Dr. Aveling borrowed sums of money from my father from time to time. I believe these were fairly considerable. But my father's needs were modest, and he was totally uninterested in money. He had never himself suffered from a lack of it, and it always seemed reasonable to him to use his excess to ease the needs of others.

As for your last question, it is true that I am privileged to be the daughter of a famous father, whose work was for much of his life the subject of controversy. It is also true that I put my own work second to his, and gladly undertake the role of transcriber and editor, a task which may well last my lifetime. But I cannot see any further parallels between my circumstances and Mrs. Aveling's.

Yours fraternally, etc.

5. From Olive Schreiner.

Ah, Dollie, does it ever strike you that our lives follow set patterns, and all our carefully reasoned decisions might just as well be made with a throw of the dice?

Can you remember how exhilarating the new freedom was, how much it seemed to promise, what a high moral tone it took? It seems that in every generation there are a few advanced spirits, innocent, idealistic, who swear to love one another, to share in all things spiritual and physical. . . . And the rest of man- and womankind goes its stubborn way, buttoned up, monogamous in theory, lecherous in fact, stingy with money and love. But perhaps man- and womankind are right after all. For the bright young spirits do terrible things to themselves and to one another, and all their dreams turn sour. . . .

I suppose that if you are writing an honest novel about love between women, you are entitled to an answer to your last question. I held her in my arms for one night. I believe it was some comfort to her. I could have been her lover but she did not want that kind of comfort, and I would not press her. She detested masculine women like Henrietta and Edith. Quite honestly, I understand her feelings—what would be the point of exchanging one kind of tyranny for another?

your Olive

6. From Havelock Ellis.

My dear Dollie,

I cannot see that my married life would be of any relevance whatsoever to your understanding of the Avelings. My wife and I have come to certain arrangements which we find mutually convenient. I might add that they are also a source of occasional distress to both of us. More to the point, we—or I—had no choice in the matter, if the marriage was to survive.

Eleanor would have been incapable of the kind of compromise I find it reasonably easy to live with. Nor did she at any time, as far as I know, find herself sexually attracted to members of her own sex, though many women found her extremely desirable. My wife had what she called a "crush" on her for a short time, but Eleanor firmly discouraged her infatuation; indeed, it was from this time that we gradually ceased to see one another, though we continued to correspond.

You must not assume that because I am a sexologist I have had a great variety of sexual experience. Indeed, my readers would probably be startled to learn just how modest my experience of women has been. I have loved two women, Olive Schreiner and my wife. Eleanor I respected, but she was far too emphatic a personality for my taste. I could not love her, in the usual sense.

Yours sincerely, etc.

2

Tussy met Aveling one June afternoon, three months after her father's death, in the refreshment room of the British Museum. He sat at a table for four. The room was crowded, and she set her cup of tea down opposite his.

Each knew who the other was, as clever young people with the same literary or political bent tend to do in London. Tussy knew that Aveling was a militant atheist, an enthusiastic propagandist for the National Secular Society, along with Charles Bradlaugh, her father's old enemy, and Annie Besant. Aveling knew that Tussy was the daughter of Karl Marx. She thought the Secularists were a fraud, and was prepared to find Aveling objectionable. Aveling had patiently worked his way through *Das Kapital,* in a French translation, and sincerely believed that Karl Marx was, after Darwin, the greatest mind of the century.

"There are very few who would agree with you."

"That's because they're ignorant fools. In fifty years there won't be a man or woman alive who doesn't know and honor your father's name."

"It's good of you to say so."

"Have I distressed you? You look so forlorn."

"I'm not used to hearing him praised by strangers."

"Then you mustn't consider me a stranger. Indeed, we met when you were a bit of a thing. You came with your father to a lecture I gave at the Orphan Working School in Haverstock Hill."

"Did I? I don't remember. No, I don't remember at all."

"It was my butterfly lecture, I'm almost certain. Butterflies and natural selection. Your father stayed to tell me he had enjoyed it. I can tell you his precise words. 'You and I have no pity for the weak,' he said. He had a great leonine head of curly black hair, a wonderful thick black beard."

"I can only see him in my mind as he was in his last months, old, ill, suffering."

"How long has it been since his death? Two or three months? You need more time, my dear. Nature is a great healer."

"Do you think so? It seems to me that Nature is a very indifferent healer."

"No doubt there are wounds which refuse to heal. No doubt there are sufferers who refuse help."

"Are you suggesting that it's my fault?"

"I imagine you have suffered a great loss. It's too early to blame yourself for a failure to recover. But eventually you will put it behind you."

"Perhaps. Tell me, Dr. Aveling, have you given up butterflies for Mrs. Besant's Secularism?"

"I lecture on botany at the Polytechnic. Will you pay me the honor of a visit?"

"Not to a botany lecture. But perhaps I'll come to one of your Secularist evenings."

"You may not find it to your taste."

"I'll tell you if I don't like it."

"Have you too no pity for the weak?"

"Certainly—I'm my father's daughter. I'll come to your next meeting, if I may."

"We meet on Sundays, at the South Place Ethical Society."

"Until next Sunday, then."

They walked to the great pillared lobby and he shook her hand warmly.

"May I?" And brought her hand to his lips.

Dollie Maitland waited for her on the Museum steps.

"Who was the *galantuomo*?"

"Why, that was Dr. Aveling."

"Not *the* Dr. Aveling! the celebrated freethinker, botanist, and ladies' man?"

"The very one. He claims to be a great admirer of Mohr. I'm not sure how serious he is."

"Take care, Tussy dear. If he's not serious we don't want him. Don't you think he's rather ugly?"

"It's not an unattractive ugliness, Dollie. Beneath the posturing and the deep looks. I rather like ugly men, anyway."

"He's an actor too, isn't he?"

"I think he knows Mr. Furnivall. Perhaps I'll ask him to the Dogberry Club. I may see him next Sunday at one of Mother Besant's evenings."

"Do you want me to come along? I can't bear that crowd. They're so unbearably serious about life. That horrible earnest little woman . . ."

"No, don't come. I'll be all right on my own."

After the meeting he proposed to see her home. Gallantly he invited her to take his arm, which she did, suppressing a smile.

"What did you think of it?"

"Do you want an honest answer?"

"Certainly. No pity to the weak."

"I think you're all very eloquent."

"Somehow, my dear Miss Marx—Eleanor—I hesitate to take that as a compliment."

"I think, to be honest, you're wasting your time."

"How so?"

"All you're doing is attacking doctrine. You strip Christianity of its most objectionable dogmas and offer it again as a harmless new religion, rational and secular. You take away the mysteries but you leave all the rest: faith, good works, love. Why do you suppose people need a religion, any religion? They'll take your sugared atheism if there's nothing better. But we want to free them from the need. We want them to stand on their own feet."

"And just how do you propose to free them?"

"They have to free themselves. All we can do is help them to see that they are not free, and to understand why."

At Great Coram Street, where she had two small rooms on the top floor of a private house, she invited him in for a cup of tea. He studied her curiously as she moved about the room, taking out cups, tea, biscuits, sugar.

"My dear Eleanor, we want the same things, you and I. It's a question of methods."

"No, I don't believe we want the same things at all."

"Surely we both want to fight dogma and superstition. We want to attack oppression at its source. We want to free people from their mental slavery."

"But you don't go to the roots of their oppression. They may be enslaved by dogma and superstition, but first of all they're victims of their economic necessities. Even if they never set foot in a Christian church, still they must sell body and soul to feed themselves."

"What would you have us do, then?"

She set the tea tray on a small table by the window and took the chair opposite him.

"Organize. Organize and educate. That is what you must do. In the face of apathy and ignorance, organize and educate. For generation after generation. It isn't enough to hold Sunday meetings in South Place for liberated middle-class ladies. You must go into the East End and talk to the people in their homes and their taverns and social clubs. You must see how they live, ten to a room, twelve families sharing a single lavatory. You must learn from them before you can teach them anything. But I don't expect Mr. Bradlaugh and Mrs. Besant to see things our way."

"No, I don't suppose they would. I would like to learn from you, though."

She smiled and looked at him appraisingly, as if considering whether or not to gamble.

"I doubt that you're very teachable, Dr. Aveling. But, if you like, you can come to our Dogberry Club next Wednesday week. We started by reading Shakespeare together, hence the name. But we're definitely expanding our repertoire. At the moment we're rehearsing a socialist 'entertainment' by William Morris, the poet, to take around to the radical clubs."

"I suppose you'll play the Republican heroine."

"No, that'll be May Morris, the author's daughter. She plays Mary Pinch, accused of stealing a loaf of bread. I play the Archbishop of Canterbury, who attends the trial as a defender of Christian morality. Do you see me in the part?"

"Hmmm . . . I should like to see you in the part."

"We meet in Ernest Radford's rooms, number 17, Brunswick Square."

18

"I'll come to see you play the Archbishop . . . if you permit me a kiss before I go."

She made no objection, and he set chaste, dry lips to hers.

"Good night, most bewitching Eleanor."

"Good be with you, Dr. Aveling."

She closed the door behind him and burst out laughing.

On the other hand, Annie Besant, Aveling's lover for a time, accused him of consorting with a group of "Bohemian Socialists" in the British Museum as early as 1882, a year before Mohr's death. So the first encounters of Tussy and Aveling may well have taken place a year earlier, and in fact, according to some sources, Aveling was present at the funeral of the great man.

Olive Schreiner was her closest woman friend. They met almost every day at the Women's Institute café on Museum Street, next door to Mudie's Lending Library. Afterward they went back to Tussy's rooms to talk.

It was Olive who saved her sanity after Mohr's death. With the patience of a skilled surgeon opening an infected wound, Olive led her to speak of her early childhood and youth. In her bewilderment—for she was cold, unable to grieve, to feel anything at all—it seemed to Tussy that everything she told Olive was false, and that Olive knew it was false, and at the same time understood the truth behind her false words. What was wonderful was that the severe judgment Tussy sensed in reserve was never pronounced. This stern moralist from whom she had no secrets never said to her: *You are to blame; you withheld your love.*

They talked about death endlessly, obsessively. Tussy admitted that she sometimes envied naïve believers who accepted personal immortality along with the rest, mystery, miracle, authority.

"Human beings want desperately to be assured of a design behind chance events. They can't tolerate the pointlessness of death. And why should they try to tolerate what is intolerable? They lie; they say 'he went very peacefully,' or 'at least he was spared greater suffering.' True, Papa died peacefully. It would have been horrible for him to live as an invalid; far better for him to go as he did. But where can I find consolation for my

19

sister's death? She died in such bitterness of heart."

"There is no consolation for her death. There is only the fact that she lived."

"I can't rejoice in her life. I see only the waste. Not only in her death, in her life."

"Her gifts live in you. You can build for her."

"She was the generous one, not I."

"Then you must build for yourself."

"How can I build, Olive? What am I to build? I have no creative talent, no profession, no learning, and no hope of acquiring useful qualifications because I must work ten hours a day grubbing away at the Museum, and drilling French verbs into the daughters of furniture manufacturers."

"Still, you must do what you can."

"No, I must do what I must. Everything beyond that is a luxury. I'm just beginning to understand."

"Women give in too readily to what they call necessity."

"It's not only women who are prisoners of necessity."

"Typically it's women who serve."

"Perhaps they are fortunate to be allowed to serve."

"Not at the cost of their own development as human beings. I wish you would fight the passiveness in your nature. Trust yourself, Eleanor, trust your best instincts. Serve if you will, but by your own choice. You must give yourself time and space to grow."

"Time! I'm twenty-eight years old. How much growing time do I need?"

"I take so much from you, Olive!" she cried once. "I give you nothing in return."

"You're in need now, and I'm strong enough to help you. In time our positions may be reversed."

"I can't imagine a time when I would be capable of helping you, dear, should you need help. It seems to me that I'm always to be the dependent one."

She recognized in Olive imaginative genius and a commensurate greatness of soul. As love yearns after the greater spirit, she loved in Olive what she knew herself to be deficient in. And so she allowed herself to lean on Olive, to use her strength as freely as it was given.

20

Though she had no intention of concealing anything of consequence from her friend, several days passed after the Secularist
meeting and Tussy made no mention of Dr. Aveling; the moment
never seemed quite right. To introduce his name might suggest
interest where there was actually very little. She would tell Olive
about him when she had something to say.

To Dollie Maitland and Ernest Radford she confided her more
mundane yearnings and fears. These conversations did not lacer-
ate her soul; they were a brightness in the prevailing gray.

They lay together, the three of them, in Dollie's room, on
mattresses covered with gay Indian cotton prints. Sometimes
they smoked hashish, which Dollie obtained from the theatre
manager at the Royalty. Mostly they talked, and tried out new
scenes, and listened to one another rehearsing, and occasionally
they slept.

Ernest slept between them now, his sweet girlish face flushed,
his mouth slightly open.

"Will you marry him, Dollie?" Tussy asked.

"I imagine so. It's more convenient in the end. Especially if
we were to have a child."

"Do you want to have a child?"

"Not for ages, of course. But one does, doesn't one?"

"I don't know, Dollie. We've had such bad luck in my family.
My sister Jenny fought against dying, but her babies just seemed
to slip away, as if they'd hardly been here long enough to care.
No, Dollie, I don't want to have children. I'm afraid—to tell
the truth, I'm afraid of dying myself."

"But, dearest, if everyone felt as you do there would be no
one to man the factories or fight in the wars or plant the flag
of Empire. . . ."

"There are more than enough women happy to breed for
cannon fodder. It's odd, isn't it, how women continue to do
what's expected of them. Do you suppose they're really stupider
than men?"

"I think your standards are too high. For women and for
men. You've been spoiled."

"Oh, Dollie, I know I don't have great abilities, but I have
some abilities, and I must use them. Jenny had great abilities,
she had Papa's fire and energy, and it was all destroyed in five

21

years, burned out of her. She was a slave to that foolish, common, overbearing man. He used her as if she were an animal or a servant, gave her one baby after another, and she had to watch them sicken and die, until she was dying herself. I believe she hated him in the end. I know she hated what he had done to her, what she had become. Do you suppose if she had had any idea of what lay ahead she would have married him?"

"One never knows, though. It's amazing how lightly one falls into these immense decisions."

"Mohr knew. He knew from the beginning. It broke his heart to let her go."

"Surely he could have prevented her!"

"Oh, you have no idea how strong she was, how willful. Especially when it came to ruining her life. Mohr was convinced that he had destroyed Mama's gifts, and one after another he saw his daughters going the same way. . . ."

"Except for you, darling."

"Except for me. No, Dollie, I won't marry."

"Nor shall I. Not for years, anyway."

"I won't throw my life away, I swear it. I refuse to be the slave to some man, to cook and clean for him and nurse his brats. . . ."

"I certainly hope you won't cook for him," Ernest said.

"Have you been listening?" Dollie said. "I thought you were asleep."

"I was pretending to sleep. I wanted to see what you and Tussy talk about when you're alone."

"Now you know," Tussy said.

"Well, if Dollie won't marry me, and you won't clean for me, Tussy, I might as well make us all some tea."

"Perhaps I'll marry him after all," said Dollie.

"On one condition: that Tussy keeps her vow. You belong to us, you see, and we refuse to let you go. We'll keep you chaste and merry. You're allowed to love Dollie and me, and no one else."

"I meant to tell you—I'm bringing Dr. Aveling along to the Dogberry Club next Wednesday. I thought he'd do very well for Mr. La-di-da. He has an amazing voice."

"I've heard he has an amazing way with women."

"I can't believe it, Ernest. He's an ugly little man with a

melodramatic style; he's serious and flattering and somewhat ridiculous, isn't he, Dollie? He looks like a lizard, with sad round eyes. He's a rather eminent botanist, and he propagandizes for Mrs. Besant, and I believe he writes one-act plays."

"Shall we worry about her, Dollie?"

"I think she's quite safe; he really is one of the ugliest men I've ever seen."

The play reading was a triumph for Dr. Aveling, who excelled at fun and games. When he arrived, hat in hand, the friends were in Ernest's large, rather elegant front room, seated on low chairs or cushions; though it was June, the curtains were drawn and a coal fire burned in the grate. Tussy introduced Aveling to the others: Dollie and Ernest; May Morris; Harry Sparling, her current suitor; Bernard Shaw. Ernest, sprawled on a rug in front of the hearth, read out a cast list.

"I thought that as a barrister I should play the villain of the piece, Mr. Justice Nupkins. Dollie plays Mr. Hungary, Q.C., counsel for the prosecution; Mr. Shaw will kindly improvise the suborned witnesses, Sergeant Sticktoit, Constable Potlegoff, Constable Strongithoath; Miss Morris, of course, plays our heroine, Mary Pinch, accused of stealing a loaf of bread; our young friend Harry is Jack Freeman, a Socialist, accused of conspiracy, sedition, and obstruction of the highway; Miss Marx impersonates the Archbishop of Canterbury; Mr. Shaw will do for Lord Tennyson and Professor Tyndall. Perhaps, Dr. Aveling, you would be kind enough to play Mr. La-di-da, accused of swindling."

"With pleasure."

"Scene one," Ernest said. "The trial of Mr. La-di-da, a worthy capitalist entrepreneur, found guilty of swindling, and released with a solemn warning not to be caught again."

"No sooner said than done," said Aveling, laughing.

Tussy said, "This is by way of preface to the trial of Mary Pinch, in which Mr. Justice Nupkins demonstrates to all present that the law is made for the poor as well as the rich."

May Morris as Mary Pinch made an affecting victim, with a hint of an Irish lilt. "My husband was a handsome young countryman once, God help us! He could live on ten shillings a week before he married me. Then the children came brisk and the wages came slack. . . . Ay, gentlemen, what if I had stolen a loaf for my babes? Are the poor to starve because there's no honest work to be had the length and breadth of the land?"

Ernest as Mr. Justice Nupkins pronounced sentence with a grand flourish. "In these days, when the spirit of discontent is so widespread, all illegal actions have a political bearing. If one act of defiance is left unpunished, society itself is threatened. Gentlemen of the jury, I ask you to think of your wives and daughters, and you will not fail in your duty to them, to your country, and your God."

Mary Pinch, sentenced to life imprisonment at hard labor, was led off defiant, and the next prisoner called to trial: Harry Sparling as Jack Freeman, the Socialist, accused of making a speech in defiance of a police ban, and suggesting, furthermore, that the Queen should be made to take in washing. Dollie, as Mr. Hungary, Q.C., waxed eloquent: "There are a set of foreigners in this country who are plotting to overturn the sacred edifice of property, the foundation of our hearths, our homes, our altars. . . ."

"How true," Tussy whispered to Aveling.

"More power to them," he whispered back.

"Scene two takes place after the revolution," May said. "Justice Nupkins, Mr. Hungary, Q.C., and Mr. La-di-da are discovered wandering about the countryside, in rags. They are brought to trial, and sentenced to six months' hard rehabilitation, so that they may learn to live as free and productive citizens under socialism."

"Delightful," Bernard said. "It should do very well for Hammersmith. They may want more blood in Hackney."

After the reading, Aveling complimented May on her stirring performance.

"May is a playwright as well," Tussy said.

"Why, I'll have to introduce you to my friend Mr. Barrett, who manages the Princess Theatre. You must come to the theatre one night next week and I'll take you back afterward to meet him. He's highly susceptible to beautiful young women."

"I'd be happy to come, but do let us keep it a secret from my father. He's not at all anxious for me to pursue a dramatic career."

"Does he find the theatre objectionable?"

"He wants to protect May," Tussy said.

"You see, my father is a truly good and great man—"

"I've heard him speak more than once," Aveling said. "And a wonderful sight it is to see him lecturing against philistinism to laborers who haven't the faintest notion of what he's talking about."

"It makes no difference to him," May said. "He's a man of deep passions. He so hates what man has done to nature that it's a moral necessity to him to speak out."

While they talked, Dollie laid out supper: Jerusalem artichokes, cheese, pickled onions, cucumber sandwiches, fresh fruit and cream, petits fours. Dollie explained to Aveling that supper was vegetarian in deference to Mr. Shaw.

Aveling volunteered: "Shelley too was a vegetarian. It's undoubtedly the case that animal food thickens the blood."

"Bernard doesn't drink, either. He has his wits about him at all times."

"Do you take no spirits at all, Mr. Shaw?"

"None whatever. Like Mr. Morris, I happen to believe my work is important to the future of the race. Dollie may choose to drown her immortal soul; I prefer soda water."

"My dear, you'll outlive us all," Dollie said.

"I fully intend to."

"I don't enjoy abstinence," Dollie said. "Of any sort."

"Then your body rules your mind, instead of serving it. At twenty-five you have the choice; at forty it's too late. Most women are ruled by their bodies, which is why—present company excepted—their work tends to be negligible."

Tussy said, "They seldom have the choice, at twenty-five or forty."

"Certainly they have the choice; they simply refuse to take it. You, my dear Miss Marx, have a choice, just as Dollie has—but I doubt that you'll last out the year, either of you. You are ripe to fall, and fall you shall, unless you take steps to prevent it. Only Miss Morris, who is so quiet and so talented, is free, because May is that neuter creature, the true artist. When she's not possessed by her muse she droops or sits quietly like a mouse."

"I don't think May is at all like a mouse," Harry protested.

"Of course she's not like a mouse, idiot," Bernard said.

"Don't be unkind to Harry," Dollie said. "He means well, and he's in love with May. You can't expect brilliance as well. Tell us, Bernard, if Tussy and I fall, who is to catch us?"

"Why, Ernest and I, of course. As for Dr. Aveling, I suspect that he's not the marrying kind."

Aveling walked Tussy the short distance to Great Coram Street without asking; it was now his right. It was his right, too, to walk up the three steep flights of stairs with her and to wait while she lit the gas and stirred the banked fire.

"You were splendid as the Archbishop," he said. "All of you were quite extraordinary, of course. But you have a certain professional edge, even in that company."

"You flatter me, Dr. Aveling."

"Nonsense. I'm a perfectionist when it comes to the stage. You must have had some instruction."

"I've taken a few lessons. . . . Shall I confess? It's always been my dream to act."

"We must see what we can do for you. I could probably arrange an audition with Madame Vezin, who is the best coach in London, even better than her husband."

"Two years ago I would have leaped at the chance. You come too late, Dr. Aveling. I am now a full-time teacher and translator, I have my father's papers to sort out. . . ."

"Let me approach Madame, then we can worry about ways and means. You must allow me to do this small favor for you. Afterward you can tell me I come too late."

"Do you think Mr. Shaw was right about you?"

"I doubt that there's much that gets past Mr. Shaw."

"Are you not the marrying kind, then?"

"Unfortunately for both of us, my dear Eleanor, I am the marrying kind. But Mr. Shaw may be right; I'm as little likely as he is to be trapped by my admiration for women."

"I don't see that there's much to admire in your average Englishwoman."

"I beg to differ! A fresh complexion, a waist you can clasp in your hands, a finely turned ankle . . ."

"Exactly. I sometimes think the progress of women is forever two steps forward and three backward. Shakespeare's women were free, but Englishwomen three hundred years later are very narrowly constrained, physically and mentally."

"Shakespeare's women are often independently wealthy. No doubt it helps not to have to worry about money."

"I'm sure it helps. But in the nineteenth century even women of independent means are imprisoned by domestic pieties."

"I don't see you as a prisoner of domestic pieties."

"That is because I'm on my own. You see, I must keep myself. I can't afford pieties of any kind."

"Don't you find the necessity of keeping yourself a kind of imprisonment?"

"Yes, it makes me mean-spirited and proud. I must always be pinching pennies on coal, tea, and sugar; I can't accept hospitality graciously because I'm unable to repay it. I bitterly resent the doors that are closed to me because of my sex. I would gladly labor without pay at the work I love, but I'm in a perpetual state of outrage at the low wages paid for teaching. I loathe teaching, and it's the only work I can get."

"Why do you paint yourself in such a bleak light? To me you seem gay and beautiful."

"I'm afraid you don't know me very well."

"Not yet. But I hope I may come to know you as well as one person may come to know another."

When he kissed her goodnight, it was the salute of one comrade to another, respectful, affectionate, and to Tussy unexpectedly moving.

Madame Vezin listened with a bored expression as Tussy recited "The Pied Piper of Hamelin," usually a great success with audiences. Her left leg from thigh to ankle trembled violently; surely the vibrations were visible through her skirt.

Madame suggested that she work on Juliet.

"Absolute simplicity; this is the great secret. I had the privilege of watching Fedotova play Juliet in Petersburg. Ah, Fedotova— there was no one like her. Her Ophelia was an experience never to be forgotten. Of course, she was a pupil of Shtechepkin; but she was also a genius. The important things can never be taught. Some are born knowing everything they will ever need to know; for the rest of us life is a struggle. . . .

"Well, we will try for three months. You have good bones; too much vivacity, but that you can learn to control. Fortunately

you are a small woman. Now you must make yourself fourteen
years old. Put everything else out of your mind; you must eat,
drink, breathe nothing but Juliet. Come back in a week and
we will see what we can make of you."

3

Just below the summit of Primrose Hill, there stands a wrought-iron and polished-oak bench, from which one can observe the full sweep of London's skyline to the Thames and beyond, pointed by the spires of Wren and Hawksmoor churches, with the golden dome of St. Paul's slightly to the left of center. It is a view inexhaustible to meditation, not least because these irregular masses of stone and mortar, monuments to church, state, and international finance, form the lineaments of a city which has been razed to the ground and rebuilt a dozen times in its two-thousand-year history.

In the foreground, the charming turrets and aviaries of the Zoological Gardens might suggest to a thoughtful observer the English genius for domesticating the wild, for taming and neutralizing passion, for pacifying the oppressed by offering them the illusion of freedom and making that illusion so like the real thing that it takes a trained eye to spot the difference. In this memorial to empire and philanthropy, the wild beasts of Asia and Africa are acclimatized to the damp native ground of sparrows and starlings; here captive beauty is free to fly, to mate, to thrive, after a fashion.

The aforementioned bench was a favorite stopping place of two persons who had just sat down on it one unseasonably warm October afternoon: a stout young woman with dark curly hair, and a trim, rather dapper man in his late sixties, she a bit winded, he obviously more fit, used to the climb. He wore a tweed jacket with leather trim, a striped scarf about his neck, and a black homburg. She wore a fringed woolen shawl over a long black skirt and gray blouse; her head was bare.

The woman was Tussy; the man was Friedrich Engels, her father's collaborator and friend. He spoke first, his tone affectionate, a barely perceptible German accent giving his speech a certain deliberateness.

"Am I correct, my dear, in thinking it is important to you that I approve of this young man?"

"I think you will like him. He writes very clearly, without condescending to his audience in the least. I believe he knows German fluently. He's an extraordinary speaker; Dollie tells me his lectures are attended by hordes of young women from Kensington. He's willing to do absolutely anything for us."

"And why has he suddenly appeared from nowhere, this extraordinary young man who is willing to do anything for us?"

She threw her arms about his neck and kissed him on the cheek.

"Dear, dear General . . ."

"You're fond of him?"

"Yes. I'm fond of him."

"And is he fond of you?"

"I believe he is. He says he is."

"Well then, let us look him over on Sunday. He will have to pass muster with Sam Moore and Willy Liebknecht. And with Nim, of course."

"Nimmy won't approve of him, I'm afraid. But she'll have to come round, that's all there is to it."

Thursday

My dear,

You are different from any woman I've known. With other women I've never felt the mystery was more than skin deep. One sees through them very quickly. But in you I sense depths and yet greater depths.

I think you will agree that there has never been any question of flirtation between us. I have never sought to possess you, to acquire your person as one acquires a choice piece of furniture. To conquer you would be to subdue a free republic, which would be repugnant to me both in moral and political terms. I have

30

desired rather to know you, and in knowing you to enlarge and humanize my own crabbed nature.

I want us to be honest with one another, comrades, equals, with all the possibilities of life open before us.

When we know each other, when we can read one another's thoughts in perfect freedom, when we gaze into one another's eyes unimpeded by the veils of convention and false modesty, then I feel confident we shall also love one another. And I believe that, when you are ready, you will come to me.

Meanwhile I want to learn all I can about you, about your sisters, your father, yourself as a child, as a young girl. About myself there is nothing to tell beyond what I have already told you. I married disastrously; I am not free, nor will I be free in the foreseeable future; I love you.

Your Edward

"Tell me about Nim, as you call her."

"Her name is Helen, Lenchen for short; Nim because that is what my niece Mémé calls her. She has been a second mother to me. When she was a young girl she had a child, whom she boarded with a family in the East End. The General always took financial responsibility for him. We were never told who the father was."

"It easily happens to an inexperienced young woman. A servant is always vulnerable."

"She was supposed to be very beautiful as a girl. I've met Freddy, her son, a few times since Mama's death. When I see him I feel so sad. He's such a kind man, but somehow helpless to deal with life or to better himself, and I feel that we are to blame; we should have done more for him."

"Today we would have our servants supplied with pessaries."

"You mustn't think of Nim as a servant—she was the heart and soul of the family."

"Still, a pessary might have helped."

"I wonder. Nimmy has a simple nature. I imagine that for her it was an act of God."

"Surely an act of man!"

"Whether of God or man, her philosophy would have been to accept the inevitable and make the best of it. I envy her, Edward. She has the steadiest character, sterling throughout.

Papa trusted her judgment more than that of anyone else."

"I'm curious to meet your Nim."

"If you say a few words to her in German, she'll think you can do no wrong."

"Tell me about your sisters."

"Jenny I idolized. Laura and I have had our differences."

Jenny was the first-born of the daughters; Laura was born a year and five months later. Then there were ten years before Tussy's birth, during which time three other children were born, two of whom died within a year of birth. When Tussy was born, the third child, the adored Mouche, was already in the grip of the consumption that was to kill him three months later. So that the youngest daughter was, in a sense, a child of sorrow.

The two older sisters were friends and allies despite their temperamental differences. Jenny was responsible, devoted to her parents, mature from an early age; Laura was wild, impulsive, selfish. Tussy, the baby of a family chronically beset by crisis, was alternately indulged and ignored, and allowed to grow as chance permitted, her education haphazardly seen to, or left to her father's library and her sisters' occasional tuition.

From an early family photograph taken on the lower slopes of Hampstead Heath, in the spring of 1864, the dark, black-browed eyes of Mohr, repeated three times, look boldly at the photographer. Laura inherited her curly chestnut hair from her mother, but the passion, the fighting spirit, the strong set of mouth and chin unmistakably derive from the handsome bearded man who stands just behind the eldest, his arm about her shoulder. Jenny, at twenty, already has the dignified bearing of a grown woman. Laura is the beauty, graceful, vixenish; Tussy, at nine, is a mischievous tomboy with knobby knees.

The three sisters had one thing in common: the dominant figure in their lives, the formative educational influence, the model of intellect, manliness, and virtue, was Mohr.

Jenny was his darling, the child of his heart. His passionate attachment was returned by her with equal passion, even after she married, after she had children. The bitterness of her life in Argenteuil, under the thumb of a penny-pinching, shrewish mother-in-law, reflected her inability to break the primary tie.

She had no desire to do so; it never occurred to her to try. No man, least of all Longuet, her husband, whose attractions faded rapidly under his mother's iron rule, could have a claim on her affection, loyalty, and duty comparable to the natural claim of her father.

Laura's marriage, on the other hand, seems to have been sustained by an excellent understanding between husband and wife, who shared the same tastes in wine, food, and politics. Mohr seems to have liked this son-in-law, and to have nobly restrained his impatience with Lafargue's errors of judgment, private and political, his romanticism, Hispanic flamboyance, and, Mohr suspected, laziness. But Lafargue never gained the intellectual respect of his formidable father-in-law, who knew from the start that his beloved daughters had, in effect, thrown their remarkable gifts away on men of essentially shallow mind.

Mohr leaned on his second daughter for her services as secretary, research assistant, translator, much as he did on Jenny, and he was in some ways more intimate with her. His love for Jenny was tinged always, after her marriage, with anxiety. He tended to depend more on Laura, who made a sure political ally, clever and daring, her politics strengthened rather than undone by domestic tragedy—for she suffered the terrible fate of women of that time, losing all three of her children in infancy or early childhood.

Tussy's relationship with Mohr was altogether different. She was merry and naughty as a child, affectionate, undisciplined; but in adolescence her happy relationship with her father was shadowed by misunderstanding. Tussy was sixteen when her sister Jenny became engaged to Charles Longuet. What could be more natural than for Tussy to fall in love with a comrade of Longuet's, a fellow Communard? Flattered by the attention of the enthusiastic and sexually mature young girl, the thirty-five-year-old exile played Othello to her Desdemona, recounting marvelous stories of heroic exploits, hazardous escapes—had he not survived to tell the tale?

Tussy promptly announced their engagement to her parents, who objected violently. They were reconciled to the hard lot of the revolutionary in Laura's case; Jenny was twenty-eight, and must do as she liked. But Tussy was another matter. Lissagaray was twice her age, and in every way unsuitable. (Imagine the scene, Mohr opening the sitting-room door on the two of them, Tussy's blouse half unbuttoned, her sweet young face flushed from the touch of a man closer to his age than hers.) Mohr laid down the law: he was not to come to the house; she was not to see him. Prompt remedies promptly taken; the matter was at an end.

Not so—for, parental opposition awakening some deeply buried resentment, Tussy sulked. And, since nobody paid any attention, in this noisy family, to sulks, she stopped eating. The sight of food made her queasy; she was fat; she was unhappy. They were busy preparing for Jenny's wedding. Nobody noticed that she wasn't eating, and so she set about starving herself more methodically, relishing the feeling of giddiness, lightheadedness, ethereality, astonished that nobody, not her mother or father, not Jenny, not even Helen, seemed to notice.

When they did notice it was too late; her body had discovered how far it could go. She knew the power of self-negation, and abandoned herself voluptuously to its heady delights. Mohr called her to him, sat her on his knee, begged her to tell him what was wrong. He could not recognize his Tussychen. Just so, she thought, gazing at him with unnaturally large, sunken eyes, testing herself curiously to see if she really felt, as she thought, no familiar tug of love for her Mohr. She was utterly detached; she felt nothing, not even the dull, aching misery that had been her constant companion for weeks.

They sent for Dr. Donkin, who diagnosed a case of nerves; there was nothing organically wrong. He recommended long walks on the Margate sands. Or, failing a sea cure, rambles on Hampstead Heath, plenty of rest, and a diet of milk, eggs, and marrow broth. Her state now officially recognized, she found herself with the faint beginning of an appetite. The color returned to her cheeks; she smiled once more and one day threw her arms about Mohr, kissed him on the ear, and confessed that she had been a wicked girl—gripped by the devil of self.

When Lissagaray asked if he might call at the house, he was granted permission, with an understanding which did not need to be spelled out. Within a month Tussy was translating his *History of the Paris Commune* into English, the two of them working each morning in the small back room adjoining Mohr's study, the interconnecting doors carefully left ajar.

34

Why Mohr?

Engels said Marx was known from his student days as "the Moor."

A year after Tussy's birth, Marx wrote to his wife, Jenny, "Ich liebe Sie in der Tat, mehr als der Mohr v. Venedig je geliebt hat." That is, "I love you, as a matter of fact, more than the Moor of Venice ever loved."

Willy Liebknecht said he was called "Moor" because of his dark complexion. Also because of his passionate nature and his jealousy.

The General had read Edward's first attempt, carefully supervised by Tussy, to render chapter ten of *Das Kapital*, "The Working Day," into clear, idiomatic English. His considered judgment, confided privately to Laura, was "worse than useless"; Aveling, he wrote her, was as yet a merely sentimental socialist. A second try, and the General gave Edward full marks for perseverance; he might, indeed, prove a worthy assistant to Sam Moore, in whose hands the translation had long been foundering. They were meeting in Engels' first-floor study; Tussy, judging Edward's chances better if she absented herself, visited with Nim downstairs. There were times when she preferred the kitchen smell of hot freshly baked bread to the dusty bluebooks upstairs, the half-empty bottles of ink, and the piles of yellowed paper.

"Dearest Nimmy, tell me what you think."

"He speaks very nicely."

"What else?"

"He seems fond of you."

"I hope he is."

"Does he always wear such a funny hat?"

"Nim darling, it's the style now. Even our General has exactly such a hat."

"If he has such a hat, he has kept it a secret from me. It comes down so low over the eyes I wonder how your man can see where he's going."

"Ah, Nim, I want you to like him. I'll teach him how to win you over."

"Don't pay attention to the silly ideas of an old woman. If

35

he's good to you, Tussy, that's enough for me."

"I'm not sure if he's good to me. I know that I feel alive when I'm with him. I feel that I can act, that I can accomplish great things. I believe in myself because he believes in me. He knows so much, Nim, and I'm so woefully ignorant."

"You're a grown woman now, Tussy. You know best what's right for you."

"I don't feel like a grown woman. . . . I feel like a child of twelve. Why is it, Nim, that you and Mohr and Mama always seemed truly grownup, wise and confident, while we children never learned a thing, and never shall?"

"You see us through a child's eyes, Liebchen. We were foolish too."

"No, you were never foolish. You always knew exactly what you wanted; you always did what you thought right. You never asked for advice. If you made mistakes there was no one to blame but yourselves; you took full responsibility for your lives. And always you had one another; there was never a moment of doubt. While we live under the double curse that we are dependent and yet solitary."

My dear Olive,

When we stayed together last summer at Bole Hill, in "our" cottage, you argued that women can be free only while they remain chaste. I agreed with you that to yield to a passion for a man means inevitably to be mastered by it in the end—if not by the sexual passion, then by the maternal passion for the child who is its likely consequence.

I cannot agree with you now, my dear, not any longer, though I cherish my freedom as you do. We are natural creatures, drawn to our kind; passion will come to us whether we will or no. To deny it when it makes its claim would be to deny the truest part of ourselves.

As for the mothering impulse, I know only this: the strongest natures have it in strongest kind. Of one thing I am sure: it takes hold regardless of sex, regardless of whether or not the child is born of one's own flesh. My father had the most powerful mothering impulse of anyone I have known. With us he was possessive, protective, helpless to deny us his time, his heart's blood, his life. With each grandchild in turn, his affections fastened on the young life; he wanted to scoop it up into his own, to hold it close to him where it might be safe. It would never have occurred to him to deny the passionate bonds of his life because they limited his freedom.

Surely freedom must lie within us, not in our circumstances. We must teach it to coexist with passion, with love.

Olive dearest, when you return I want you to meet Dr. Aveling. And I want your candid opinion, as an arch-critic of Men, of his merits and demerits. I think he is a good specimen—but will await your informed judgment before committing myself.

I miss you, dear. I depend on you more than you can ever know—return soon to your own

E.

4

39 Newman Street

My dear Eleanor,

Will you come to me here, this morning—two flights up, second door on the right. I am kept in by my miserable old kidney ailment, but I won't give up our daily chat. Don't fail your long-suffering

Edward

He was in his dressing gown; she thought he looked pale.

"I've brought you some buns."

"Ah, I knew you'd come."

Books and papers lay scattered on the kitchen table, were stacked against the walls, entirely covered a small writing desk. A coal fire burned in the iron grate; two comfortably worn armchairs were placed to either side of the fire, with a low table between them, also covered with papers.

"Shouldn't you be in bed?"

"I do feel a bit faint."

She laughed. "Did you really mean to wait on me? Get into bed and I'll make tea."

"You're very good."

"Nonsense. It's no more than I'd do for any friend."

A red velvet curtain separated the sitting room from the inner room, which contained a large bedstead, a chest of drawers, and a washstand. She brought tea and sat by the edge of the bed. He leaned back against the pillows and shut his eyes. He shivered suddenly.

"Is it very bad?"

"Bad, yes. Very bad."

He held tight to her hand. She watched him tenderly; he looked careworn, thin, vulnerable.

"Tell me what I can do for you."

"It should pass in a minute."

"Do you have these attacks very often?"

"Every six weeks or so. No doubt I shall die before I'm forty, like most men of creative genius."

"I didn't know you had creative genius."

"The truth is I haven't a spark. I'm like the parasites I lecture about to my young ladies, a grub, a cockchafer. I live on the genius of the illustrious dead, I reflect their brilliance. I'm a fraud, Eleanor, from start to finish."

"Poor Edward. I could have guessed as much."

He kissed her hand and held it to his cheek.

"Will you come again tomorrow?"

"Perhaps I can work here for an hour."

"Yes—you mustn't neglect your work."

She bent down and kissed his forehead. "I don't like to leave you like this. Shouldn't you have someone to stay?"

"I'll be all right. Mrs. Jones brings me dinner and looks in now and then."

"I'll come tomorrow. Don't get up—I'll let myself out."

The next day she brought her books and a small parcel containing a change of clothing. She thought Edward looked worse.

"You're to stay in bed, and I'm going to work at your kitchen table, if I can make some space. I have to go out at two to give lessons, then I'm coming back here and staying the night. You can't be left alone. I've told Mrs. Jones that I'm staying."

"Have you, indeed. And where do you propose to sleep?"

"I'll sit up in a chair. I did it for many weeks when Papa was ill. I refuse to hear any argument."

"I won't argue with you, then. I'll do as you say. I'll be meek as a lamb."

In the morning he seemed recovered, in one of those surprising transformations that Tussy was to witness frequently later on. He leaped out of bed, fresh-cheeked under the three-day stubble, his eyes clear; it was Tussy who was worn, exhausted from a sleepless night. He insisted that she go home to sleep before her lessons, after which he proposed to take her out to dinner.

One way or another, they began to spend most of their days and often their nights together. Olive was away, but her other friends—Dollie and Ernest, May Morris, Clementine Black— she put off with vague excuses. She missed a lesson or two, then three in a row; her work at the Museum ground to a halt. As for Edward, he seemed always to be free. She took to working in his rooms in the morning; then they would separate for the afternoon, she to teach, he to lecture or coach pupils for their matriculation exams. Afterward they met for supper, then back to his rooms or hers for a late coffee. If they talked in his rooms until two or three in the morning, she would stay, sleeping on an extra cot Mrs. Jones thoughtfully provided when he was ill.

Throughout these weeks of intimacy they were chaste as brother and sister, and she began to long for the moment when he would touch her.

"Did you know, Edward, that you have a reputation as a seducer of virtuous women?"

"Not virtuous women, my dear; only actresses and the like."

"I think I shall proclaim to the world that you have another character altogether, temperate, self-disciplined, ascetic."

"Perhaps my asceticism is enforced."

"How should it be enforced?"

"Dear sweet Eleanor—what an innocent you are. I might have contracted a social disease."

"Surely not! I trust that you're not serious."

"No; the truth is that I'm waiting for you. You must come to me of your own free will."

"And suppose I prefer us to remain as we are?"

"That's your privilege, my dear."

"How patient you are!"

"I have nothing to lose by being patient, and everything to gain."

"I'd like to have an imperious lover, who would sweep me up in his arms and carry me off to another world. . . ."

"You deserve a lover who will keep you firmly attached to this world. My dear Tussy, you want a lover who delights in the flesh and respects its necessities."

She stood before him in her sensible dark clothes, her hair pulled back in a bun, her loose blouse surmounted by a neat white collar, her long skirts just clearing the tops of high-buttoned walking shoes. She looked exactly like the current un-fashionable version of proud, candid womanhood, fearless before mysteries. Yet she was hardly a young girl. For the first time (it seemed to her) he looked at her closely, not at her intelligent eyes, but at her full woman's body, deliberately taking its mea-sure, and she quailed before something clinical, experienced, and cold in his gaze.

"Hold me, Edward, kiss me, be kind to me—you frighten me. . . ."

"There's nothing to be frightened of, my dear. I'm sure you'll make a very good pupil."

Dearest—

I cannot believe in my good fortune! that I should be flooded with happiness in this way . . . Walking down Fitzroy Street I caught myself smiling at something you said last night, half hugging myself with joy at being alive. . . . Everything I see about me is transformed by your having been here, and seen, and touched, the cup you drank from, your chair. . . . I seem to see you still, to hear your voice, to feel your hand caressing my cheek. I have never felt so whole, so *complete.* . . . It still seems miraculous to me how all difficulties melted away; indeed I cannot even remember what it was to imagine difficulties.

You were right in thinking that I was afraid to love you. I have disciplined my heart for so long now that cowardice has become habitual to me. Love seems to me such a marvel, so undeserved, that I fear to seek it out. That it should against all expectation seek me out, transfiguring my world, liberating my spirit—this is your doing, Edward dear, your private making of miracles, which I accept now as my right. . . . I shall not let you go!

They decided to set up house together in rooms on Great Russell Street, opposite the Museum; it seemed pointless to main-tain two establishments. On the first night that Tussy returned to her rooms and slept alone, she felt as if she had been exiled to a foreign land; that she was self-exiled made no difference. She belonged to Edward; she belonged in his bed. Her body curved to his, moved to his motion, rested in his repose; her place, henceforth, was by his side.

Did he feel equally bound to her? It never occurred to her to doubt it. It was he who suggested that they live together; it would be cheaper, he pointed out, and far more convenient than ferrying books and clothes and tins of tea back and forth across Soho. They could not marry; well and good, they would announce to their friends that they were married in fact if not in deed, and leave it to the world to respond as it saw fit.

For their "honeymoon," with a gift of fifty pounds from the General, who sought thus to set to rest his uneasiness, they took rooms at the Dog and Partridge, just outside Wirksworth, on the edge of the Derby Dales. They were not far from Shottle, Belper, and Alderwasley, and within a day's easy ride of Biggin, Hognaston, Cross o' the Hands, and Mugginton. A few miles further north were Brassington, Tissington, and the lush glens and waterfalls of Dove Dale, the "Happy Valley" of Samuel Johnson's *Rasselas*.

Olive Schreiner took a cottage nearby at Bole Hill (just past Whatstandwell), where she was joined for a week by Havelock Ellis. Almost every day the friends took long rambles together in the Dales, or picnicked beside the tow paths bordering the River Derwent. Aveling recited Shelley's poems in a voice of rich, low, and penetrating timbre (the poet himself has been described as having the voice of a cracked soprano). Olive, Havelock, and Tussy discussed controversial issues in which literature, psychology, and politics mingled: the status and physiology of women, parliamentary reform as against a workers' revolution, free love as against marriage.

They flung themselves down one afternoon on a stretch of grass along the river, under the shade of a willow, and laid out a picnic lunch provided by Olive: roast chicken, veal and ham pies, green Derbyshire cheese, a loaf of bread, radishes, fresh butter, boiled eggs, strawberries, thick Derby cream, a flask of red wine. Before them stretched the broad, shallow river, flecked and dappled with sunlight.

"If we could only hold on to this moment," Olive said.

"I can imagine a very pleasant pastoral life for a week or

42

two," said Tussy. "Eating and drinking, and lying in the sun."

"And making love," said Edward.

"Why not?" said Olive. "With a book or two—"

"Oh, if you're going to bring along your books—" said Havelock.

"No books permitted," said Edward. "A loaf of bread, a jug of wine, and thou—under the elderberry bush."

"I would need my books," said Olive.

"It's a typical English idyll," said Havelock. "I imagine that's why it appeals to you, my dear Olive; you have nothing so cozy as this in the veldt. But we English slip much too easily into a pastoral somnolence; we hate to work, and we hate even more to think. As a thin-blooded Englishman I would be afraid to try it for more than two or three days. A week at most."

"I can't share your fears," said Edward. "But then I'm Irish."

"Are you a Republican, then, Dr. Aveling?"

"Indeed I am, Miss Schreiner, and have been for years. I marched for O'Donovan Rossa, and count O'Leary and Parnell among my friends. You see, on my mother's side I'm a son of the Connacht. That's why I relish me wine and me song and me bit of a frolic."

Conversation turned to Shelleyan notions of communal love.

"I agree in principle," said Edward. "Or perhaps I should say I agree in practice. I myself am the least possessive of lovers."

Tussy said, "I should think love which is not possessive is a rather shallow kind of love."

"On the contrary. It is possessive love that is shallow, fixed, limited, afraid of dilution, unconfident. My love for you, dearest Eleanor, liberates my spirit, turns me into a freer, more loving person. It enables me to love others, where before I was too stingy with love, fearing to lose where I owned nothing. I am a rich man, now."

"You're a persuasive advocate, Dr. Aveling," said Havelock. "But you are ignoring fundamental differences between men and women. As a woman is a receptacle for love, it behooves her to be possessive. She is rightly jealous when she is left empty, and another woman receives what is her due. But the man, as the giver of love, can be prodigal with his gifts. Possessiveness has no physical meaning for him. He has no cause to feel jealous, since he is not being deprived."

"I agree with Havelock. I think you're playing a dangerous

game, Dr. Aveling. I tell you this quite frankly, because I love Eleanor."

"Should I feel jealous of your love for Eleanor?"

"I would respect you for such a feeling."

"Admit it, Edward. You're a little jealous of Olive, aren't you?"

"Not a bit of it. If anything, I'm jealous of Dr. Ellis. I would like to love you too, Miss Schreiner, but you won't let me near you."

"Let us try and be friends first, Dr. Aveling."

"With all my heart."

Tussy lay on the bed fully clothed; Edward sat beside her. He put his hand on her belly.

"How is thy receptacle tonight?" He laughed.

"Did you pay Olive for our share of the picnic?"

"She didn't ask."

"Oh, Edward, she can ill afford—"

"You can settle with her tomorrow, then."

"Yes, of course. But you make me feel as if I must cover for you; on your own you would let her pay for everything."

"Leave it to me, then. But I must do these things my own way. I won't be bullied."

"Am I bullying you?"

"You're being disagreeable."

"You've known all along that I'm not the most agreeable of women."

"I hoped you'd improve under my tutelage."

He bent down to kiss her on the mouth. After a minute she pushed him away.

"I'm really very tired, Edward. I feel tired down to my bones."

"You'd better sleep, then. Hadn't you?"

"I don't feel sleepy. . . .You're so clever about people, Edward, but you're wrong about Olive and Dr. Ellis."

"How do you mean, wrong?"

"They're not lovers."

He burst out laughing. "Why didn't you tell me?"

"I think Olive is rather . . . uncomfortable about it. It's not her decision. I think they've tried."

"Are you suggesting that the distinguished student of sexual mores is impotent?"

44

"Olive didn't say as much, but . . ."

"Or perhaps only impotent with her?"

"I believe he's a virgin."

"And so all this talk about love is purely theoretical."

"I'm sure he loves Olive very deeply."

"What a set you are!"

He knelt over her, pressing her body down with his, and whispered fiercely in her ear.

"I won't give in to you, Tussy. I'll show you what love is, my girl, what it comes down to in the end for the butcher and baker and Joan and Harry. Love is flesh and blood, it always has been and always will be. It's a stiff prick and a slippery cunt for you and me, and the very same for your poets and philosophers. Even for Dr. Havelock Ellis, I daresay. And Miss Olive Schreiner."

Havelock claimed to notice a strong smell of musk about Eleanor.

"Do you suppose it's because she's Jewish?" he asked Olive when they were back at Bole Hill.

"I hadn't given it any thought."

"They do smell different, you know. Their metabolism is more rapid than ours, hence they exude a pungent axillary fragrance. Their diet is well known to be extremely spicy."

"I'd never noticed that Eleanor eats differently from us. I think she's miserable."

"She didn't seem miserable to me. She seemed quite cheerful. She laughed a lot—she was almost giddy, in fact."

"I wish I could like him, for her sake. Detestable little man."

"I thought he was rather entertaining."

"He's all veneer; there's no substance to him. Or if there is one can't get hold of it. One can't get past his manner. I don't like the way he looked at me, out of those staring eyes."

"My dear Olive, he can't be held accountable for the shape of his eyes."

"He saw exactly what our relations are. He was being deliberately provoking."

"I can't agree with you. He was entirely affable to me, just as he's been all week. And our relations are a very complex matter, hardly to be pinned down."

"Do you think so, Havelock? Could you put a name to our relations?"

"Why, I would say we have a relation of the deepest friendship."

"Friendship only?"

He clasped her small hands between his own.

"Ah, Olive, you know that I love you."

"Forgive me, dearest. I know you do, as far as your nature allows."

"Would you rather we were lovers, in the physical sense?"

"I'm not sure, Havelock. I want you to hold my hands, like this, and confide to me your inmost heart and mind. I know this is a kind of love . . . we are a kind of lovers. I doubt that the other kind can be forced. Indeed, I'm sure that it can't be forced. Isn't it a cruel joke of Nature's, that a woman's love can be forced, and not a man's?"

"Are you hinting, my dear, that if you could you would rape me?"

She kissed his hand and nibbled at it.

"Certainly I would try. I wouldn't give up so easily!"

"Ah, Olive, you shame me. . . .What a poor thing I am for a woman like you."

"No, dear, we're very well suited. You deny me your sex, but you force me to be free, and I'm grateful for that."

"You're content for us to be comrades?"

"No, never content . . . but reconciled. As for Dr. Aveling— I do believe I hate him!"

5

First-Year Biology, South Kensington College for Ladies
Lecturer: E. B. Aveling, D.Sc.
Lecture One: "The True Scientist"

What distinguishes the true scientist from other men?

His respect for Nature—that is to say, for Life—in all her manifestations, great and small.

The true scientist observes and records the visible features of the natural world, studying her face with the attentiveness of a lover. At the same time, he penetrates beyond the surface of life to its structure, seeking to identify the invisible forces that drive and form all that we see.

It is given to one or two in each generation to make the great speculative leap that infers from the visible effect its invisible cause in nature. Such a one was Isaac Newton, who inferred from the movement of falling bodies the force of gravity. Such another was Charles Darwin, who inferred from the fossilized evidence of extinct varieties of life and the variation among living species, the great chain of evolution.

Those of us who follow these great ones can only observe the rule of science: Study Nature, honor her, as other men fear and honor God. Nature is our preserver; Nature is our indifferent destroyer. It is she to whom we devote the only form of prayer science acknowledges: a ceaseless effort to understand.

And let us not forget that we too are subject to Nature's laws, "so careful of the type she seems, so careless of the single life."

47

The human qualities which define us—curiosity, the drive to master our world, the longing for fame—are no more and no less than Nature's means of ensuring our survival as a species. For note well: she cares not what illusions we fondly cherish, nor what false gods we worship. The sacrificial rite of the savage, the Deist's faith in a beneficent creator, the Christian's belief in personal immortality, suit her as well as any other fables, so long as mankind continues to serve her, our true mother, mistress, friend, whose law is eternal strife, whose sole certainty is change.

Let us approach our studies with humility, then, and in a spirit of reverence. Out with those old hags Dogma and Superstition! We seek the maiden Truth, where she wanders alone and unbefriended in Nature's vast solitudes. Fare forth, travelers! we have a long journey ahead.

The ladies, mainly twenty and under, were captivated, and attendance doubled at the next lecture, in which Dr. Aveling spoke to the following effect:

What have we learned in the three hundred years since Copernicus taught us to regard the sun as the center of our universe? in the fifty years since Lyell's geological studies disproved the dogma of special creation? We have learned that *nothing is but that which is.* . . .

Has our faith in humanity been destroyed by the knowledge of our personal insignificance? Not by a jot or tittle. For our materialism teaches us what the wise Greeks knew all along: that the world is created, ruled, and driven by love.

Our fathers' theology identified desire with the principle of evil, and taught us to repress our instincts lest we be damned forever. Modern science teaches us to live today, to trust our bodies, to follow our instincts, for they are the vehicles of our heritage, the guardians of our future. It is our instincts that instruct us to preserve ourselves and to perpetuate our species. To say "No" to our instincts is to say "No" to Life itself.

As the course progressed, several students became enthusiastic converts to the new science of materialism, atheism, and love. And from time to time a worried mother could be seen in the back row, assiduously taking notes on asexual reproduction among the free-living platyhelminths, and the autumn spawning of the lugworm.

"They've cooked up a cock-and-bull story between them," Tussy told Dollie. "I'm afraid they mean to force him to resign."

"Surely he'll put up a fight!"

"Oh, Dollie, allegations of this kind are almost impossible to disprove."

Young girls have tended from time immemorial to misconstrue the kindness of their instructors. Teachers, like physicians, are peculiarly vulnerable to accusations of sexual impropriety; it takes only one hysterical virgin to cast a cloud over a man's reputation.

"Edward has a natural genius for teaching. No doubt his pupils come under the spell of his personality. One or two are bound to mistake his interest in their mental development for . . . something else."

"What on earth do they accuse him of?"

"These mothers . . . There are three separate letters to the governors, the most bare-faced lies. Unfortunately, in each case it's simply Edward's word against the girl's. It's disgraceful— as if a grown man, a D.Sc., would go about seducing his seventeen-year-old students! As if he had the time, let alone the inclination, to make assignations, to set crafty traps for innocence . . . as if he would relish the fumbling in the dark, the stratagems and excuses, the risks . . . as if a man whose days are devoted to scientific research should find anything to interest him in these foolish, spoiled young women!"

"Oh, Tussy. What will you do?"

"Why, we'll go on as usual, I suppose. What else can we do?"

Edward was offered leave without pay until the matter should be resolved. He resigned on the spot.

Tussy, not to be outdone, felt it only proper to inform her school governors of her new living arrangements, and to submit her resignation. Rather to her surprise, they regretfully, but "under the circumstances" etc., accepted.

Thus at one stroke the Avelings, as they were now to be called, exchanged the relative security, monotony, and predictability of salaried employment for the hazards of freelance work.

49

In practical terms, their joint income was halved just as expenses, rather mysteriously, seemed to quadruple. Their livelihood was to depend in the future on occasional teaching and journalism, commissions for textbooks and translations, Tussy's share in the Marx papers, and Edward's ventures into the theatre.

Since the General supported Tussy's sister Laura and her husband Paul, along with Jenny's children, Edward saw no reason why he and Tussy should not also appeal to Engels' purse. To this sensible proposal Tussy was adamantly opposed; it was the occasion of their first real argument.

"I must stand on my own feet."

"But you shall stand on your own feet. It's a matter of getting started."

"I will not be indebted."

"But why not, my dear? If your sister Laura can accept gifts graciously, if they are given cheerfully, with no strings attached, why should it be so hard for you?"

"I think she's very wrong—but it's entirely her decision. She and Paul live very well on the General's charity; it would never occur to them to do without wine or servants. It's not Paul's fault; every project he's begun has come to nothing. But Laura could work. She's extremely capable."

"Perhaps she doesn't wish to shame her less capable husband."

"No, I think she really doesn't care about money."

"Do you care about money, then?"

"I couldn't live on the profits of Ermen and Engels. I won't be a parasite. I refuse to live on the earnings of other workers; I must keep myself."

"Then you turn yourself into a wage slave. You chain yourself to the system you want to destroy. Surely you must be free if you are to free others."

"I can't purchase my freedom so easily."

"And you would have me be a wage slave as well."

"I fail to see why we can't live within our means."

"Very well, let us live within our means. We have two rooms; we can rent one to lodgers. We can live on dry bread and watered beer, and after a week we'll be screaming at each other like Jack and Polly, and I'll be after thee with a broken bottle and thee'll be after me with the bread knife. No, Tussy, I'll not have you on these terms. You'll have to give me leave to beg and borrow enough to see us through the next few months."

"You can do as you please."

"Indeed I shall do as I please."

"I don't wish to know about it."

"Never fear, what you don't wish to know you won't be told."

One consequence of their straitened means was an early decision not to have children, at least for the foreseeable future. This decision, difficult to carry out only a generation earlier, had been made relatively simple by the development of the rubber sheath, which, displeasing to the true voluptuary, yet had the incidental advantage of protecting the wearer against venereal disease.

Though a joint decision, it was Tussy who bore the emotional brunt of it; Aveling had the easier part. He was not the sort of man to urge a woman to bear his child. A keen biologist, he took a detached view. The species would reproduce itself; whether or not he had a personal share in the process was a matter of indifference to him. Nor was he the sort of man to prevent a woman from having a child; had Tussy at any point changed her mind, he would have gone along. Indeed, he would have been curious to see what a child of his might turn out to be like, given the Marx heritage. And fatherhood might have softened him; he might have experienced in it a love that seeks no advantage, that sustains without devouring its object. A child might also have changed the nature of his relationship to Tussy, constituting a bond of a more permanent kind. Loving the child, he might have allowed its mother a safe corner of his heart.

For Tussy the choice was never a real one. She must work; therefore she could not have a child, at least for the present. She was twenty-eight years old. But she had no desire to bear a child; she was afraid of pregnancy, afraid of dying. She had nursed her sisters' babies; she was a kind of foster mother still to Jenny's surviving children. Such mothering instinct as she had was fully employed.

It was only ten years later that her childlessness came to seem a radical deprivation.

51

6

Havelock Ellis's *Studies in the Psychology of Sex* were taking shape as an anthology of thinly disguised case histories, anthropological research, and cullings from obscure German and Scandinavian sexologists. He depended on his women friends to supply him with the less esoteric bits, and something sweet and candid in his manner encouraged frank discussion of matters about which he had no first-hand experience.

"I am convinced," he told Tussy, "that the next century will see sexuality restored to its central place in human experience. It is the root and flower, the source and substance of our lives. Yet most people live in ignorance of the body's needs."

"Perhaps it's just as well that they remain ignorant."

"You can't mean that seriously. Why, when we read Shakespeare or Sophocles or the Bible, the delicacy of our age must surely seem an aberration. There is, after all, nothing more intrinsically liberating, more fully human, than the coupling of a man and woman. Don't you agree?"

"I'm not so sure. For a man, the sexual act is liberating; it's a means of asserting his mastery. For a woman, the sexual act compels and reinforces her subjection to the man. Each time she receives him she is more inexorably bound to him."

"I don't see why the sexual act, for a man, need be an expression of mastery. It's also an act of homage. The woman, in permitting a man to enter her body, is not a subject bound to her master but a queen graciously and freely acknowledging a gift freely given."

"Oh, I don't know, Havelock. To me your relationship with Olive is very beautiful. You are true comrades. You are on terms of absolute equality. You respect Olive for her wisdom, her imagination, her sensitivity to the inner life. She respects you for your acute powers of observation and analysis, your responsiveness to the ideas of others. You've agreed to refrain from sexual relations, yet your minds are entirely open to one another. I can't imagine that you would be more honest with a sexual mate. You make no demands on each other, you don't invent nonexistent slights or injuries, you have no reason ever to lie to one another. . . . Ah! how I envy you!"

Olive, meanwhile, was coming to believe that women must renounce men altogether if they wished to be free. Their freedom lay in a new sisterhood.

"We must love one another," she said to Tussy. "We must do without men for a while. Until we learn to respect one another we shall not be able to lift ourselves from our degraded state. As long as men remain more interesting to us than women we confess ourselves their inferiors."

"Admit the truth, Olive. You think it's hellish to be a woman."

"I try to fight against that feeling. It's true that at every stage in a woman's life, when she longs to be fully human, to experience all that there is to be experienced, something reaches out and says, 'No—this isn't for you, off-limits, unsuitable, *verboten.*' And the things she wants most passionately recede even as she pursues them—education, a profession, independence. . . . It's the woman's curse, the conviction that she is incapable of standing on her own feet. Life whispers that a woman needs a helper, someone to lean on. Men feel this too, but circumstances force them into the world, and they learn that they can stand on their own."

"I don't think life is any easier for men; it's as much of a struggle. But I've never identified particularly with women. We were always different, my sisters and I. My father was our entry into the world, and he never doubted that we would somehow absorb everything he knew; he had the highest expectations for us. We were so entirely outside the bourgeois world that we had the illusion that we could do virtually anything we pleased. To be a revolutionary is like being a Jew—you know that you have to live by your wits. And you take a certain pride in being able to find your own way."

Tussy passed Olive's views on to Dollie, somewhat mischievously, as she knew Dollie had no intention of renouncing men or embracing a new sisterhood.

"We have higher standards for members of our own sex," Dollie said. "My closest friends are women, but in a room of mixed company, I would rather talk to any man, no matter how unpromising, than any woman. We tend to find something touching and vulnerable in men, while with women we make no allowances for weakness of character or intellect. This seems to me natural and right."

Tussy disagreed with both her friends.

"I make no distinctions of sex. To love and be loved is all that makes life worth living. One loves the human being, not the sex."

"Admirable," said Dollie. "But difficult in practice."

Dollie admitted that she was grossly ignorant about the conditions ruling most women's lives; perhaps she had no right to have opinions about anything.

"I have no idea what the practical choices are," she said. "Not for women like us—for the others."

Tussy was patience itself. "The choices are so few that the very idea of choice is probably irrelevant. The uneducated woman can sell her labor as a cleaner, factory hand, or seamstress; she can sell her person, as a prostitute, a mistress, or wife—or, if she is shrewd, she can arrange to be maintained on the labor of other women, servants and nursemaids. The educated woman can sell her knowledge as a governess or schoolteacher. But only in the last case is her wage likely to be more than the cost of subsistence."

"But schoolteaching is so mean, so joyless, so degrading to the spirit and imagination! You omit the only kind of work that I would find at all satisfying, the work of an artist."

"How many of us can hope to be artists, true creators? That isn't a real choice for most of us—it's everyone's dream, but it happens only as a fluke, by the sheerest accident."

"I can't agree with you. Surely if the talent is there, all one needs is study, perseverance, a little luck."

"Perhaps for a man. But a woman is also the prisoner of her body. Her most creative years are the years of her fertility. If she is to have a fighting chance as an artist she must be chaste, or at the very least she must refuse to have children. But a man need not deny his sexuality in order to create. He will be a greater artist for being a complete human being, a lover, a husband, a father."

"Surely a woman can live as a complete human being, can love, and still create."

"Then why are there so few who succeed? so few who persevere?"

"I can't believe that love inevitably destroys a woman and makes it impossible for her gifts to thrive. I don't feel destroyed because I love Ernest; I feel happy and energetic. I have the drive of two. Since we've married I've become disciplined, productive, self-confident. . . ."

"Oh, if the man is weak . . . then it's an altogether different story."

7

She did not go back to Madame Vezin; she was not an artist and never would be. She was a socialist; her life belonged to others. Serving was also a vocation, indeed a necessity if one was to preserve one's self-respect. What kind of worth had a life devoted entirely to selfish ends? Art was a luxury, a secret vice, to be harbored, hidden, resolutely suppressed. *We must educate and organize*, she had told Edward. Now that their lives were joined, their work must begin in earnest.

They joined the Social Democratic Federation, an uneasy alliance of English social democrats and "internationalists," that is, Marxists, many of them European. The first object of any political group with more than three members is to acquire or to found a journal. Edward was already editing *Progress*, the Secularist monthly, as the official editor had been imprisoned for "blasphemous libel." He was therefore an obvious choice for the new SDF journal *To-Day*, aptly named for all time. There were also long-established journals with substantial, deceptively neutral titles, like *Modern Thought, Nineteenth Century*, the *Fortnightly;* these were open to provocative articles, and offered a means of reaching the enlightened but uncommitted middle classes.

When the SDF executive voted to enter candidates in local elections, the Avelings volunteered their services as fund raisers. It was a great asset to know something about voice projection, especially when hecklers got out of hand. Tussy might never make a Juliet, but she could reduce a crowd of hard-fisted miners to tears with her recitation of "The Cry of the Children." They worked out a routine: Tussy recited Mrs. Browning's verses or Nora's great speech in *A Doll's House,* then the candidate spoke for ten minutes, and Edward finished with a rousing rendition of Shelley's "Ode to the West Wind." When the socialist candidate for Bradford came in second in elections to the City Council, it seemed to Tussy that she was putting her dramatic gifts to the best possible use. She was in great demand as a speaker, and when Edward's teaching duties kept him in London, she toured the slums of the Midlands, secretly gratified by her ability to speak directly to ordinary working men and women, who unaccountably took her to their hearts.

Her course as an activist was clear. All efforts to create a sense of working-class solidarity helped to prepare for the coming struggle. Every issue, however small, which appealed directly to the self-interest of the workers, which could serve as a rallying point for agitation, demonstration, and ultimately for strike action, must be pressed in terms which were always one step ahead of the minimum concession employers were disposed to grant: the ten-, then nine-, then eight-hour day; union recognition; minimum pay.

But the Avelings had a long-range commitment as well, to the revolution, the overthrow of capitalism, and the triumph of the working classes. Therefore, however they might grieve at the suffering caused by (for instance) the "Great Depression" of 1884–87, or the intransigence of employers toward efforts to limit working hours and to prevent a fall in wages (the usual method of coping with diminished profits), they also welcomed these events as they contributed to the polarization of rich and poor.

And an inevitable duplicity clouded their relations with the workers, who, in accordance with correct Marxist principles, were encouraged to lead union activity, the Avelings keeping well in the background. For every victory on a specific issue— the ten-hour day, for instance—entailed the danger that the conflict would be defused, organization slacken, and the natural sheeplike docility of the English worker, fed by a few crumbs from the capitalist table, set back the class struggle fifty years.

On the other hand, it seemed to Tussy that concrete gains in the workers' lives did not in practice weaken solidarity; for every issue won, a dozen new issues rose to take its place. Furthermore, it was by no means clear that the workers' cause was strengthened by misery; indeed it seemed that success increased their strength and militancy. She therefore allowed her natural sympathy with the workers full play, rejoiced with them at each victory, suffered at each defeat. She laughed at Aveling when he gloomily predicted that certain union leaders had an eye on political office, and would eventually make themselves respectable as Liberals; he didn't know them as she did. Their class loyalty was absolute, in victory as in defeat, in comparative comfort as in the grimmest poverty.

Within a short time the Avelings had a solid reputation as a team; their names on a program were virtually guaranteed to attract a sizable audience and stir it to enthusiastic response. Their success in the North of England, in Yorkshire social clubs and Lancashire workers' institutes, led, through the General's discreet prodding, to an invitation to America, expenses to be paid by the Socialist Labor Party in New York. This American expedition—a twelve-week tour of thirty-five cities and towns—was to be at once the high point of their joint political career and a paradigm of what some might take to be their ultimate failure.

From Tussy's letters from America.

1. To Olive Schreiner.

New York is the dirtiest, noisiest city I have ever seen. Commerce rules, from the elevated railroad rattling overhead to the garish advertisements stretched on wires along the streets. The natives are either embarrassingly friendly or rude beyond belief. I have the uncomfortable sense of being stared at wherever I go. You told me once how you cringed when you walked into town and the colored girls pointed at you and laughed because you weren't wearing stays, and how cruel it seemed to you to be laughed at by the very persons whose wrongs you felt so keenly. Well, I am tougher than you were, or I should have cried myself to sleep every night of our first week here. Not only do the women point at me, they say what they are thinking in their loud, penetrating voices. They assume that anyone who looks "foreign" or odd must also be deaf, and an idiot.

The children look like wizened little men and women; their faces are quite hard. . . .

2. To Laura Lafargue.

How protected we are by our family, our friendships, our ordinary associations! The connections between social forms and underlying economic forces which are politely obscured in England and on the Continent are here open for all to see. Each man is out to take what he can. All are looking for what they call "the main chance." Do you know that wonderful passage in Caxton? "That city is well and justly governed in the which no man may say by right, by custom, ne by ordinance 'this is mine.' But I say to thee certainly sithen this custom come forth to say 'this is mine' and 'this is thine,' no man thought to preserve the common profit so much as his own." The words should be inscribed above the City Hall of New York as a reminder that individualism is not everything!

Edward is collecting a glossary of the odd phrases one hears, and I shall send you some of our favorites as I have time and opportunity.

3. To the General, to be saved for possible publication.

Capitalist America is both like and unlike capitalist England, and it is difficult to know whether the likenesses or the differences are more significant in the long run. There is more money to be made here, but the gap between rich and poor is as great as it is in England, and the degradation of the poor far worse, because it is the common feeling, shared by the poor, that they are entirely to blame for their poverty. And the complacency of those who are comfortably off must be seen to be believed. They are convinced that they are wealthy through sheer merit, not only as businessmen but as human beings. This seems to be the natural consequence of egalitarianism, in a world which knows no scarcity, and in which there is no belief in communal values. It is up to each man to acquire as much of the world's goods as he can. Material success becomes the goal of all, because it is apparently within reach of all. If you were to suggest to the average American that someone might be successful in a particular sphere—the arts, let us say—and that his way of life might show no material improvement, the American would be totally baffled. As for the possibility that anyone might deliberately choose not to live in comfort, this is a notion totally alien to Americans. Though the cities are foul and the streets impassable, physical comfort is regarded as essential, and the standard in the ordinary middle-class private dwelling is astonishing to English eyes. Yet the comfortable lives of the middle classes seem totally untouched by the misery that surrounds them, and on which their comfort depends.

It is hard to say which is more terrible, the misery of the industrial poor in their urban tenements, or of the rural poor in their roadside shanties. I think the latter, because in the cities some of the poor, the children at least, can escape. The struggle for survival in a great city sharpens the wits of the inhabitants, and the city itself is a school from which some few learn enough to equip themselves for a freer life than their parents enjoy. But in the fields and farms of rural America parents and children alike seem trapped in ignorance, apathy, a soul-destroying passivity. Of the rural poor, those who suffer most are the migrants, driven from one region of this immense country to the next to eke out the bare necessities of life. And of these migrant poor the worst-off are the Negroes, many of whom remember their lot under slavery as a more bearable because more certain existence.

The cruelest part is that no one cares. The prevailing ideology so glorifies individualism that it is left to the wives of businessmen to engage in "charity"—truly crumbs from the rich man's table. And here, even more than in England, an activity delegated to women is sure to be regarded as essentially unimportant.

In conclusion, there seems to be no awareness either among the wealthy, as they compete to increase their wealth, or among the poor, who accept their lot with the docility of dumb animals, that the nation is a whole, in which all suffer if a part is diseased.

4. To Laura.

Our lectures have been wonderfully well attended. We had six hundred in Paterson, New Jersey, a small, dreary manufacturing town across the Hudson River from New York, and over a thousand in Bridgeport, Connecticut, a factory town literally smothering in its own foul chemical waste.

I send you some American slang which may amuse you. Here are my favorites: "Piece" for "thing" or "person" (as in "she's a nice piece!"); "lunch" for any intermediate feeding between breakfast, dinner, and supper; "dump" for "get rid of"; to "give it away" for to "let on"; "jump" for "flee" or "cut and run"; the "flimflam game" for "ringing the changes." Public signs have a bold directness: "Keep out" for "No admittance"; "Keep off" for our polite "Visitors are requested not to, etc." But this is a true people's democracy, and social distinctions, breeding, and the forms of polite discourse must all go the way of titles and rank. Probably a good thing too; it just takes "some getting used to," as my American friends say.

5. To the General.

We arrived in Chicago to find our friends in a state of great excitement. Eight anarchists are imprisoned in Cook County jail, seven of them sentenced to death on trumped-up charges of murder. You know that last May the Pinkerton men shot seven workers in cold blood, and the anarchists called a meeting in Haymarket Square to protest. The meeting went along peaceably until the end, when the police charged, and someone threw a grenade which killed a number of policemen. The eight who were arrested had spoken earlier at the meeting, or had been associated with its planning; there is no evidence to suggest that they had explosives, or were even present when the bomb was thrown. But of course everyone knows that anarchists throw bombs, on occasion, and the city officials want revenge; hence the arrests.

Of course, we could hardly let the opportunity slip. Over two thousand people came to listen to us talk, ostensibly on the British trades union movement, and they cheered wildly when I accused the government of committing judicial murder. I can't believe they will allow it to go on; it is such a clear case of injustice, and Americans above all people hate injustice, when they see it for what it is. Wherever we go we are cheered and fêted; overnight we appear to be famous as the defenders of the "Haymarket eight." The bourgeois press gives us front-page coverage, and is not unsympathetic. It appears certain that the executions will be postponed, which will give us time to mobilize support both here and in England and the Continent.

What pleases us particularly is that we are in the delightful position of defending to the authorities those liberal democratic principles which they claim we "revolutionaries" oppose—the right to a fair trial, the presumption of innocence, the right to assembly, freedom of speech, etc. etc.

6. To the General—not for publication.

I have the unpleasant task of describing our final meetings with the New York virago, Mother Wishnevskaya. She in effect accused Edward of pocketing the money for the trip for his personal aggrandizement, and there is now to be a full-blown investigation. The bourgeois press has already given the accusations full play, and Edward must write an answer, however reluctant he is to dignify the charges by doing so.

What a miserable business! They hold three things against us, as far as I can see. First, Edward attacked the Germans for exclusiveness, and implied that until the movement became truly American—*and English-speaking*—it would have a limited effect. Second, we refused to support the feminist demands of the New York chapter for the suffrage, equal rights, etc., because we feel they distract attention and energy from the working-class movement. (These ladies are bitterly anti-male; they act as if they would really prefer a world in which men simply withered away, and it is impossible to talk sensibly to them. They are also woefully ignorant; one ardent young suffragist I spoke to had never heard of Mary Wollstonecraft; she knew vaguely that George Sand wore men's clothes and was Chopin's mistress, but could not name one of her books.) Third, they object to our support of the Chicago anarchists, on the grounds that we should allow our enemies to destroy one another without interference from us. I find this a repellent doctrine, especially since the victims could just as well have been socialists as anarchists; it would make absolutely no difference to this government. Besides, as Edward quite rightly points out, the cause enlists the sympathy of the vast majority of the uncommitted, and it would be foolish for us not to take advantage of the issue to widen our own support.

Still, the business of the funds is extremely unfortunate. And, since the money is already spent, it appears that there is very little we can do.

8

On their return from America, Dr. Aveling thought it prudent to withdraw briefly from politics. Helped along by Tussy's frequent absences in provincial centers of the industrial North, the career of "Alec Nelson" began to burgeon. There was no point in confusing art with politics; hence the pseudonym, which served more than one useful purpose in a world where masks and disguises are all part of the game.

A clever reviewer, especially in the precarious world of the theatre, soon becomes indispensable to his associates. In theory above influence, he is nevertheless open to certain pressures; he is bound to be courted by those who stand to gain by his favorable notice. Aveling believed that the critic's role was not only to discriminate between the good and the second-rate, but to encourage the vigorous growth of the arts. A connoisseur of beauty, he liked to allow his enthusiasms a chance to establish themselves before time (and empty houses) forced them off the stage.

He was a familiar figure at the stage door; leading ladies made a pet of him. Ugly, short, solemn, sarcastic, Alec Nelson hardly cut a romantic figure. Still, in a world of handsome, vain, somewhat effeminate leading men, he was a diversion. He had the rare faculty of understanding the insecurity to which the most successful actress was prey; he could feel on his pulse her fear of aging, her jealousy of the beautiful young girl on the way up. He showed the affectionate, ironic camaraderie of someone in the trade.

When, under the influence of wine, late hours, loneliness, camaraderie crossed that artificial boundary separating the friendly kiss from the invitation to bed, he turned out to have remarkable staying power, a rarity in men of the theatre, he was told more than once. Gallantly he attributed his prodigious size and endurance to the charms of the lady in question. But, like other talents, his amatory skill was a matter of natural ability, training, and self-control. In proof of which, he performed equally well for Tussy, who was unimpressed, having little to measure him against. Wounded vanity suggested that he must find other means of corrupting her.

Only six months after the Avelings returned from their triumphant tour, Ernest proposed to Tussy that she should leave Aveling and come to live with him and Dollie, married now for a year and happily ensconced in Brunswick Square.

"Dollie isn't prepared to risk her friendship with you. But I must say what I feel. I care for you, Tussy, more than for anyone except Dollie. If you hate me for what I say, so be it."

"I couldn't hate you for anything you might say to me, dear."

"Still, you have the right to conduct your private life as you see fit."

"It would seem so."

"Ah, Tussy, don't throw yourself away. You're too important to us. We can't stand aside and watch you destroy yourself. . . ."

"What exactly do you have against Dr. Aveling?"

"I wish I could give you a bill of particulars. . . . I don't like his atheism, for one thing."

"Why, what are you and Dollie if not atheists?"

"Granted, we're all agnostic, at the least. It's not a matter of belief."

"What is it, then?"

"It's that whole crew, Bradlaugh, Mrs. Besant. . . . it's the preaching I find objectionable, and the self-righteous priggishness. Your father despised them."

"Edward has broken with them long since."

"Yes . . . now he preaches socialism as an atheist, and atheism as a socialist; he's even converted Mrs. Besant. I fail to see how it serves any useful purpose."

"Do you doubt his sincerity?"

"It seems to me that he finds his current brand of morality singularly convenient."

"We all suit our beliefs to our needs."

"Not you, Tussy. You make things as hard as you can for yourself."

"It's his private life you object to, isn't it? It's not his atheism."

"Very well. It's his private life I find . . . not objectionable, exactly; I don't know anything definite to object to. Unsavory. Suspicious. There are unsettled questions, rumors. . . ."

"You can hardly convict a man upon rumors. You, a barrister by training."

"I'd like to be able to set the rumors to rest, in my own mind at least."

"Are you in such a good position to examine another man's private life?"

"Oh, I know I sponge off Dollie, and I'd rather write poetry than practice the *jus* . . . But I don't actually harm anyone."

"Do you think Dr. Aveling actually harms anyone?"

"I'd like to know more about his first marriage. I'd like to know why he gave up his fellowship at King's. . . . I'm sorry, Tussy."

"What if I told you that I have asked Edward about each and every one of the rumors that, as you say, refuse to settle?"

"I wouldn't believe you, quite frankly."

"I'm stronger than you think. I'll make you a proposition. Write an article setting out your views on the Secularists. Edward will publish it in *To-Day*, and I'll answer you in the next issue. You know I can't quarrel with you and Dollie. Let us agree to differ."

"Don't hate me for speaking out."

"Why should I hate you? It's not the first time I've been advised to love or not to love . . . as if one had any choice in the matter!"

"Surely one has a choice."

"Only in the eyes of a father or a brother. And, since I never had a brother, you do very well as a surrogate."

"I could have been more to you, Tussy."

"No, dear. Never. We're too much alike. We're both soft and sentimental; we see the other side too readily. You see, Edward has the metal I lack. It's true that he seems aggressive and hard, and they're not likable qualities. But they're what I need. I need to be toughened, otherwise I'll continue to sway this way and that. I can't get on with anything, I fritter my life away. . . . It's no good, Ernest, I can't live on my own, I'd go completely to pieces. Everything you say may be true, but none of it matters."

Edward continued to take a professional interest in May Morris; he supervised her tentative efforts at playwriting, and introduced her to his theatrical friends. Thus it was Edward who broke the news of May's surrender to Harry Sparling.

"I'm deeply disappointed in her," he told Tussy. "Harry is a nonentity, even as an expert on Arthurian legend. I'm positive she's going ahead with it only because her father disapproves."

"I don't see that it's anyone's business but May's that Harry is a nonentity. If he is a nonentity."

"It's certainly her father's business if he's to end up supporting them both."

"Nonsense—May will support them. She's already a first-class embroiderer; she could easily establish her own workshop. She'll certainly be able to support them until Harry establishes himself."

"And what if Harry fails to establish himself?"

"Oh, he's bound to do all right; May's father will see to that."

"It won't last, mark my words. May has no tolerance for the second-rate, any more than you or I do."

"I can't imagine what standards you're applying. We're all amateurs in the arts, you and I as much as anyone else. Truthfully, Edward, you can hardly claim that *Lovers' Meetings* is first-rate theatre. Amusing, perhaps, mildly entertaining, but hardly first-rate."

"I hadn't realized you thought so little of my creative efforts."

"If you take the larger scale of value—"

"Shakespeare or Sophocles, for instance?"

"All I mean to say is that we shouldn't be so hard on poor Harry, just because he's something of what my East London friends call a *schlemiel.*"

"But, you see, I have a stake in what becomes of Miss Morris. It hasn't been very long since the beauteous May was quite happy to take my arm on her way to the theatre—not that she was one of those who succumbed. But she came close to it, I assure you. Now, aren't you fortunate to have succeeded where so many tried and failed?"

As their lack of money became chronic, Tussy arrived at a principle which she was never to abandon: accept any work that offers. Work was a means to an end, subsistence, keeping afloat. If it was more than this, if it offered food for mind and spirit, if it turned out to be creative work rather than drudgery, so much the better. But she expected very little; why should she be different from a thousand others?

Fortunately there were times when duty and inclination coincided. Swan Sonnenschein, the General's publisher, had undertaken an ambitious project of publishing the complete works of the leading European modernists. George Moore, the Irish novelist, and a close friend of Olive's, asked Tussy on Sonnenschein's behalf if she would translate a French novel of the realistic school, by a writer largely unknown in England. The pay was a generous ten pounds, enough to pay a quarter's rent. The writer was Gustave Flaubert; the novel, *Madame Bovary*.

With the bills mounting daily, Tussy had to fight to suppress her eagerness. She confessed to some apprehension; she had no literary style of her own. But she would do her best to provide a literal translation, grammatically correct, and as idiomatic as she could make it without falsifying the original.

As she submitted to the discipline of translation, concentrating her mental energy on searching out exact equivalents for Flaubert's precise phrases, a submerged part of her began in a curious, unpredictable way to identify with his heroine. She, Tussy, suffered with Emma Bovary, languished, yearned, brooded over her undeserved misfortunes. She too addressed her man enviously: You are a man, and therefore free. She too turned on him contemptuously, angrily, in the classic cry of the resentful housewife: *You, a man, can't possibly know what it is to be busy all the time. . . .* Like Emma she was clever but uneducated, talented in a small way, restless, easily bored; she too adored greatness, beauty, grace. Forgetful of her true self, she knew her soul stifled; she too hungered for love.

Yet as a translator she shared the double-edged vision of the author, who, even as he identified with the passions of his heroine, dissected and analyzed her corruption. The novel, Tussy saw, was a study not only of a woman but of an entire society ruled by greed, driven by the bourgeois myth of progress. In Flaubert's world not only women but men were prisoners of their foolish desires and limited ideas. Tussy found in the politics of the novel her own politics confirmed: aristocrats and liberal democrats were alike governed by self-interest, their so-called principles a justification of self and class.

Solutions had no place in art, of course. The author was more interested in the observation and diagnosis of disease than in its cure; he left his heroine no recourse but self-destruction. Life was intolerable; better to end it than to struggle on without hope. Tussy was congenitally optimistic about the future, and strong enough to recover from temporary setbacks. But her own views about life receded as she followed Emma Bovary's degeneration step by step. One door after another was shut, every recourse exhausted. Scandal threatened; she faced utter ruin, total exposure. The question of love and the question of money twisted one upon the other and became indistinguishable in Emma's poor confused mind. Tussy translated literally from the text: "Suddenly it seemed to her that fiery spheres were exploding in the air like fulminating balls when they strike, and were whirling, whirling, to melt at last upon the snow between the branches of the trees. In the midst of each of them appeared the face of Rodolphe. . . . *Alors sa situation, telle qu'un abîme, se représenta.* . . . Now her situation, like an abyss, again presented itself. . . . She went straight to the third shelf—so well did her memory guide her—seized the blue jar, tore out the cork, plunged in her hand, and withdrawing it full of a white powder, she began eating it. . . ."

Tussy, writing feverishly, her heart wrenched by the wrongs suffered by this possessed woman, in her deepest being assented to her death. What choice had she? She had exhausted every possibility, every avenue of help. *Alors sa situation, telle qu'un abîme, se représenta.* No escape, no hope. Therefore the eating of the white powder, the only escape, the only hope.

She handed her translation to George Moore a month after he had given her the text. She felt that her life had been altered. For the first time it seemed to her that translation was not hack work, but a true vocation. As she redrew Flaubert's precise, balanced, ironic phrases, she too, by virtue of her fidelity, was an artist.

In a preface she tried to communicate what she understood,

as a socialist and a woman, of this study of romantic illusion and bourgeois reality. Yet she had an intuition that in fifty years no one would read the book as a political indictment. Especially since the message of the novel, if it had a message, seemed to be: *a plague o' both your houses!*

When she was finished, the work receded, and her identification with Emma Bovary paled, became a dim, uncertain memory. With undiminished energy she rededicated herself to the liberation of the oppressed—her father's cause and mankind's—binding herself ever more closely in political and journalistic zeal to her husband-in-name.

The Haymarket anarchists were executed on November 11, 1887, a year after the Avelings returned from America. Tussy couldn't believe the Governor would refuse to issue a last-minute pardon. The world had seen and protested, hundreds of thousands had marched, written letters, signed petitions. Why, she and Edward had collected over four hundred signatures for a cable on the last day but one. Everyone had signed, everyone had contributed; they knew it was cold-blooded murder. Yet the authorities remained unmoved. The people's democracy extorted a tremendous price for the exercise of freedom.

For Tussy it was a brutal demonstration of the power of government, established institutions, the propertied classes, *that which is.* When one was among friends, it was easy to forget that public events were still to a large extent determined by choices made by men in power. Regardless of the force exerted on them from outside—economic pressure, the persuasive force of a thousand signatures, the condemnation of the national and international press, the threat of demonstration, strikes, the breakdown of public order—those in power were still free to act as they chose to act, unless and until they were removed from power. How to gain power—how to take power—was still the crucial political problem. As a servant of scientific socialism, Tussy believed that her task was essentially to interpret and to assist to birth processes which were inevitable in the long run. But belief in the inevitable triumph of the working class was increasingly difficult to sustain.

It turned out that Aveling, a scientist before he became a socialist, hadn't sent the cable after all, having recognized sooner than anyone else its utter futility.

9

It was inevitable that the intense, careless happiness of her first months with Aveling should pass. Change is fundamental to life, the only certainty, Aveling repeatedly told his students; it is the nature of passion to alter, as it is the nature of more tangible things to age and decay.

Not that their sexual passion had altered appreciably in the four years they had been living together. But recently they seemed to have no time to spend with each other, and the time they did spend together was taken up with business, committee meetings, plans for provincial tours, last-minute editorials for *To-Day*, stratagems for obtaining a few pounds here or there, for postponing the grocer's bill, the rent collector. Indeed, Tussy sometimes wondered if she were not fated to reproduce her parents' desperate juggling act of pawnshop, butcher, coalman; if it were not she, rather than Aveling, who arranged for them to owe more from month to month than they could possibly repay in a year.

Their nights were often spent apart; political meetings tended to run late, and if Tussy came in first she'd collapse exhausted, awakening sometimes at eight in the morning to find that Edward had not yet returned. Where had he been? It was a matter of pride not to ask. And, if she asked, her pride humbled for the moment, the answers were worse than silence, transparent lies rolled off the tongue with no serious intention of deceiving her. It was not her business to know where he had been—those were the terms on which they had joined their lives, those were the terms under which he had agreed to love her.

Did he love her? He claimed to love her; he was often loving to her in manner, demonstratively so. Love is an unreliable quantity at best, a matter of being convinced, at a given moment, that one loves, or is in love. He loved her, he affirmed when pressed—but in freedom, not possessively, not exclusively. Why lie to her, why lie to oneself? He was that rare being, a lover who made no claims, required no vows of fidelity.

She was free as well, of course. He had no objection if she fancied one of their many friends for a night or two—Ernest Radford or poor dear Freddy, or Shaw, for God's sake.

"You say things you can't possibly mean."

"I'm perfectly serious. What do they say on the boulevards? 'Absence makes the heart grow fonder.' 'Variety is the spice of life.' And so it is, Tussy. But you close your eyes to that side of love."

"For good reason."

"No, you can't have good reasons for denying the common human pleasures. You make yourself a prisoner, Tussy, not I. I want you to be free and happy."

"Yet you make my hours bitter as gall. . . ."

"What rubbish—sheer melodrama. I've told you I love you. I'm here to prove it. What more could any woman want?"

"I have no idea what any woman might want. I only know that I'm miserable."

"Yes . . . I forgot that you're not any woman. You're different. You're one of the others. . . . But not that different, Tussy. Let us not delude ourselves. You're not that different from Mary and Sally and Polly Hawkins and Joan Higgins and Henrietta Smith. Not even you, Tussy Marx."

She sat in the warm kitchen drinking Pilsener beer, and Nim fussed about her.

"Do sit down, Nimmy dear, so we can have a proper chat."

"Was Edward pleased about the notices?"

"I suppose so. I haven't spoken to him yet."

"Is he off again?"

"He's very busy. I really can't expect him to report to me every two hours."

"Doesn't he come home at night, then?"

71

"Oh, Nim, darling, you know we don't live like other people. I've explained it all to you. Don't make me go through it again."

"You can explain away; I'm too old to understand such explanations."

She fought the impulse to rest her head against the massive chest of the older woman.

"Were you never in love, Nim darling?"

"When would I have had the time to be in love? When I was nursing your poor mother? when I was sitting up with her poor sick babies?"

"You could have married, Nim."

"Oh, I had hundreds of beaux. I could have married half a dozen of them, I suppose. And what would all of you have done without me, I'd like to know?"

"You could have had your own life."

"Ah, Tussy, when will you learn that people do exactly as they please? Do you think I didn't know what I was doing? Don't you think I stayed with a free heart? Your mother and father were all the love I wanted. Why, I was the only one of us with any sense."

"Nothing's changed, then. You're still the only one with any sense."

"Laura's sensible enough, when she keeps her temper."

"Meaning that I'm not, even when I keep my temper."

"Ah, Tussy, it's not your wild Irish rages I worry about, it's when you're quiet, like this. Quiet, and sad . . . it's as if you've lost the will to fight."

"I'm tired, Nim. I'm tired of fighting. I can't sleep at night; somehow I never feel properly rested. Sleep seems so delicious to me. If I could have one night of a really deep, dreamless sleep, I'd feel better, I'm sure of it."

"How long has it been going on, then?"

"I don't know, really. Perhaps from the beginning. It's as if I've awakened only recently to something I've known for a very long time. And it's something so awful, so unmanageable, that I'd rather not be awake; I'd rather it lie unrecognized as it did before. . . ."

"Dear child, I'm only an ignorant old woman, but I don't think he means to hurt you like this."

"Oh, Nim, if I could believe that—"

"It's his nature, Tussy. He can't help it."

"That's exactly what I've told myself. And I believe it's true, in a way. But . . . oh, Nim, there's more to it than that."

"Tell me, darling. Tell your Nimmy."

For answer she embraced her old nurse, shut her eyes, and allowed herself to be rocked and petted. How much simpler love was for them, she thought, for Nim, for Mama and Mohr; the comfort of children, everything in its place, a loyalty beyond question, through thick and thin. How fortunate they were to be spared an illusory, oppressive freedom; to be tied to one another with bonds of steel.

I can't speak about it to anyone, she thought. Not to Nim, not to Dollie, not to Olive. I'm not sure in what it consists. I have never been sexually shy; I doubt that there is any form of sexual cares or union which is inherently degrading. Yet I feel degraded, fouled. In every caress I sense Edward's intention of humiliating me. Horrible as it is to admit, I can't discover in his lovemaking any motive of love, any desire other than that of using me to gratify his physical needs.

If this were all, I could bear to be thus used, for his sake. But I am half convinced he means to punish me, for what offense I am ignorant, to demonstrate to me over and over again some truth essential to our relations—that I am a woman, and therefore a thing to be used, who must be disciplined not to feel, to act, to question. Or perhaps that as a woman I am deluded in regarding the sexual act as an expression of love; I must learn that it is an appetite like any other, that takes its satisfaction where it finds it.

Tussy found Bernard working in the reading room of the British Museum, Henry George's *Progress and Poverty* open before him.

"Come have a cup of tea," she said. "I need to talk."

In the refreshment room, "I want to be free," she said. "I want to be my own woman. Help me."

"Leave him," Bernard said.

"Never. I can't leave him. I refuse to be defeated."

"Then I can't help you. You're like all the others."

"Do you despise me?"

"Of course not. Perhaps it's not important that you be free."

"I think it is. I can't live like this."

"You could have a child."

"It's easy for you to say."

"Women are fools. How can you expect reasonable people to pay attention to you?"

"Why do I feel like such a child, Bernard? I have no faith in my abilities, no confidence in my judgment."

"Poor Tussy. You're still suffering the effects of your father's death. But you'll have to come out of it; you're on your own now. We're all orphans, Tussy. Sooner or later."

"I feel sometimes as though I shall never stop wanting them. Yet you can have no idea how much I fought them when they were alive. I cut myself off from them completely. I was so hard to my mother. . . . I can't bear to think of it."

"Mothers take no notice. Your tea is cold."

"Shall you ever marry, Bernard?"

"If I do, it won't be your sort of marriage."

"I have no sort of marriage."

"If it were up to me, babies would be bred in the laboratory and reared in nurseries. We'd all be free then, Tussy, not just you and me but the great unwashed."

"Free for what?"

"Why, to write our books. Sex is the great enemy of intellectual progress—which is why there's been so little of it. Until men and women choose to sleep alone we shall see no improvement in the race."

"You're the one that's the child."

"I never pretended otherwise."

"Ah, Bernard, why is it so much easier to love our friends—"

"Than our wives and husbands? Because our friends are free to come and go, while our spouses represent property, and tend to depreciate in value."

"It seems most unfair that I should have the restraints of marriage without the name."

"Leave him, Tussy. Walk out. Slam the door behind you. Live—be free. Love him if you must, at a distance. Save yourself. But don't come to me for help—there's nothing I or anyone can do for you."

Tussy suspected that Aveling's flirtations with actresses were casual, short-lived; a matter of a few kisses, an embrace in a darkened theatre, the fondling of a breast, a thigh pressed between the folds of a silk dress. At worst, fornication under the railway arches at Charing Cross, against the walls of the Embankment late at night, or in Miss Smythe-Jones's narrow bed. A man who quite frankly admires the female body, and has anatomized it professionally, can be forgiven for taking what is on offer.

Suffering from a mixture of guesses, hints, and half-hearted denials, she reasoned thus: it is quite possible that he loves me, after his fashion. I can't expect him to change his nature, which to an outsider might seem cold and indifferent. Whom does he care for if not for me? Does he not depend on me to provide a kind of home, peace and quiet for work, intelligent talk, comradeship in bed? I have no rights over him, after all. We are joined in freedom, we can separate in freedom, each to go his own way. He would not stay unless he cared for me, after his fashion. I am wrong to doubt, to take his absent-mindedness for indifference, his rather cruel humor for a sign that he is weary of me, and wants to break loose. What binds us together if not the beliefs we share, our joint decision to work for a better life for all, to educate, agitate, organize? We are true partners, true comrades. And, despite all, true lovers.

Aveling was quite willing to shrug off his affairs with actresses and the like. He preferred Tussy, on the whole, though she could be troublesome. He found her interesting; he admired her grasp of history and literature, her skill in languages, the rather remarkable talents she took for granted. And he was enthralled by her circle, not her irritating women friends, like Dollie Radford, Olive Schreiner, and the formidable Clementina Black, but the socialists who met at the General's dinner table, Stepnyak, Willy Liebknecht, Karl Kautsky, Eduard Bernstein. He was humbled by their cosmopolitanism, their physical bravery, their easy familiarity with philosophy, political and economic theory, the full range of European thought. They made him feel an amateur, incurably English; he was eager to learn from them, and they tolerated him for that reason.

Tussy's suffering he took philosophically; she was bound to

suffer, whatever he did. It was woman's lot, woman's choice. He had very little sympathy for her wrongs, and was merely amused by her anguished silences, her heroic efforts not to reproach him. If she wished to be his comrade, she must take the rough with the smooth; there was bound to be more of the first and less of the second as time went on.

Who was present at 122 Regents Park Road for the celebration of the General's seventieth birthday? August Bebel, Willy Liebknecht, Paul Singer for the German Social Democratic Party, Stepnyak, Tussy and Edward, Louise Kautsky, Pumps, the General's niece, and the devoted Schorlemmer, also known affectionately as Jollymeier.

What was consumed? Sixteen bottles of champagne, twenty-five bottles of claret, twelve dozen oysters.

From whom did the General receive fraternal greetings? From the National Council of the French Workers' Party, the Russische Sozialdemokraten of Berne, the Leipzig Stadt und Land, the Klassenbewusste Bergleute of Bochum, the Arbeiter Verein of London. Also from W. Morris and F. Kitz for the Socialist League; from R. B. Cunninghame Graham, W. Parnell, H. Champion, and Tom Mann for the Labour Association of England; from Keir Hardie for the Ayrshire Mine-Workers' Union; and for the Austrian Socialist Workers' Party from Popp, Adler, Hoffmann, Kreutzer, Winnig (Vienna), Mackart (Innsbruck), Sieg (Linz), Nemecek (Prague), and Zednicek (Prossnitz). And many others.

What did the General conceive to be the greatest dangers confronting socialism in this the last decade of the nineteenth century? The greatest danger, he believed, was nationalism, and the prospect of national and ultimately global wars on a scale hitherto inconceivable. The second great danger, ironically enough, was the success of the trade-union movement, with the resulting bourgeoisification of the working classes.

What did he conceive to be the great hope for socialism? The sincere fraternity established once and forever between the French and German proletarians. For he believed that the alliance of three great Western nations, France, England, and Germany, was the condition for the political and social emancipation of all Europe. That alliance could be achieved only by a united international proletarian movement. If successful, it would put an end for all time to the wars of governments and nations. He hoped to see the groundwork laid within his lifetime.

Olive went back to South Africa to preach a new sisterhood. After six months Tussy finally had a letter from her.

My dear Eleanor,

I am to be married January 14th to Samuel Cronwright, a gentleman farmer of Durban. We plan to make our home in Pietermaritzburg.

I hope you will visit Havelock from time to time. Be kind to him, for my sake. He fought to keep me, but I could not stay on his terms.

It seems right for me, now, to commit my life to my homeland. We have so few genuine choices in life that those we do have— the choice of a mate, the choice of a home—we owe it to ourselves to consider from the most comprehensive view. I sincerely believe that the future you are working for has a greater chance of materializing here or in a raw young country like America than in England. Foreigners often mistake English tolerance for a genuine openness to new ideas. But the English are tolerant only because they believe themselves to be quite safe; they have centuries of successful accommodation behind them. The Englishwoman is quite content with her cottage and her garden, her role on parish committees and charitable boards, her access to a few carefully chosen professions; why should she risk losing what she has by a foolish militancy? The Englishman would rather have his Saturday pay packet and his tavern pint than a new society. You and I can have little to do in a country that values common sense above imagination, comfort above justice.

Cron is an honorable, kind man, the best man I know. He loves me, and at my stage of life that seems a good and sufficient condition for marriage.

Havelock and I loved each other as brother and sister. We had—and still have—an understanding that I shall never have with anyone else. But even now I find that I begin to forget him.

I write from a full heart. I really think grief will be my portion henceforth, inseparable from whatever happiness and domestic joy I may find in my new life. But I know that it is right for me to be here.

We have agreed that I am to keep my name; Cron wishes to be known as "Cronwright-Schreiner."

Wish me all good out of your own goodness and generosity— and let me know that you do not feel abandoned by your

Olive

She had no sooner read the last words than she felt abandoned. She wrote to Havelock and proposed that they should dine together later in the week. Only she and Havelock, of Olive's English friends, knew her intimately, loved her, would find their lives narrowed by her absence. Havelock must be devastated, utterly lost; she hoped that his native English good sense, so underrated by Olive, would pull him through.

Three weeks passed before he wrote back.

Dear Eleanor,

I hope you will forgive me for not answering sooner. I have been extremely busy, as I'm sure you can understand. I have a paper to give next March in Frankfurt, and the publishers have been pressing me for the next installment of "Auto-eroticism among the Bantu," an important and delicate subject which requires utmost concentration on my part. Besides, I am in process of moving to the country, as I find that the distractions of London make it impossible to work.

I'm afraid I can't see any time clear for us to meet until after Easter.

Olive's life is of course her own concern, but I frankly can't see her submitting cheerfully to the domestic restraints of marriage.

I have taken the liberty of giving your name to Ernest Rhys, who is looking for someone to translate two or three of Ibsen's plays. I am sure you would have no difficulty mastering Norwegian, which I am told is a fairly simple language, with close affinities to English and German. If this appeals to you, I gather the pay is quite reasonable.

As ever,
Havelock Ellis

She read the letter twice, looking in vain for some sign of affection. Even the commission at the end seemed not an act of friendship so much as a distant recognition of her pecuniary embarrassment. She had gone to Havelock in kindness to him, not out of her own need. She knew he was busy; she too was busy, frantically busy, busy to no point or purpose, it often seemed. What were friends for if they could not make room in a busy schedule for one another?

It struck her that she had become, by virtue of her unhappiness, one of those tedious sufferers who are gradually shuffled off by their friends and acquaintances, with varying degrees of politeness: meetings postponed with vague excuses, letters left unanswered, invitations neglected or ceasing altogether. It was as if unhappiness was an embarrassing disease, a social burden fatal to amusing conversation.

But Havelock had moved on. Rumor had it that he was in love and intended to marry. His letter was innocuous, after all. Still, it was a clear signal that he was no longer someone she could depend on.

Though he might be imperceptive about human relations, Havelock was right about the Norwegian language. With a copy of a Norwegian grammar, and French and German translations in reserve, Tussy found it fairly easy to produce a literal translation of *Fruen fra Havet*, which could then be manipulated to produce readable lines.

For instance, "Er—er vi alene i huset nu?" became "Are—are we alone in house now?" then "Are—are we alone at home now?" Similarly, the hero's touching assessment of his wife, with its layers of misunderstanding: "Du er en aerlig natur, Ellida. Du har et trofast sind" became "You are an honorable nature, Ellida. You have a (true) (steadfast) mind," and finally, "Yours is an honest nature, Ellida—yours is a faithful mind."

Not all of it was so straightforward, of course. But the language had a simplicity and grandeur, like Anglo-Saxon or medieval Latin, which gave the sentiments a melancholy weight and conviction. Certain lines reverberated in Tussy's imagination:

"Nu går snart den glade sommertid til ende. Snart er alle sunde lukket."

"The glad summertime will soon be over now. Soon all ways will be barred. . . ."

She had to concentrate all her conscious attention on the linguistic task. But as she translated Ibsen's play she found herself repeating the curious experience she had had while translating *Madame Bovary*, sharing at one moment the detached, ironic viewpoint of the author-physician, and in the next identifying wholly with the passions of the heroine. Her own troubles dropped away and she became Ellida; she, Tussy, was *Fruen fra Havet*—the Lady from the Sea—whose natural element is the limitless, the infinite, the passional, who sickens and dies when she is transplanted inland.

When Ellida cries to her husband, "My own true life lost its bearings when I agreed to live with you," it was a short step for Tussy to apply the words to herself: my own true life lost its bearings when I agreed to live with . . . Edward.

As Ellida despairs: "When you have once become a land-creature you can no longer find your way back again to the sea, nor to the sea-life either," it was tempting to rewrite the lines: "When you have once become entangled in lies you can no longer find your way back to the truth; when you have once begun to compromise, it is impossible to make a fresh start; when you have cast your lot with a weak and dishonorable man, you are no longer permitted to associate with free, noble, untainted human beings."

Strangely enough, if Dr. Aveling was in certain ways like Dr. Wangel, Ellida's husband, "Alec Nelson," was strikingly like the Stranger, "den fremmeck mand," who comes to take possession of Ellida. The "Alec Nelson" who was an artist, bound by no civilized principles, obedient only to the passions that ruled him—did not he too have cold, dead eyes that changed with the color they reflected, of sea or sky? Was not he too a man impervious to reason, argument, fact? Did not his secret power over her have the effect of dissolving her will, her inmost being?

How easily Ibsen could have made a tragedy out of his heroine's dilemma! Instead he chose to offer her freedom. And Tussy, understanding too well the grip of the Stranger over Ellida's deepest being, saw as the climax of the play Ellida's success in expelling her lover: "To me you are as one dead. I no longer dread you. And I am no longer drawn to you." For Tussy this seemed a happy resolution of problems that in her own life remained insoluble.

It was impossible for her to expel the past, impossible to cancel her attraction to evil.

It was impossible to choose, impossible to renounce.

It was impossible for her, in Ibsen's phrase, to acclimatize herself.

Where was the physician, what the medicine that could set her free?

10

While Tussy struggled to translate Ibsen's masterpiece, Edward dashed off half a dozen one-act plays, freely mixing farce, melodrama, comedy, pastoral, romance. He placed the most promising, *The Perfect Gentleman*, in a lunchtime spot at the Princess Theatre. Miss Smythe-Jones played the ingénue, Edward himself the rakish hero. Rehearsals lasted well into the night, and Tussy took on more and more of Edward's political committee work.

In their rooms on Great Russell Street, ten minutes from the theatre, Edward was optimistic, exceedingly pleased with himself and the world.

"It's our chance to get clear once and for all. We're booked at the Princess for three weeks, along with a melodrama by O'Keefe. Then there's a possibility of an American tour. All I need is a foothold, I'm convinced of it. Success breeds success; it's the law of the theatre."

"The other side of it being that failure breeds failure."

"No, that doesn't apply in the theatre, only in real life. Nobody remembers failure in the theatre. You fail one day, are forgotten the next. Theatre folk are like children; they're incurable romantics. They always think tomorrow will be different. They believe in impulse, miracles, magic. And every now and then it happens, the magic works, the miracle occurs. For us too, Tussy. I count on it."

"I wish I could be equally optimistic."

"Then come to a rehearsal."

He seldom asked her to attend rehearsals. Tacitly she assumed she was wise to shut her eyes to his theatre life. But in spite of severe misgivings she went along the next day.

She sat frozen through the first scene, in a state of growing wretchedness. It was all there, on stage before her, badly acted, unconvincing, crude: the susceptible, shallow young girl; the attractive rake, cynical, experienced; the girl's defenses brought down easily one by one; Mama appeased, Papa deceived, Sister brought in as an accomplice. By the end of the second scene the game was won. It was clear to Tussy that Miss Smythe-Jones was smitten by Edward; every curve of her provocative little body was an invitation.

She began to grow angry, her anger swelling until it seemed that the pressure within her head and in her breast must have release. She left the theatre and walked toward Trafalgar Square, then to the river, hardly aware of where she was going. She walked for hours through a fine rain, until the water seeped through her boots and her skirts became heavy with moisture. Past the Embankment, she kept on toward Vauxhall, and across Battersea Bridge, where she stopped and stood looking down into the swirling gray water. Her eyes followed the debris carried along by the tide—charred timber, drums of oil, fragments of a wreck further upriver. She was stirred by a memory, a story of one of the true English heroines, who had stood on this very bridge, at the same spot perhaps, and stared down— how far down it was!—thinking the blackest thoughts of hell. . . . Mary Wollstonecraft had thrown herself from Battersea Bridge, abandoned by the man she considered herself married to in spirit if not in name. Her skirts had borne her up, and she was rescued by rivermen. Tussy shivered . . . she would never have had the courage.

Someone tapped at her shoulder.

"Are you all right, miss?"

She nodded and walked on quickly, across the bridge and into the mean streets of Battersea, long terraces of gray brick houses, two up, two down, built right to the footpath, only fifteen years old but already in a state of disrepair, chimney pots hanging loose, front windows broken or boarded up. The poor in Battersea were different from the East End poor, they were tough Irish workmen who came with the railways, the women slatterns by the age of thirty, with half a dozen or ten children, always another on the way. They shut the door on you with a curse if you dared to knock, but they needed help as much as the East Enders, or more. As for political consciousness, they knew only a crude hatred of Them, the British, the Jews, the land owners . . . a start, perhaps. Still, Tussy felt a great weariness as she trudged down the endless identical roads. What help could she give? What business had she offering help to anyone? If a woman had the energy to struggle with ten squalling brats and a drunken husband, what business had she to interfere? People seemed to have an infinite capacity to adjust to their conditions; some survived, some sank, but it occurred to very few that there were other ways of organizing their lives. What did it take to make someone rise up finally against intolerable oppression? Recklessness, a conviction that there was nothing more to be lost, indifference to death . . . above all, an overmastering anger. . . .

If Aveling was cruel to her in later years, he could point out, with some truth, that he served her in the way of a substitute. There were others, living and dead, who came first.

"Prove to me that I come first," he said, bent on mischief.

"How can you ask . . . ?"

"I want you to admit the true state of affairs. You are committed elsewhere, Tussy. Your father's wishes still have force. If your sister Laura called, you would drop everything and go to her. Even Freddy has more of a claim on you than I do. Well, I too have my little . . . interests. Let us agree to be free agents."

"You've always been a free agent."

"Exactly. I intend to continue as before."

"Have I asked you to do otherwise?"

"Not in so many words."

"Then why do you torture me?"

"My dear Eleanor, there is more than one way of making your feelings known. When you wait up for me at night, when you ask me to account for five quid here or ten quid there . . ."

"I merely asked whether you had repaid Karl Kautsky."

"I think you can trust your Semitic friends to collect for themselves."

"Sometimes I can't understand you at all."

"I'm sure you understand me very well."

"Oh, you are cold, Edward! I can't bear it when you use that tone to me."

"Then stop questioning me. I warn you, if you continue to question me about how I spend my time, whom I spend my time with, how much money I owe and to whom, it won't only be my tone that you find objectionable."

"Are you threatening me? Are we in practice for a new melodrama? or perhaps a new farce?"

"You're very beautiful when you're angry . . . a righteous angel of our secular Lord—an angel of Humanity. You breathe fire and ice; I can positively smell your wrath."

"Why is it that nothing I can say or do makes any impression on you?"

"You're quite wrong, my dear. I'm full of admiration for everything you do and say."

"Nothing touches you. I believe you really don't care whether you hurt people. It makes no difference at all to you what people think of you."

"Didn't Mohr teach us that? Didn't he quote Dante at us? *Segui il tuo corso, e lascia dir le genti.* Take your own way, and let people say what they like . . . It is my motto as well."

"Oh, Edward, you are a parody of him!"

He turned pale, and looked at her with what, to her horror, she took to be undisguised hatred.

"A hit, my dear, a palpable hit."

"I'm sorry, Edward."

"Not at all. The cat's out of the bag. Ain't it, now?"

"I said that I'm sorry."

"I'll remember. But don't you think it would be overdoing it for both of us to be virtuous? I've promised not to interfere with you, I support you in everything you do, I work like a nigger for you. . . ."

"Yes, you work very hard."

"Then you must allow me to play now and then."

"I can't prevent you."

"True. You can't prevent me. Then let us live for our pleasure, you and I."

"What pleasure can there be for me in our life together?"

"Why, the pleasure of loving and of being loved, for your

excellent mind and your healthy body."

"My barren body."

"Your choice, my dear."

"Yes. My choice. My fate."

Dearest Olive,

I am so glad that you are happy in your new life, secure in your love for your husband and his love for you! It is right that you should be content, fulfilled—truly at home. Perhaps it's a mistake to think too closely about the important decisions of our lives. When the right moment comes, the decision is taken for us. It feels right, it *is* right—and we assent to it un-questioningly.

I'm convinced that people need a single focus to their lives. There must be something tangible, felt in the blood, that binds one to this world, some indissoluble tie, some passion that pre-sents itself not as a free choice but as a necessity. Otherwise everything one does seems infected with a terrible pointlessness; the reason for going on, from day to day, evaporates. It becomes a burden to pick up the pieces of one's life each morning.

If I thought the time would come when I would be unable to love, that I would never again be startled by a sudden rush of happiness, that I would cease to hope confidently for mira-cles—for is not every change a kind of miracle? and do we not have evidence every day of the banality of the miraculous? If I no longer believed in life, then I would be lost indeed, Olive dear.

But you are right—things are very bad between Edward and me. I can't tell you how bad; I am half afraid to find out. We shall go on, somehow, because we must; the bond that joins us can't lightly be broken. Yet I wonder sometimes if I am not imagining it all, if I have not invented this Edward, with his thin, hard mouth, his eyes that never regard me, his iron will. Surely I have invented some monstrosity of a false lover out of a perverse need of my own. The real Edward is gentle, loving, kind, a friend and companion; he is only temporarily absent, forgetful of himself. Let me believe this if I can—let my faith create the real Edward out of the false.

Meanwhile I receive a singular education. I shall have every womanish sentiment, every romantic illusion driven from mind and heart; slowly I am learning to restrain each affectionate impulse, to pretend to an indifference I can never feel. I know now what it is to be dominated without love, to feel my will dissolve in the presence of a stronger will, inflexible, unreasonable, immune to pity or remorse.

Ah, my dear, what am I to do? Help me, counsel me. I fear the worst.

not sent

It seemed to her sometimes that she represented all women injured by men, used, abused, deserted, cast aside; left for younger women, for drink, for whoring, for male companionship or the love of boys.

For their sake, if not her own, she must steel herself to endure.

She sat slumped in a chair by the fire, staring into the glowing coals. Though she was wrapped in a blanket, with a woolen shawl over her knees and another around her shoulders, she was shaken by waves of shivering. Dollie knelt at her feet, chafing Tussy's cold hands between her warm ones.

"How could you do such a dreadful thing to us, Tussy? How could you even contemplate it? Can you imagine how Ernest and I would have felt? We'd never have been able to face each other. . . . Oh, Tussy, you came so close—you'll never know. It was pure chance that I stopped by. I was going to go straight home after I finished at the Museum, and then I just thought I'd look in for a minute. . . . I was worried because you weren't at the Museum yesterday, and I thought perhaps you were ill. But you always tell me not to give in to my foolish fears, and it was late. So if I hadn't remembered the script Edward wanted us to look at I would have walked right past."

"Would that you had!" (Her voice harsh, strained, despairing.)

"Tussy, dearest, don't say that, I can't bear to think of it. There are one or two times in our lives when the gods are with us. . . . Don't I always come when you need me? Didn't I fly to Margate when you were so dreadfully ill, and your poor father had no idea what was wrong with you? Didn't I nurse you through those terrible nights?"

"I can't tell you how delicious it was to go down, knowing that I was sinking and need never rise again."

"You don't know what you're saying."

"When I came back and knew I had failed, and saw that it was you who brought me back, I hated you. I don't think I can forgive you."

"Why did you do it, Tussy?"

"I cannot live without love."

"But, darling, we love you, Ernest and I—"

"You have each other."

"Olive loves you. Olive needs you. You know she does."

"Olive must make her own way."

"But Laura—Jenny's children—"

"Laura's life is with her husband. As for the children—yes, it's very hard. But they're not my children. Jenny left them, after all."

"Not of her own choice, surely."

"How do we know? What do we know about these matters? Less than nothing. She hated her life."

"Oh, Tussy, you're talking such wild nonsense! I refuse to listen."

"I've never thought more clearly. It's all very plain to me. I see things I never saw before. I was a fool, Dollie."

"You were a fool to frighten us so."

"I was a fool to pretend that I was happy, that I could be happy, ever."

"But I've seen you happy, Tussy. You and Edward."

"You saw me pretending to be happy."

"You've forgotten, dear. You've forgotten those first months."

"I've forgotten nothing."

"What shall I tell Edward when he comes back?"

"He's not coming back."

"What do you mean, he's not coming back?"

"He's gone."

"Gone where?"

"Oh, how do I know? He's gone up to Newcastle or down to Dorset, or perhaps he's just down the road making love to Miss Smythe-Jones—what difference does it make? Oh, Dollie, why couldn't you leave me to die?"

"Swear to me you'll never try it again. I won't leave you for a minute. Ernest and I will stay with you day and night. We won't let you out of our sight, unless you swear to me by all we hold solemn that this is the last time."

"I'll swear anything you like." *But next time I'll do it properly.*

What kind of understanding could they possibly arrive at?

An attempted suicide clears the air for a time, brings matters to a crisis; it cuts to ribbons the polite lies which allow dupe and deceiver to go on from day to day, behaving as if neither suspects what the other is doing or thinking.

Tussy's suicide attempt informed Aveling, in so many words: I cannot—or will not—live without you.

To which Aveling's reply, after due consideration, was: Very well, then I shall stay with you.

This shifted the grounds of their union, as each of them recognized. Their "marriage" was, thenceforth, a matter of necessity for her, of accommodation and convenience for him.

Edward's agreement to stay was, they both knew, a concession, wrung from him by Tussy's desperate gamble. What concession was Tussy prepared to make in return?

She was prepared, without saying as much, to close her eyes to his philandering. What he did when he was away from her was his own business. She would neither ask nor expect to be told. When they were together he was her husband and trusted comrade, as before.

This somewhat precarious arrangement could work only under certain conditions. Edward would have to balance his double life so that he was "home" rather more than he was "away." Tussy would have to discipline herself to leave him free in spirit as well as fact. Both of them would have to change in radical ways, he to assume responsibilities for which he had little talent or inclination, she to moderate her need for love.

Shaken by the sight of Tussy near death—for he did not want her to die, and certainly not on his account—Edward determined to try to change. For three weeks he nursed her, unfailingly considerate, gentle as a woman. When he gradually resumed his normal life, he gave advance notice of any absences, returning always as promised. What was required of him was not much more than a surface courtesy. Tussy was more vulnerable than he had thought; he would make a genuine effort not to hurt her.

For Tussy, the change required was more difficult, striking

89

as it did at her deepest nature. And the kinder Edward was to her, the harder it was for her to discipline her heart. How could she stifle her newborn hopes, her resurgent faith in miracles? She knew that she must expect nothing; indeed, she expected nothing. She sternly denied herself the luxury of loving him. But, when she was surprised by an affectionate kiss, when the old habits of passion reasserted themselves, when he caressed her with a tenderness that seemed to acknowledge all her suffering—then how could she remain cold to him?

"He needs to be free," she told Dollie. "He needs to be free as you and I need to be rooted in the ground. It is his deepest belief—that man is a being who strives to be free. He is convinced that all social progress lies in the emancipation of mind and body."

"Isn't it what you and I believe as well?"

"I'm no longer sure what I believe. I think that human beings need to form permanent ties. I know that I need to be able to hold someone in my arms, and to be held. To me the thought of freedom without love is like a bottomless pit. It would be the tyranny of self. I'm not strong enough to live without love."

"Do you think Edward can live without love?"

"Very easily. He's not a loving person, Dollie. He can love or not, it doesn't matter to him very much one way or the other. It's not a central part of his nature."

"Then why is it so important to him to—"

"To have other women? That's pleasure, it has nothing to do with love. His pleasure is very important to him. He's like a child; he sees no reason why he can't take what he wants."

"I wish you had never set eyes on him!"

"Don't say that, Dollie, not if you love me."

"What kind of life can you have with a man whom you know to be unloving, childish, irresponsible . . . ?"

"Why, the best kind of life I can hope for. You don't seem to realize that Edward wants to stay. He insists on it. It's his decision, not mine. For one thing, he doesn't have the money to set up on his own. He's in debt; he can't possibly manage without me."

"You're surely not going to pay his debts!"

"I most certainly am. I can hardly leave him to borrow or beg, or worse."

"Whatever do you mean, 'worse'?"

"I'm trying to be realistic. It's not easy for me, Dollie. Don't ask me to explain."

"Is there something you haven't told me?"

"Nothing . . . nothing that I know of for certain. But it may be that Edward needs me as much as I need him."

While Edward continued to be cooperative, Tussy thought it might be a good idea to itemize their resources, so that they could rationalize their income and expenditures.

Her income broke down into teaching (about fifteen hours a week at two and six an hour), translation (five pounds for each commission), and "hacking," mainly for Miss Zimmern.

(What exactly did she do for Miss Zimmern? Her letters mention serving as a *préer*, that is, summarizing sources, and writing reviews on assignment, presumably splitting the fee with the signatory. The catalogues of the British Museum—the same heavy volumes, with handwritten entries, that Tussy used for her "research" a century ago—reveal that one Helen Zimmern, occasionally in collaboration with her sister Alice and others unnamed, produced over twenty-five volumes between 1877 and 1894, including the lives and works of the German philosophers Schopenhauer and Lessing, translations from the Edda, and short stories translated from Norwegian, German, and Italian. Presumably Tussy had a hand in some or most of these works; she received five shillings for every thirty paid to Miss Zimmern.)

Edward's income was harder to itemize. His teaching was erratic, a great rush when the London matriculation exams came up, falling off afterward; he had several science textbooks commissioned, at seven or eight pounds each; he reviewed regularly for the *Drama Review*, at five shillings for a review; his plays occasionally brought in some funds.

Edward's resources were complicated by the fact that some of his work was commissioned in advance, some paid for on completion, and his plays usually required some investment beforehand. The truth was that all his income as it materialized had already been paid out or promised; he lived on what he borrowed. Tussy usually had some cash on hand, since she spent only what she earned. The problem, she knew, was to prevent her small income from being swallowed up in Edward's debts. They agreed, as a sensible precaution, to keep their accounts entirely separate.

Edward's financial affairs were further obscured by the fact that he was treasurer of several organizations with overlapping directorates. Since the kindly William Morris made good any deficit of the Socialist League or other groups in which he played an active role, it was always possible to "borrow" small sums from the petty cash. And, since Edward's expenses were often incurred while he was engaged in unremunerated political work, it seemed reasonable to draw on the petty cash funds of one organization or another, if he spread out his indebtedness.

This side of Edward's life he decided to spare Tussy, as her puritan sense of accountability would undoubtedly disapprove.

11

She saw Havelock Ellis one day at the Museum, his straw-colored hair glinting orange in the light that filtered through the high domed window of the reading room. They had tea together and he told her about a remarkable woman whom he was hoping to marry.

"Of course, like many women of genius, she can't tolerate nervous excitation. It shall fall to me to smooth her way."

"Will you have the time?" Tussy asked. "You have so many other commitments."

"It shall be my vocation to study her needs. Her gifts are so far superior to mine that there can't be any question of apportioning time. Besides, you know that I have a good deal of the feminine in my nature. I find it easy and natural to serve."

"Has she enough of the masculine in her nature to enjoy being served?"

"She seems to me wholly womanly. But there are those who consider her—well, mannish. She dresses in a way that could be construed as mannish."

"I wish you well in your adventure, Havelock."

"Thank you, Tussy. It hasn't been an easy decision for me. Marriage has never presented itself to me as the ideal arrangement for someone of my temperament. I'm naturally lazy and disorganized, and work only under extreme pressure. My needs are few; I have no taste for luxury. It doesn't seem quite right to ask someone to share the kind of ascetic, irregular life I prefer.

Yet we all seem to pair off, eventually. The world goes by twos, for better or worse."

"So it seems . . . Do you think Olive had any case at all for her dream of a sisterhood?"

"You see how long it lasted! Olive has a passionate sexual nature—it was absurd for her to renounce men. Her reaction was predictable; she married a sober bourgeois pillar of the community, a frontiersman, by God! It would make more sense in a way for me to remain single, as I have far less energy than Olive, and I find sexual relations extremely enervating. They hardly leave one time to think, let alone to carry out serious work."

They talked for an hour, until their talk became desultory. Tussy found it impossible to say, as she would have said a year ago, "Come along for a meal"; or "Why don't we meet next week?" He didn't ask about Edward; he didn't ask Tussy about herself. He probably felt it pointless to ask in the conventional way; and he simply did not have the time for true intimacy. Tussy's troubles were boundless, appalling; he knew it without asking. His own life absorbed him utterly, at the moment.

She doubted whether she would see him again.

The Museum became a sanctuary, the Museum tearoom the only place where she could breathe freely, laugh, return to the easy comradeship of her youth.

Bernard accused her of working as hard as he did.

"You're a prisoner of the work ethos, Tussy. Don't you see, you're as bound to your wheel as your uneducated sister is to her oaf of a husband and thirteen squalling brats. You obey the secular commandment *Thou shalt work* as blindly as a cart horse towing a barge along the canal, that can't see the barge it pulls and knows nothing of its destination or purpose, only feels the tug of the rope and the prod of the stick wielded by the equally ignorant boy who walks alongside."

"That's unjust, Bernard. If I felt my work had no social pupose I'd give it up and do something else."

"Something equally fruitless and underpaid, I imagine."

"I think it's rather presumptuous for people like us to complain of working too hard or of achieving too little. We complain from a position of immense privilege, you and I. We know nothing of the grinding misery of the true workers. Clementina and I went to visit a family in Hackney—ah, Bernard, I can't describe the horror of it. A woman lying naked on a pile of straw, barely covered by a dirty shawl, a baby at her breast who looked more like a wizened old man than an infant, five children sitting about apathetically, their eyes dull, their bellies distended. The eldest, a girl of seven, made a pitiful effort to neaten the room for our visit. The husband is a docker and can't get work, a respectable man, with no fight left in him, no will, no hope. What they live on I can't imagine—the rotten greens and worm-eaten potatoes the children beg from the costermongers, half a loaf of stale bread, the gift of an equally destitute neighbor, for these people share the little they have. . . . Oh, we know nothing of the real misery of life."

"If we knew enough of the real misery of life we'd be no use to anyone. Why don't you come to Victoria Park on Sunday? We had over three thousand last week."

"Perhaps I'll come and listen to you."

"Come and talk. Talk to your sisters in Hackney, a woman speaking to other women. Tell them they have nothing to lose. If Annie Besant can preach to the converted—"

"I doubt that the miserable creatures I've seen starving in one room go to Victoria Park on a Sunday."

"Perhaps not. But the word spreads. It's their only hope."

"Do you think my suffering family in Hackney will be helped by your preaching?"

"That particular family, and others like them, may have to be sacrificed. If you save them now—and possibly they can be saved, at a cost—then you jeopardize our only chance of changing their conditions of life. The meek have always had more to gain from religion than from politics."

"Better for them to die, you mean."

"What have they to live for? Yes, better for them to die, and for others to witness and publicize their deaths. Better for their heads to be borne aloft by the mob in their vengeance. Better for the people to be roused from their stupor."

"Perhaps I'll come on Sunday. But I won't say what you want me to say. I'll say we must do both; we must save the starving children, and we must become our own masters. Not a child shall die that we may liberate our souls, but the fat, sleek horses of the rich, the bought women in their furs and diamonds, these shall be sacrificed; the bankers and mill owners and bishops, the governors of charitable foundations and their ladies' committees, these shall fall in their pride and complacency."

"Bravo, Tussy . . . your father's daughter!"

She went to Victoria Park on the following Sunday. She spoke for ten minutes, was applauded for fifteen, was hugged by red-faced women of immense girth and stature, fed cups of tea by withered crones with beetle eyes, she was pulled and plucked at by ragged urchins who wanted to touch the lady who was the daughter of the man who had promised them the world. She plunged into work in the East End, took her translating to the library of the People's Palace on Mile End Road, a small-scale but exact imitation of the great reading room of the British Museum. She gave free English lessons to immigrants, and lectured to attentive evening meetings on the New Unionism, the ten-hour day, the lung disease that ravaged the match girls of Bryant and May's.

Among the poor of the East End she found herself drawn with a curious mix of attraction and repulsion to the Jews, who alone of all those swarming thousands seemed able to survive as an identifiable group. In the meanest Jewish home, one of the miserable scrawny children would be singled out as the family scholar, and everyone else, parents, brothers, sisters, willingly sacrificed to send him to the *melamed,* the local teacher of Torah. Behind this passion for the one chosen son lay an instinct for group preservation, a recognition that the essence of human activity is not physical but mental and spiritual. If one child could be saved to study Torah, then all members of the family shared vicariously in a common life extending back as far as history, forward as far as the imagination could conceive.

Inevitably, the question would arise on her third or fourth visit—a secret twinkle in the eye, the pressure of a warm sweating hand on her cool dry one—"And you, Liebchen, you're one of us, no?"

At first she denied kinship. But as the scene, touching or amusing at first, irritating later on, was repeated in as many variations as there are modes of human recognition, Tussy became convinced, *yes, she was one of them,* a throwback to her rabbinical

96

ancestors on her father's side, those Trier scholars disowned by her father's father for prudential reasons, scorned by her father for ideological reasons. She studied her face in the pier glass—strong, prominent features, more character than beauty or charm, the nose assertive, definitely long, a Semitic nose without doubt; the eyes dark, lustrous, set too close together, the heavy brows almost meeting; her thick dark curling hair a giveaway. . . . Yes, she was a daughter of Abraham. The secret blood denied by the male was carried in defiance by the female, and she would give it recognition.

She asked discreetly among her friends; Clementina confessed that she had never been claimed as "one of us," though she was welcomed effusively and treated (to her embarrassment) with the deference befitting a great lady. So the poor, ignorant Jews of Whitechapel knew; they had recognized something deep in Tussy's nature which was obscure to her intellectual friends. They knew her out of an intuitive knowledge that transcended language, nationality, class, sex. They were true democrats, these Jews, despite their unctuous deference, their submissiveness, the touching of the cap. The long-suffering acceptance of their condition as the most scorned of outcasts was merely an act, designed to placate the thick-witted but powerful philistines among whom they found themselves. It never touched their secret pride, their ambition for their children, their contempt for the second-rate. Almost against her will she came to feel very much at home with them. Though she had full intended to help them change their lives, to educate and organize, increasingly it was they who served her. They offered her an education in singular contrast to that materialist ethos in which she had been reared, and which Edward embodied in thought and deed.

Without her full awareness or consent, her sympathy with the Jews spilled over to affect her sense of her mock marriage. As she became more and more "Jewish," she came to see her relationship to Edward as a discipline of the soul, an obscure test of faith, of love. The Jews expected no reward in this life or the next; their faith in their stern God was an act of will, a voluntary acceptance of a solemn compact whose origin was only a dim tribal memory. Let God turn a stony face to their prayers, let him rain down plague and pestilence, their faith altered not a jot, even to the sacrifice of the first-born. In human

affairs they reserved the right to act according to their conscience, to judge good and evil. Yet in a deeper sense they accepted suffering; life, they knew, was an ordeal, a trial which
they were fully prepared to endure without question. And
Tussy, hating suffering, ready to fight against injustice, found
in herself an unsuspected strength to endure.

Yet it occurred to her, in her weariness, that her ordeal was
by no means necessary. From one point of view, she had been
cursed in meeting Aveling; he was a man diseased, rotted by a
sickness of the soul. Had she loved any other man—and in this
city of two millions, even among the hundreds who formed
her acquaintance, it would have been possible, surely, to love
one other—she might have had a happy, fruitful life, instead
of this dreary slogging on, day after day, joyless, loveless, solitary.
What the outcome of her trial might be, what benefit it might
eventually yield to Edward or herself, was anybody's guess.

Through her half-drugged sleep she heard the door open, and
slam shut. She heard him stumble through the sitting room,
knocking against a table in his progress to the bedroom. In the
dead stillness of the early morning she heard him remove his
clothes, draping them clumsily over a chair. He urinated into
the chamber pot, a loud, long stream, dribbling off, then another
last short trickle.

She lay on her side of the bed, turned away from him, her
knees pulled up toward her chest, her bare arm covering her
face. Drink made Edward amorous, seldom incapable. Wherever
he might have been earlier in the night, he liked to finish off
in her, and through her heavy sleep she considered turning toward him, to get it over with. Her body, inert, still yearning
to sleep, refused to obey her waking mind, and she stayed as
she was when he fell into bed beside her.

With a delicacy strange and touching in someone drunk he
lifted her cotton nightdress to her waist, freeing it gently underneath her. He lay with his face on her buttocks, and caressed
her between her legs, stroking her rhythmically. He never spoke
to her when he caressed her; she heard instead monitory voices:
there's hell, there's darkness, there's the sulphurous pit . . . In spite
of herself she burned, clamped herself on his fingers, rode his
hand like a hobby horse. With his thumb he pressed her anus,

rubbed it, entered it painfully. She tried to turn toward him, but found herself held as in a vise between his knees, powerless to move, his hands now gripping her waist, pressing her down, his penis sweeping along her cleft, hardening, pressing each time more forcefully at her, penetrating her fractionally, then entering her from behind with a slow pressure unbearable to her, stretching her in a slow rotary motion until she could receive him, pumping to reach more deeply while she was held immobile, speared, until she heard her breath issuing in a scream that was like the scream of childbirth, and it was over, and he rolled away from her, already asleep, to judge from his breathing.

"Did you mind," he asked the next morning, or rather afternoon, as it was almost one when he rose, and she had already been out at work for three hours. "Are you very sore?"

"It's bestial," she said. "You are bestial."

"I thought you might like a touch of variety. I assure you it's only painful the first time. Like most things."

"There won't be a second time."

"Well, if you won't there are others who will. No doubt it's a special taste. You can pass it on to your friend, Dr. Ellis. Or is he only interested in urinary pleasures?"

"I have no idea what he's interested in."

"That's not so, Tussy, my love. Your indiscreet friend Miss Schreiner told you all about it, in strictest confidence. I remember, if you don't. Your lover of nature, your worshiper of female beauty and intellect, asks his ladies to urinate in front of him, or on him, perhaps, preferably out of doors, while he muses on mountain streams and waterfalls. I remember it very well because it struck me as quaint at the time."

"Olive is right. Men degrade us. The best of them. The worst of them."

"No more than men degrade themselves. We drag you down, you pull us up. We're in it together either way. No damage done—I've not injured you, have I, now? Truthfully?"

"I would not mind anything you did to me for love. What you did to me had no love in it."

"It's a word, Tussy."

"Not for me."

"You delude yourself. It's a word as *God* is a word. As *good*

99

and *evil* are words. Useful words to those in power, false comfort to those in need. No more than words to those who know better."

"What if I am one of those in need? What better comfort can I find?"

"You know what I have to offer. You don't seem to like it very much."

"I loathe it."

"Then find someone with more agreeable manners. I won't offend you in that way again, I promise. Or in any other."

12

He was gone the next morning. It was the first time since her suicide attempt that he had left without giving an address.

It would have been a good time for taking stock, but the day after he left she was called to Regents Park Road. Nim was ill. She lay in bed, her face to the wall; she refused to tell the General what was wrong. When Tussy arrived, her son Freddy was sitting with her, twisting a bit of string in his hands, his face a mask of fear.

"What is it?"

"She won't say. She's like an animal that knows its time is near."

"You don't have to whisper," Nim said. "I'm not deaf."

"What's troubling you, darling? What's wrong?" Tussy said. She leaned over the bed and smoothed the damp gray hairs on Nim's forehead. The old woman's eyes were half closed, and her skin had an unhealthy yellowish tinge.

"Send him away."

"You'd better go, Freddy."

"I'll wait outside," he said miserably. "I'm no use to her."

"Now tell me, Nim dear."

She stared straight ahead of her. "I've started bleeding again. Between my legs."

"When did it start?"

"A week ago."

"Oh, Nim darling, why didn't you tell the General? Why didn't you tell Freddy?"

"I'm ashamed, Tussy. At my age."

"You should be ashamed, not telling anyone. I'll ask the General to call Dr. Donkin."

"I won't have a doctor. I won't have a man poking about inside me."

"Nonsense—you'll have the best medical attention in London."

"It's no use, Tussy. *He* knows. He knew as soon as he came in that door. I saw it in his face. No need to talk about it."

"Don't say such things, Nim. Don't frighten me so. Dr. Donkin will have you up and about in no time."

Her voice had a false edge of confidence; she really was frightened. It was seven years since Mohr had died. Imperceptibly she had relaxed her guard; in the last year she had been wholly absorbed in her own misery. She had forgotten the rules; one had to be eternally vigilant.

Nim spoke slowly, breathing hoarsely between the words. "You'll take care of him, Tussy. He's a good boy. But he needs someone to look after him."

"Of course I'll look after him, Don't fret, darling. We'll look after each other, Freddy and I."

When the doctor came, the old woman, true to her word, refused to allow him to examine her. She had pain in the left groin, and Donkin told the General he suspected a uterine tumor. She complained of insatiable thirst.

"She can sit up for an hour if she feels strong enough," Donkin told Freddy. "Don't let her give up."

"She'll hang on," Freddy said. "You don't know her. She's tough as nails."

But she turned her face to the wall and refused to speak to anyone. To Tussy it seemed that she was offering her prone body to the slow poisons that had invaded it, while she withdrew as far from the scene of her agony as she could, deep inside to some sheltered place where she could be alone, remote from her pain, from their fear.

During the days that followed, Tussy spent as much time as she could at Regents Park Road. Freddy was there every day, leaving at night to work the midnight shift at a tool-fitting plant in Hackney. He was always the same, gentle, self-effacing, stoical. What was his life like? Though she had seen him once or twice a month for eight years, since her mother's death, Tussy had never been to his home. She was not even sure where he lived, or with whom.

"Where are you living now, Freddy?"

"I've got myself a room on Bishop's Place, off the Caledonian Road. One of the lads has a room there, and we share a basin and a cooker. Four shillings a week, and I can have little Freddy with me on the weekends. *She's* agreed to that."

"She lets you see him, then."

"Oh, it suits her; she has a gentleman friend weekends. I wouldn't be surprised if she let me have the boy during the week as well. I could manage, being home days."

"But you want a proper flat, with some privacy."

Why did he expect so little? To Tussy he seemed beaten down, hopeless; she couldn't understand his passiveness. He didn't have an ounce of bitterness or anger in him—and such good reason for bitterness, so much cause for anger.

The General was not his father, she knew. Which of the dozens of refugees who had passed through Dean Street had it been? For Nim it was ancient history; she had finished with it once and for all thirty-five years ago. A "fall"—a single lapse—and the hapless consequences: the swelling belly, the stern disapproval of the lady of the house, dear Mohme, incapable of taking a light view of these matters. The child must be boarded out, his name not to be mentioned henceforth, the incident closed. The General paid, of course, as he paid for every disaster that threatened their family. And for Nim, stolen visits to Hackney, annual small presents from Mohr and the General, a conspiracy of silence. Mohme's children she loved, while her own child was the object of continual anxiety.

Even now, Freddy's very presence irritated her, his hangdog apologetic look, his clumsiness, his slowness. It was Tussy she wanted close at hand.

One warm October afternoon, when Nim seemed to be resting comfortably, Tussy walked with Freddy across the road and to the top of Primrose Hill. Yellowing leaves from a giant sycamore drifted past them.

"You never saw our old house," Tussy said. "We used to walk here and back two or three times a week; up Regents Park Road, across the railway bridge, two minutes' walk up Haverstock

Hill, and we'd be home. . . . I can remember racing across the bridge, bursting with a piece of news for Mama, an urgent message for Mohr. . . . Sometimes it's all very clear to me, and at other times it fades or alters. . . . I have to recreate it or it vanishes altogether."

They sat down on the wrought-iron bench where, on a similar afternoon seven years before, Tussy had told the General that she had met the man whose life was henceforth to be united to hers.

"There's nothing in my past I'd want to hang on to; it could all vanish like those leaves, as far as I'm concerned," Freddy said. "Except for Nim and the General, and you and Laura, and my boy."

"We should have been there more of the time. For you, I mean."

"No, you wouldn't have wanted to know me back then; you wouldn't have had much to say to a lad like me."

"Oh, Freddy, if you knew how I hate the things that divide us! Your life could have been so different—it could have been anything you wanted it to be."

"No, Tussy, you mustn't think my life could have been very different. You mustn't blame yourself for anything that's gone wrong for me. I'm not that badly off; I've got my boy, and regular work, and a roof over my head. There are many who are worse off than I am. Oh, I'd be the first to admit it's lonely living by myself. But I'd rather live alone than have the fighting and lying, the cheating on the side, and see my boy torn to pieces. . . ."

"I doubt whether I could live alone. Even to end the fighting and the lying . . ."

"It's different for you and Edward. I know you have your ups and downs, but you can talk about whatever's wrong, you can work it out between you."

"Edward and I don't talk much these days. . . . Oh, Freddy, I haven't told a soul, but he's been gone for a week, and *I don't know where he is!*"

"But he must be at the miners' conference in Ayrshire . . . didn't he tell you?"

"I suppose that's where he is, but no, he didn't tell me, not in so many words."

"It's a bad time for him, Tussy." He hesitated. "Maybe I shouldn't be the one to say it, but he keeps things from you. It might be better for you to know."

"What sorts of things? He hasn't—oh, Freddy, he hasn't tried to borrow from you?"

"Not from me."

It dawned on her suddenly. "Oh God—not from Nim, surely?"

"Only as a loan, until Christmas."

"She didn't give in to him, did she?" She was trembling with rage. Nim's small savings, that were all she had after years of patient scraping and scrimping. They had been given freely a hundred times over to Mohr and Mohme; what she had carefully set aside for the last few years was meant for Freddy.

"I think she sent him to the General. If she gave him anything it wasn't much. You know she'd do anything for you and Edward."

"It wasn't for me, I assure you. Edward has far better things to spend other people's money on. I beg you, Freddy, find out how much it was. I'll pay it back, every shilling of it. Oh, I feel fouled, shamed . . . to have my dear Nim abused!"

"I should never have told you, Tussy; she made me swear not to. I thought it would ease your mind to know. He must have been in a spot, with nobody else to turn to."

"No, you don't know him, Freddy. He borrows a few pounds here, a few pounds there, conveniently forgets about the smaller debts unless he's reminded, then postpones repaying them until he's reminded again. Most people give up eventually. They're embarrassed to keep dunning him. The list is infinitely expandable, but he must have met two or three refusals. You don't know how often the General has come through. He thinks Edward is like himself, someone who likes good food and drink and women, and sometimes overdoes things out of *joie de vivre*. But he's wrong, Edward isn't like him at all. The General is genuinely pleasure-loving, and his kindliness overflows onto others, he wants everyone to drink and be merry. But with Edward it's not pleasure; it's like a disease. There's a calculatedness about his pleasure, and a self-hatred. . . . Don't try to stop me, Freddy, why shouldn't I tell you the truth? You are utterly truthful with me, why should I hide anything from you? Why should you think that Edward is decent, or humane, or honorable? He's not decent, humane, or honorable, and he despises people who are; he thinks they're fools. Perhaps he's right; perhaps it's foolish to hope that people can be moved by anything other than greed and lust. Edward respects one virtue, which he calls honesty, but it's not what you or I would recognize as honesty. It consists of stripping every illusion, every last shred of dignity, from those who have nothing else to sustain them; it's a brutal honesty that stops at nothing to get its way, that erects Self into a religious principle and says, This God and no other will I serve. He's a devoted man, my Edward, as fanatical as any Jesuit, and as crafty and unscrupulous. But he could have spared Nim—he could have spared me that humiliation."

Freddy patted her clumsily on the shoulder.

"Come, I'll take you back. You're not yourself, Tussy. You're upset, worn out . . . you need to rest. You don't mean what you're saying."

"Oh God, Freddy, you'll make me weep . . . all it takes is a kind word. See what you're doing to me, in public, too."

She allowed herself to sob, hiding her face against his chest, while he held her awkwardly, and looked sternly at two children rolling a hoop through the wet leaves.

They rose finally and made their way slowly down the hill, Tussy leaning on Freddy's arm. She neither confirmed nor denied what she had said earlier; he was free to think what he liked. He took her confidence as a solemn trust, a bond to be honored henceforth; when she needed him, he would be there for her.

On their return, the General called Tussy into his study.

"You see how I am surrounded." he said, gesturing toward the papers piled on desk, bookshelves, floor. "In this box are Lassalle's letters to Mohr, which I have promised to edit for Dietz Verlag; here in this carton are my notes for the history of the International; most important, in these boxes are Mohr's manuscripts for volume three, with my attempt to decipher them. On top of which, the doctor as you know has forbidden me to read or write by gaslight, and I must agree with him that it is necessary for me to conserve my eyesight. Now, my dear girl, what am I to do? If I could split myself in two, and be the Engels of forty and the Engels of thirty, I would still have work for two good lifetimes. The question is: Can you and Edward undertake responsibility for some small portion of this colossal task?"

"You know I'll do what I can," Tussy said. "I can't speak for Edward."

He looked at her shrewdly. "I think you can, my dear. Edward will do what you say, and more. I'll ask him myself, of course. I don't question his willingness, only his proficiency at German."

"Oh, he's proficient enough."

"Then, if there are two of you, and you can give me two mornings a week, perhaps we can make a dent in this Everest."

How could she hint to him that there were difficulties that had nothing to do with proficiency in German? If the General, with his experience of men and women, couldn't see that her life was in a shambles . . . or perhaps he saw, and had decided that her problems were trivial, surmountable, not worth serious discussion.

She said that she would begin copying as soon as she finished her translation from the Edda for Miss Zimmern.

He sighed and shifted to a more comfortable position. He didn't look well, Tussy thought; his skin, always sallow, was drawn, and drained of color; though his eyes had their usual kindly gleam, he looked tired.

"If it were copying alone . . . You see, my dear, Mohr did not finish one subject and go on to the next. No, he went backwards, sidewards, he found it impossible to resist the tempting digression. Instead of proceeding sensibly with volumes two, three, and four, I should be revising volume one for publication in four parallel columns, with Mohr's qualifications, footnotes, afterthoughts set out against every paragraph of the published text."

"How can I be of most use to you?"

"Perhaps I can give you some of the Lassalle correspondence to copy. There is the matter of notes and a tactful preface. Old quarrels set down for posterity have a certain parochial flavor . . . But what fire we had in those days! Every sentence blazes with conviction."

"Surely we know more now."

"Ah, we know less, if anything. Events happened so rapidly then, and of course in exile we had perspective, we could see

107

the sweep of history in one European country after another. Now progress is very slow, and we must be patient. . . . It becomes very difficult to see beyond the immediate pressure of local issues. Paul's election, for instance, which is of immense importance to Paul and Laura, but in the long run, I'm afraid, of little consequence."

"How unfair that it all rests on your shoulders! You've always been so good, so uncomplaining."

"I have no choice; there is no one else. Having conducted a lifelong dialogue with Mohr, I am fairly confident that I can follow his thinking. Unfortunately much of what he left is raw data, jottings from obscure historical sources of dubious accuracy. . . . Don't misunderstand, Tussy, I'm not complaining now. I simply want you to know what the difficulties are. Sooner or later I am going to have to pass the work on. You and Edward are closest to me, and closest to Mohr; it is only proper that you should know what is involved."

"It makes our work in Whitechapel seem trifling."

"Mohr believed that theory and practical work must proceed together. The practical work may seem slow and unrewarding, but it's necessary work, Tussy—never forget that."

If it was necessary work—which she doubted—did it therefore validate her life, and her life with Edward? It occurred to her that the General, talking with such frankness about his difficulties, was trying to tell her something which his delicacy forbade making more explicit. How much did he know? Sly old codger, he knew more than he let on; he knew whatever there was to know.

"Even if you see no results, Tussy, even if we seem to be moving backward rather than forward, remember that you are teaching the poor and the oppressed that progress is possible. I'm convinced we shall see changes beyond our wildest hopes, in your lifetime if not in mine. Twenty-five years from now Europe is going to be turned upside down, Tussy, and you and Edward will have played your small part in making that new Europe possible."

One morning the General presented her with a small box neatly tied with pale blue ribbon.

"You might like to have these," he said.

They were her sister Jenny's letters to Mohr, written when she moved to Paris with Longuet after amnesty had been granted to the Communards.

Tussy read them over, grieving for her dead sister as if the ink on the letters were fresh. Though she had visited Jenny in Argenteuil, she had seen her as a child does, who assumes that all is as it ought to be. She was now the age Jenny had been when she wrote the letters, and she understood for the first time the full cruelty of her wasted gifts.

"I cannot get used to this separation," Jenny had written her father—not a child torn from her father's bosom but a grown woman of thirty, happily married, knowing perfectly well that it is a daughter's lot to leave her parents' house and to go with her husband.

Indeed, it was her mother who counseled her to leave, for the sake of her husband and the children she would later bear him. And the daughter, obedient like all good daughters to her mother's instructions, wrenched herself from parents, sisters, friends, country, traveled with her husband to his native home, to his own anxiously waiting mother, and watched outraged as he submitted to his mother's indulgent control. In the bitterness of exile, she began to breed. Contemptuous of her husband, she focused her love, her frustrated ambitions, her ever-present anxiety about her aging, ill parents on each infant as she nursed it into life. Her husband was of no interest to her unless he was suddenly taken ill; then her early love flooded back, she was tenderness itself for a day or two, until the crisis passed. At night he took her in the dark, sucking at her nipples, rooting in her loins, as eager and mindless as a dog mounting a bitch; he couldn't leave her alone.

Jenny, in thrall to her babies, burned to be released. Unable to read a book, her life consumed by household chores from dawn until midnight, she imagined a single hour—a pure space all her own—in which she might once again be a serious, thinking human being.

But she had acquired the terrible habit of self-denial. The first denial presented itself as a necessary compromise: she denied herself time for selfish pursuits like reading and writing, useless activities which mattered to no one but herself. If there was a minute to read, it must be used for proofreading Longuet's new journal; a moment to write and it must be snatched for a letter home. Then, when her dear mother lay ill, dying of cancer, her instinctive reaction—I must fly to her immediately—on reflection seemed selfish; her duty lay with her babies. And so she denied the passionate longing of her heart. She could not leave her brood; certainly not with Longuet, and Madame Longuet volunteered to help in a way which made it impossible to accept. The servants were impossible; not for a minute could she imagine trusting them with her little ones. She was the only one who understood them, who could manage them—Johnny's tantrums, poor Harra's asthma. How could she possibly abandon them to Longuet's absentmindedness, the servants' incompetence, Madame Longuet's cold efficiency? Oh, she might release Johnny to his father for a day's outing, or send Harra to Madame Longuet for dinner. But she must be with them at night and when they woke in the morning; she must ensure that they had at all times the proper mixture of indulgent love and firm control; she must see that Harra was not agitated, Johnny not allowed his own way.

For there was no reason for her to dream that she would be taken from them without warning, and that they would be in the care of others not for a night or a week but for the rest of their lives.

Adoring her brood of infants, wholly absorbed in their growing pains, their illnesses, exhausted by their ceaseless demands for attention and care, she had one word of advice to the sister twelve years her junior, whose life was still her own.

Don't allow yourself to fall into the woman's trap, as I did. Fight to be free. Be yourself; live for yourself.

Leave him, leave him, sang the bells of St. Margaret's. *Stay and work, stay and work,* rumbled the new rolling stock of the Great Northern. Surely the General was right, their joint labors justified their lives together. Amatory squabbles were temporary and insignificant, political education a contribution, however small, to historical progress and the liberation of the masses.

Yet her friends were also right; she must break free or life was not worth living.

Why was it so difficult to break free? They were not legally bound; she was self-supporting; she had friends, comrades. And now she knew that in Freddy she had a last refuge; she need not be alone.

Why then could she not make a clean break, remove herself from Aveling's presence, start fresh as if he had never existed?

She forced herself, while he was gone, to consider coldly, clinically, the possibility of doing just that.

The first truth she had to face was that the decision was hers, and hers alone. If she removed herself, and all trace of her life, from their rooms on Great Russell Street, he would make no effort to bring about a reconciliation. And, in spite of the General's flattering references to their common work, their working lives were now so distinct that each could carry on undisturbed without the other. If Edward's political work threatened to impinge on hers, he would, she suspected, have little hesitation in abandoning it for more amusing or profitable ventures.

She tried to imagine him returning to rooms emptied of all sign of her existence, her books, clothes, pictures. . . . Would he feel regret? guilt? More likely, relief that the break had been made cleanly, with dignity, by her choice rather than his. No doubt he would briskly set to work to make his life comfortable, to close any gaps her absence left. Probably he would install his current lover to keep his bed warm and his house neat.

Even as she considered his probable response, she saw the difficulty. She could not prevent herself from following him in imagination, jealous, possessive, critical. She was still in thrall to him. Though she might remove herself physically, she was as bound to him as ever.

It was far better to free herself in spirit, which she could only do by staying, by confronting him with her existence, her love.

Edward came back a reformed man. He embraced Tussy as if there had been no quarrel, no unforgivable exchange; attended dutifully on Nim, and remained closeted for hours with the General.

Why did she brood continually on the past? She was mistaken, she was inventing it all; Edward's blithe good-humor was a demonstration of her pettiness in resurrecting old quarrels. He had forgotten; therefore what she remembered with such bitterness had never occurred.

111

They made up a schedule for the next few months: party meetings in Brussels and Frankfurt; a week in Paris with Paul and Laura; regional labor conferences in the Midlands and Lancashire; possibly a second American trip in six months. Edward was efficient, enthusiastic; he contemplated entering as a candidate for a by-election in Hornsby.

In bed he wooed her tactfully, with the considerateness of a bridegroom for his virgin bride. He held her to his chest, stroked her hair, and talked to her in a voice she hardly recognized:

"Shall we start over, Tussy? Shall we show them that it's possible to start over? They think we're finished, intellectually bankrupt, but we can prove that they're wrong, we can force them to swallow their words.

"Do you remember how we knocked them out at the beginning? Fire and ice, the two of us . . . I was the only one who knew you were trembling, your knee shaking like a leaf.

"We can't give up, you and I. Not now, not when we're needed more than ever before. The funny thing is, we're irreplaceable. We're not much use separately, but as a team we're terrific, we fit hand and glove."

And, to prove his point, rode her until she felt her hard resistance splinter into a million shards, and she was one with him, as she had been at the start, and as she would continue to be as long as her body clung to his with the tenacity of instinct overriding intellect, common sense, and such pride as remained to her.

At the same time, Edward's financial embarrassment seemed to have resolved itself. That is, he had enough money to cover his expenses, with something left over for occasional presents— preposterous presents: hothouse flowers, exotic blooms; champagne.

There were things Tussy preferred not to know about. Still, it took all her ingenuity to avoid drawing connections between Edward's relative prosperity and his solicitude, between his tenderness to her and his weekly visits to the General. It was clear to her that the General chose that they should remain together, for the sake of the movement, and for her sake as well, she supposed. He had decided that she wanted or needed Edward to stay. Once he had decided upon a course of action, the General took all measures necessary to assure its success.

He knew the value and use of money, exactly how much was needed to buy things or persons, to bring about a desired end. He was certainly prepared to pay. And, though Tussy tried not to think about it, the only question she had, really, was how much she had cost him.

13

Olive returned from South Africa alone. She took two mean rooms in Middleton Buildings, hundred-year-old tenements facing onto a dark, narrow court between Foley and Riding House streets, not far from Oxford Circus. She would stay for three months, she said, perhaps longer. She thought she might train as a midwife at Middlesex Hospital, the grim turrets of which were visible from her window.

"It hasn't been a success," she told Tussy. "He's a very good man, kind, considerate, attentive to my every wish. But I make his life miserable. He can't understand what's wrong. He planned everything so carefully."

"Your letters sounded so happy," Tussy said.

"Marriage doesn't suit everyone. I found it very difficult to be with another person continuously, to have to consider his needs before mine, to talk to him when I would rather read a book. I was totally unable to work. He had a studio built especially for me on the farm, a hundred yards from the main house, fitted up with bookshelves, a desk, comfortable chairs. I couldn't bear to enter it. When I saw how unhappy it made him, I forced myself to sit in the studio he had carefully designed for me, for hours on end, chained to the comfortable chair, my mind blank. I developed asthma; we had to give up the farm. It was like taking his life's work and tearing it into little bits."

"Perhaps you needed more time."

"You must understand that I loved him. I love him now, as

much as I can love any man. But if I can't work I'm no use to anyone."

"Shall you be able to work in London?"

"I won't know until I've tried. I may have destroyed whatever talent I had. The baby's death was very hard. Hard for me, even harder for Cron. I was unable to weep; in the end I was probably relieved. But he couldn't believe that it had happened, he was crazed with grief. And I knew there would never be another."

"He sounds like such an admirable human being," Tussy said.

"What I can't understand," Olive said, "is why I felt incomplete without the experience of marriage. That feeling of incompleteness doesn't pass with marriage; it's worse, if anything. I felt that I must split myself into half a dozen different persons. I think now that the experience of wholeness that we long for, and seek in another human being, is the rarest of gifts . . . perhaps only an illusion. We *are* incomplete, imperfect, solitary. That is our real condition, that we must learn to live with, and out of which we must create what happiness we can, for ourselves or others."

She had a shadow, a silent girl from the slums of the Minories, whom she picked up in the Berwick Street market one day, and who lived with her, attending to her bare needs. In the evenings she sat at Olive's feet, and Olive stroked her hair, and read to her from her *Dreams*.

May Morris too admitted to Tussy that her marriage was under a strain.

"I can't understand what it is about Harry. He is so talented, he has a fine, sensitive ear for poetry, he's genuinely artistic, but somehow he refuses to make anything of his gifts. He refuses to take the initiative. Papa has given him all kinds of work, and he's perfectly happy to do as he's told. But he can't seem to carry through any project on his own."

"I think it would be very hard for any man to satisfy your father's idea of a proper son-in-law for his darling May."

"It's true that he suffers terribly from Papa's temper. You know Papa is incapable of dissimulation. He really doesn't think much of Harry. And oh, Tussy, I fight against it, but I begin to feel more and more like my father's daughter. I become terribly impatient with Harry too. . . . Why does he have so little appetite for life?

"The truth is, I don't feel at all like 'Mrs. Sparling.' It isn't me at all."

"Give yourself time, May dear. You have to learn to 'acclimatize' yourself. There's nothing natural or simple about marriage, after all. It's a choice we make, that we must learn to live with. The fault can't be entirely on the other side."

Why she should want her friends to remain married was an oddity that puzzled nobody. Was she not a living demonstration of the instinct to hold fast?

There came a time when a single thought began to intrude itself and, having established uneasy residence, came to dominate her consciousness.

He's not worth it.

It has all been for nothing.

He's not worth it, was never worth it.

This thought was more dreadful to her than the knowledge of his philandering, and of his carelessness with other people's money.

She needed reassurance. She needed someone whom she trusted to say firmly, authoritatively: Whatever Edward's faults—and admitted, he has many and grave faults—he is, not necessarily a good man, or a great man, but a man worthy of respect.

There was the General, who could and did say to her: Edward means well; he tries very hard; he contributes what he can.

But the General saw too much, and what he said to Tussy was of limited help. If he considered Edward worthy of respect, it was because Tussy had chosen him.

There was Nim, who told Tussy that Edward could not help what he was, or alter his nature. This was no help at all to Tussy. Nim had a poor opinion altogether of men; in her eyes Edward was no different from most. They were big babies; they needed to be coddled, and cosseted, and fed. Mohr himself she had seen through; underneath his violent rages he had been as tender-hearted as a young girl, and as helpless to deal with the real business of life. To consider a man unworthy of love one

116

had to have very unrealistic expectations of the man, and a very high opinion of oneself. What did women live for if not to care for their men, and to make life more tolerable for them?

Olive might have argued against this rather old-fashioned view, but Tussy was reluctant to talk to her women friends about Edward. They had given up on him; on her as well, she sometimes thought. Dollie had a child and was expecting another; her life had become tediously infant-centered. Olive was strangely remote since she had returned; though she talked freely about her own life, she seldom asked about Tussy's.

With their political allies, it was essential to simulate complete confidence in Edward. With his theatrical colleagues she had nothing to do, except for Bernard, who had given his opinion once and did not like to repeat himself.

Still, she raised the subject indirectly; or rather, took advantage of an opening in Bernard's conversation.

"You people," he said—Europeans, he meant, or Jews—"can't see beyond your noses. For all your intelligence, or possibly because of your intelligence, you don't understand the first thing about this country. At the first hint of revolution, the English workers will rise as one man and fight to the death to defend their oppressors. Revolution is French and Jacobin, and your true red-blooded Englishman wants nothing to do with it. In fifty years England will be safely in the grip of a native socialism which is reformist and benign and utterly unlike the authentic thing."

"More's the pity," Tussy said.

"Possibly. But the point is that the English are now ready to accept reform, on a scale that amounts to revolutionary change. It's extremely important for us to get it right now; otherwise later generations will feel obliged to discover socialism for themselves, and who knows where that might lead us."

"You're abandoning us, then. Like everyone else."

"It's not I who abandon you. You're cutting yourself off from us. You refuse to recognize English realities. Your father understood them very well; he would have seen very clearly that the greatest industrial powers, that is, England and America, are moving not toward revolution but toward accommodation. Far from becoming polarized between rich and poor, both ends are leaning toward a vast amorphous middle, with ample resources to sustain life at the bottom and promote capitalist expansion at the top. We should be flexible enough to change our strategy. For the time being we withdraw from active agitation among the masses, and concentrate our resources, which are in the end our intellects, on analysis and education. Miss Black, who knows more than any of us about the actual conditions of the poor, sees very clearly what we must do—push for legislative reform, the election of Members, the recognition of unions."

"I admire Clementina's work as much as you do. But I don't believe that she's given up on the revolution, not for a minute."

"Ah, it's the same old story, Tussy—you cannot break the primary tie. Your father never hesitated to change his mind. His intellect was essentially analytic and critical, self-critical as well as critical of others. But you adhere rigidly to his last formulations, as if by relinquishing them or altering them you would be betraying his charge. Can't you see that the rigidity is in you, not in him? He would have wanted you to trust your own judgment. English capitalism has changed; you can't apply the analysis of forty years ago."

"Even if you were right—which I don't admit—I fail to see how my attachment to my father should affect Edward's political views."

"Oh, Edward's another case entirely. He likes system, and he's completely free of sentiment, so that there's no reason for him not to hold to a hard line. He has a peculiar brand of Marxism; it's quite original, really."

"Do you respect his thinking?"

"Not as an analysis of English society."

"Do you respect him as a scientist?"

"He's an excellent popularizer. Or was—he hasn't done anything substantial for some time."

Do you respect him as a human being?

This was not a question she could ask Bernard, for whom people were interesting or uninteresting by virtue of their talent and wit. Edward had been moderately interesting to him up to a year ago; now she suspected that that was no longer the case. He might be ticked away for future reference as a minor character in an "Unpleasant" play; but social relations, like political relations, were virtually finished.

118

Nim had given up. Her mind wandered; when she spoke it was in German, in a voice that belonged to her childhood. There were times when she failed to recognize Freddy; Tussy she always knew. The General looked in on her each morning, but did not stay.

She sat bolt upright once, and said in a querulous, childish, voice, "Ich muss nach Hause gehen," then fell back, exhausted.

Tussy, bathing her forehead tenderly, brooded about Nim's life. She had served Mohr and Mohme unquestioningly, nursed them in illness, shielded each from the other's temper, provided food, good cheer, and such elements of order and cleanliness as their complicated lives were susceptible to. Had she kept any corner of her life for herself? The question had never arisen.

Yet Mohr had always maintained that Helen, born to a different sphere of life, could have achieved anything she had set her mind to; she had intellectual and human gifts of the highest order.

Had she no regrets? no suspicion that her life might have been other than it was? She loved them; they were her family, and their love was her reward. But wasn't their love for her essentially self-centered? She gave them her life; they accepted her gift. It was hardly a fair exchange.

Not that human relations were ever democratic. But it would be quite wrong to use another human being, to accept her life as one's right, simply because she offered herself to be used.

Or perhaps there were no rights and wrongs in the closest relations, those of mother and child, husband and wife. There was no justice in love, no equality, no freedom of choice. A mother could not deny her child, though the child might deny its mother.

Tussy studied Nim's face, still beautiful in age, her broad forehead creased into a hundred lines, like fine china crazed by use, but retaining its original shape and strength, her hooded eyes half closed, her mouth partly open to ease her breathing. She had provided for each of them a warmth that was always there, to be counted on; and the child in Tussy still took comfort in her unfailing presence.

In the three-roomed flat on Dean Street, Soho, the two young women had divided the functions of family life: Mohme continually pregnant, often ill, in the grip of a life-consuming passion for the Jew who had wooed her, a German *haute bourgeoise*, for seven years; Helen competent, serene, infinitely ingenious at marketing and cooking for indefinite numbers of hungry mouths, dealing with irate tradesmen, nursing the crying infants, tending Mohme when she took to her bed with migraine headaches, soothing Mohr when his boils and carbuncles and weak kidneys made him irritable beyond endurance. Until a small fault briefly altered the pattern of their lives, creating a disturbance which must very soon have presented itself to each of them in the same light. ("Of one event that occurred that summer I shall not speak"—so wrote Mohme in her "Notes Toward an Autobiography"; nor did she speak of it in life, more than once, and then, Tussy guessed, very much to the point.) The child was registered, "father unknown," and soon afterward disappeared from their lives. Nor had Nim ever given a sign that she would have wished things to be arranged differently. Those she served came first; anything to do with her own life was secondary. Freddy was her problem; she would deal with him as she could.

Yet after Mohme's death he re-entered their lives, still very much in the background, quiet, ill at ease, but plainly occupying a space within the circle of Nim's love, along with Tussy, Laura, and Jenny's children. If there had been injustice done, neither he nor Nim seemed aware of it. Only Tussy was convinced that there had been a radical error. And because she was the only one who felt that a wrong had been done, she also felt in some obscure way that the guilt was hers, and hers alone.

There was no recompense she could make now. And perhaps no recompense was needed. For Nim seemed content to have her son and Tussy by her bedside, in their last attendance on her, and to take pleasure in the General's morning visits, and the daily messages of love from Laura and Paul. There was nothing wasted about a life whose loving care of others was thus recognized and returned.

As she watched Nim's life ebb, the dear features lose their mobility, the strong hands grow cold and resistless to touch, Tussy was seized by panic at her own unconnected life, its center rotten, its days consumed by futile tasks, purposes imposed from without. What anchor was there for her, of person or belief?

She held to the dead, the dead and the dying, but they could no longer provide sustenance. She clung to the necessities of her working life—the meetings, conferences, the writing of manifestoes—desperate expedients to postpone that moment when she must face, alone, the terrors that awaited her.

Nim's death was prolonged, unbearable; her poor racked body seemed perversely to choose this last moment to fight.

"Can't we do something?" Freddy begged Tussy. "Can't we shorten her suffering? No one is meant to suffer like this."

They increased the morphine, to little effect. Though her suffering had no point or purpose, it seemed that it must play itself out.

"She wanted to go peacefully," Freddy said. "For your sake, Tussy. She thought always of others. Why can't we make it easier for her?"

But Tussy was drawn to Nim's death agony as if she must share it, possess it as her own; she breathed with the failing breath of the old woman, her chest was racked by convulsive gasps, her hands too trembled and clutched the coverlid. She couldn't talk to Freddy, except to say, once: *"This is as close as we'll come to knowing."*

To knowing what? That nothing else matters; only this solitary, bitter struggle between the body's instinct to live and the forces of disintegration and decay.

After much consultation among the interested parties—the General, Freddy, Tussy, Laura—they decided to bury Nim with Mohr and Mohme, in the southeast corner of Highgate Cemetery. Tussy spoke at the grave, to the following effect:

"Her life was given to the service of others. Not once did the thought of self interfere with her devotion to those whose lives she enriched so immeasurably. Taken from her native land as a young girl, wrenched from family and friends, she created a home abroad, whose doors were open to all who were in flight from tyranny or oppression. She had the rarest human gifts, the sterling virtues of integrity and loyalty, united to unfailing good sense and warmth of heart. It is fitting that we who loved her lay her to rest with the two dear comrades with whom she united her life."

Freddy wept inconsolably. Tussy, weeping also, led him away from the grave and embraced him, standing apart from the others.

"I have no one, no one at all," he said.

"We'll make it up to you, dear. Somehow. I promise by all that I hold sacred. I won't let you down."

Edward began to take an interest in Freddy. He urged him to stand for election to his union's executive. They needed an ally on the executive, and it would be good for Freddy to take a more active role. It was true that he had no one; his wife was moving out of London to her people in Wolverhampton, and taking the boy with her.

"You need to build up his confidence, Tussy. He's too deferential by far. He has the timidity of someone who doesn't know his true name. He underestimates his abilities, he defers to his seniors in rank, he gives way immediately if challenged. We have to teach him who he is. I'll undertake to reform him if you'll do your part."

"What would you have me do?"

He thought, or pretended to think. "For a start . . . you could find out who his father was."

For a long time it had been assumed that the General was Freddy's father. But for almost as long, at least since Nim had come to live with the General after Mohr's death, Tussy had known that his relationship with Nim had never been other than that of affectionate comrade in the service of the family Marx. He assumed financial responsibility for Freddy, on Nim's account, as he assumed financial responsibility for Mohr's daughters and their husbands and children. But that Freddy could be his son was unthinkable. Most likely the father had been one of the numerous German exiles who stayed briefly with the Marx family in Soho, then disappeared from sight in America or Canada or South America. Tussy saw no point in raking up the past; better for Nim's secret to die with her.

And Edward did not bring up the subject again. What he did, instead, was to encourage Tussy to spend time alone with Freddy. When Freddy came for dinner, Edward was mysteriously delayed, then turned up at midnight, distant and preoccupied. He urged Freddy to stay the weekend; when Freddy agreed, Edward discovered an engagement that required his presence overnight in Newcastle or Leeds.

Little by little Edward allowed Freddy to take over his function as Tussy's political ally. When Tussy spoke in Victoria Park, it was Freddy who followed her on the soapbox; when she lectured at the People's Palace, Freddy met her afterward and saw her home from the dark, rat-infested alleys leading off Mile End Road. It was Freddy who handed out leaflets, addressed envelopes, protected Tussy from importunate admirers, the mad and the peculiar. Tussy found him comforting and dependable, and she knew she filled a gap in his life. But what Edward's motive was in throwing them so much together puzzled her.

What did he think of Freddy? She asked him point blank.

"I think he's improved greatly. Yes, he's coming along very nicely."

"Coming along for what?"

"It's good for you to have him on hand. He adores you—he'd do anything in the world for you."

"He'd be better off with a wife."

"He could live with us. We need a larger flat; we could get one large enough for the three of us."

"Would that please you?"

"It would mean that I needn't worry about you when I have to leave you alone."

"Do you worry about me when you leave me alone?"

"Of course I worry about you. I worry that you might do something . . . foolish."

"Foolish? Or inconsiderate?"

"Certainly it would be inconsiderate for you to do something foolish. If you take my feelings into account."

"And extremely inconvenient."

"Why must you take that tone? You sound like an aggrieved wife—which you're not, not by any means. Not aggrieved."

"Still, you like the idea of being able to leave me."

"I have no choice, if I'm required to be elsewhere."

"You like the idea."

"I neither like nor dislike the idea."

"That's honest, at least. I wonder sometimes what it is that makes us cleave to one person and no other."

123

"Habit. Fear. We attach ourselves to what is familiar; we fear what is unknown. Some of us, at any rate."

"But not you, Edward. The familiar bores you."

"To a degree. I may have a lower tolerance for boredom than other people."

"I bore you. You might as well admit it."

"Why do you push so hard, Tussy? Can't you leave well enough alone? We agreed to be honest with each other; we can hardly agree never to bore each other. If I find you boring, at times, I'm prepared to deal with it. I don't expect you to change."

"You're prepared to tolerate me as I am."

"Exactly."

14

TUSSY'S WEEK.

Meetings: Monday, Editorial Board, *Time*, to plan the next issue. R. B. Cunninghame Graham on labor legislation; Annie Besant on women's trade unions; Stepnyak on Russian liberalism; William Morris on medieval guilds; a short story by Clementina Black; a short story by Alexander Kielland, translated from Norwegian by Eleanor Marx-Aveling; Israel Zangwill on the East End Jews; poems by Ernest and Dollie Radford; a poem by Baudelaire translated by Laura Lafarge; frontispiece by Walter Crane. Wednesday, Executive Council (nonvoting member), Gasworkers Union.

Paid work: Research for Miss Zimmern, ten hours; typewriting (a newly-aquired skill), ten hours; two lectures for the Educational Alliance ("The New Ibsenism"); lecture for the Croyden Workers' Institute, "The Legal Eight-Hour Day."

Unpaid work: English lessons for Jim Thorne; two mornings for the General; debate at the People's Palace with E. Belfort Bax: "Feminism and Socialism"; addressing envelopes for the Gasworkers, the Wade's Arms, Poplar.

Visits to plan: W. Liebknecht, tour of the Midlands; Bebel, tour of workingmen's clubs, East London.

Correspondence: International report on party congresses.

Engagements: Monday, visit Olive; Tuesday, dinner with Dollie and Ernest; Wednesday, tea with Clementina; Thursday,

opening of new bedroom farce by Alec Nelson at the Royalty;
Friday, Freddy; Sunday, supper at Regents Park Road.

She began to turn more and more to Clementina, whose life
seemed to have a stability, a quality of cool, aristocratic poise,
absent from her own. Clementina was unmarried, but had access
to as much family life as suited her with her sister Constance
and Constance's husband, Richard Garnett, whom they all knew
through working at the Museum, where he was assistant keeper;
Constance was librarian at the People's Palace. Clem and Constance had a sisterly closeness, an intuitive way of thinking and
feeling together. No friend, no mere husband, could lessen the
bond. Clementina's work was disciplined and orderly; she wrote
every morning from nine to one, and devoted the afternoons
to visiting the poor, to research or political organizing. She lived
with a younger sister in a gracious but modestly furnished flat
on Bedford Place, off Russell Square, five minutes' walk from
the Garnetts'.

From Clementina Tussy felt assured of a steady, uncritical,
undemanding affection. She was intelligent, sympathetic, very
English. She seldom asked about Edward, or about those sides
of Tussy's life which she did not actually share.

When they were together, they were independent, self-suffi-
cient friends, and it was as if this was the common, natural
pattern of adult relationship; it seemed entirely reasonable for
two single, unattached adults to meet and work together, and
to separate at night, each to her own private world, for neither
to intrude on the other's innermost self, to threaten to consume
the other. If there was something virginal and passionless about
Clementina, it was something she, Clementina, felt entirely at
ease with. Tussy never had the sense that she was paying a
severe price for the discipline of her life, that she had fought
a life-and-death battle to suppress her instincts. No, her nature
was equable, her emotions temperate, and her equanimity freed
her to lead a useful, productive life, satisfying to her and of
benefit to others.

"I wish I had more of your calm," Tussy said. "So much of
the time I feel that I am seething within, and it's only an immense
effort of will that prevents an explosion."

"It's not a quality to envy, dear. It's really a kind of depriva-

126

tion. I can't feel things as intensely as I ought; something in me immediately takes a critical, ironic stance that puts me at a safe distance. Possibly it's because of the way we were educated, my sisters and I, taught always to analyze our feelings before expressing them. In the end it creates a kind of library mentality. I make a very good researcher. But then you are a superb researcher, without sacrificing the power to feel."

"Only because I discipline myself to work. But it goes so against the grain; I feel so impatient with myself, and even more impatient with earlier workers whose ground I have to cover again. There's nothing professional about my work. I have no habits to fall back on; I have to force myself to assume a critical detachment. I half think it's a matter of blood—you have to be born into a rational way of perceiving the world. But with us the burning conviction always came first, and the indignation. My earliest memories are of being indignant—about Ireland, about the brutalization of the poor, the unfairness of life. And nothing has changed, life remains unfair, and I feel the same outrage. But I know now that nothing is achieved by indignation; passion has to be harnessed and used. And inevitably those who are most skillful at harnessing the passion of others are free of passion themselves."

"I can't believe that it is wrong to feel outraged by injustice. I know the families we visit, the Orlevskys and the Brauns, need your outrage. They tolerate me, but they adore you, Tussy; you're the high point of their week. They believe in you; they have more faith than you give them credit for."

"No, Clem—they're kind to me, they try to cheer me up. I learn more from them than they could possibly learn from me. I am continually amazed by the dignity with which the poor accept their suffering. They have no hope that their lives will change materially; sometimes I doubt whether they want their lives to change. Their horizons may be narrow, but they know the meaning of comradeship, the love of man and wife, the joy of childbirth; they know how to face death, which is such a familiar part of their world. I wonder what we achieve when we try to make them understand how they are exploited and abused. Will they be happier when they see how deeply wronged they have been, they and their children?"

"You idealize them, Tussy. I doubt that the poor suffer with more dignity than the rich, or that they're kinder to their children, or more loving to their husbands and wives. There's nothing ennobling about poverty. The Brauns aren't typical. You're allowing one unusual Jewish family to distort your view of the whole of the East End. You know as well as I do that the misery of the poor is total, degrading, and unrelievable."

"But oh, Clem—what of the misery that has nothing to do with poverty or physical hardship? I sometimes think that if we were to rid the earth of poverty, if science were to cure all the physical illnesses that waste the young, if we could ensure that no one starved, that all had work, if we could end war and the savagery of war, we would still not make a dent in the sum of human suffering."

In January, 1890, the eminent Liberal monthly *Nineteenth Century* published a manifesto opposing the extension of the suffrage to single women over thirty. The writers of the manifesto professed to welcome the expansion of opportunities for women in higher education and medicine; they approved women's activities on school boards, workhouse commissions, public charities, etc. But the sphere of government, they argued, including finance, military affairs, and foreign trade, traditionally the province of men, was unsuited to women by reason not only of their physical inferiority to men but also their peculiar moral virtues, for instance, tender-heartedness, sympathy, and sensibility. The manifesto was signed by 104 notable women, including a score of duchesses and honorables, and several wives of distinguished men, Mrs. Matthew Arnold, Mrs. Arnold Toynbee, and others. Among the signatories were ten women staff members of Girton College, Cambridge.

The editors of *Nineteenth Century* endorsed the manifesto, arguing that female suffrage would have incalculably destructive effects on family relations and domestic harmony. They appended a tear-out sheet for additional signatures, to be sent to Parliament while the bill was under debate.

It was felt that countermeasures were in order, and a campaign was mounted by several women prominent in education and the arts. The March issue of *Nineteenth Century* carried a persuasive letter refuting point by point the arguments of the anti-suffrage camp, signed by, among the two hundred others, Tussy's good friends Elizabeth Garrett Anderson, the founder of the first hospital to be staffed entirely by women, Frances Mary Buss, founder of North London Collegiate and Camden School for Girls, and the novelists Clementina Black and Olive Schreiner. Tussy's name was conspicuously absent from the list.

Clementina had her first real argument with Tussy.

"You should be with us on this as you are with us on the Legal Eight-hour Day. When reform has so slim a chance, how can you ally yourself with our enemies?" A Newnham graduate, she was personally affronted by the fact that half of Girton declared against female suffrage. "It's the successful women who keep their sisters down. Their niche is secure; we threaten them with the prospect of a truly open society. Why is it so important to them to keep the numbers small? They fight against allowing married women to study or teach; fifty years from now they'll fight with their dying breath to prevent the other Cambridge colleges from opening their doors to women."

Tussy told Clementina bluntly that Girton College and Cambridge University were of no interest to her; they were vestigial enclaves of academic privilege, cut off from the only knowledge that mattered, the study of real life. The liberal reforms so dear to the middle classes—extension of the suffrage, the widening of educational and vocational opportunity—would benefit the middle classes chiefly, and perhaps a very few others; they left untouched the fundamental, deep-seated oppression of the masses, men and women alike.

To prove her point, Tussy wrote a pamphlet on "The Woman Question," signed with her name and Edward's, since on this matter if none other they agreed entirely, and it seemed useful to present the pamphlet as the product of "a man and woman thinking and working together." In it they cogently argued against the middle-class delusion that progress could be achieved by liberalizing existing systems.

"We will suppose all women enabled to vote," they wrote, "every calling open to both sexes. The actual position of women in respect to men would not be vitally touched. For not one of these things touches them in their sex relations. Without a larger social change, women will never be free."

Dollie, who had little interest in the suffrage or in higher education, but who hated the idea of violence of any kind, asked

Tussy to explain further. Why need the sex relations of men and women be oppressive? She did not find her sex relation with Ernest oppressive; on the contrary, they had an excellent understanding based on mutual respect and affection.

"The prostitute grants a man temporary use of her body in exchange for a fixed sum; the wife grants her husband lifetime rights over her body in exchange for lifetime maintenance. You may not feel that your relationship with Ernest can be reduced to this kind of exchange, since you maintain Ernest, and you don't feel that either of you has 'rights' over the other's body. But the law doesn't recognize your private, idiosyncratic arrangement; in the eyes of the law, Ernest is obliged to support you, to assume your debts, to transact all legal business for you. If you refuse him connubial rights, he is no longer obliged to support you; nothing could be clearer."

"I still don't see why I should feel oppressed. Ernest and I have no intention of going to law; we're perfectly happy to work out matters for ourselves. I don't see that our marriage is a form of prostitution; indeed, I don't see that marriage and prostitution are necessarily connected at all."

"Oh, Dollie, you amaze me. If middle-class girls must be kept pure for marriage—and they must be chaste, or their husbands have no proof of paternity—then their working-class sisters must be available for use. . . . You surely don't expect middle-class men to remain chaste; it would be contrary to nature, and would serve no useful social purpose. No, our girls must be divided into those who are reserved to procreate, and those available for purchased pleasure. You couldn't sustain marriage without prostitution; you wouldn't need prostitution if marriage ceased to exist. Every woman who marries in effect condones the sale of her sisters in prostitution; she is submitting to a system that denies women education and all but the most menial employment lest it interfere with their functions of breeding and sexual service."

"Then why do you argue against extending education and professional training to women?"

"I don't argue against extending higher education to women— why, women like us would be the first to benefit. But it's a mistake to think that because a few women are admitted to London University and Cambridge the oppression of the masses is going to be materially altered. Unless the system is changed from the roots up, the few women who succeed will simply become like men. They will inevitably be more concerned to protect their small stake in the system than to change it."

"It still seems to me that Clementina and Olive are fighting for things that matter, and that have a chance of success, and that you're setting yourself against them."

"They're distracting attention from more important issues. Working men and working women have more in common than working women and middle-class women. Besides, middle-class women make poor leaders for a truly revolutionary movement. They'll always settle in the end; they're frightened by violence, and they're repelled by real misery."

Tussy shared her father's scorn for what the General called the "hysterical effusions of bourgeois and petty bourgeois women careerists," for instance, Mrs. Wishnevskaya—now Miss Kelley, since her divorce—and her friends in the New York branch of the SLP. Women were welcome in the socialist camp as long as they behaved themselves and did not push the feminist line too hard. In fact there were few women who were utterly reliable; they tended to be difficult from start to finish, temperamental, self-aggrandizing, erratic. Tussy was virtually the only one who could be counted on, and she was an exception, in every way.

Though she had come to England only for a few months, Olive showed no sign of wanting to return to her life in South Africa, her kind, devoted husband, her comfortable, well-furnished house, the servants, the round of visiting from family, friends, and her husband's professional colleagues and their wives. Instead, she systematically stripped herself of bourgeois trappings, not only the husband and home she had left behind, but property of all description—clothing, furnishings, even books. She dressed only in black; her meals were spare. She developed an awkward new symptom, a susceptibility to choking fits—a kind of spasm of the esophagus, which once it had started was virtually impossible to stop until it had worn itself out. She had always found it painful to eat with other persons present; now she avoided all social engagements whatsoever. She sought to revive the creative springs that had dried out in the harsh glare of the African sky—to penetrate to the mystical essence of her life.

And she allowed her passion for women to flower. Suppressed for so many years, it seemed to flow from her in greater strength and purity, a powerful longing that sustained her in her difficult, solitary hours of writing or meditating.

Havelock Ellis was struggling to write a long essay on "inversion" in women, for his second volume of *Sexual Psychopathology*. He asked Olive for the privilege of an afternoon's conversation.

"When I think of the great artists of the past," she told Havelock, "Raphael, Leonardo, Michelangelo, Rembrandt—and there is not a single woman among them; when I think of the composers whose art has given happiness to so many, and there is not a single woman among them; then I feel a despairing grief for all the women who have achieved nothing noteworthy, who have added nothing to the history of the race, to thought, art, scientific knowledge. And when I read through the list of those who have qualified for entrance to Oxford and Cambridge and London University, or to medical schools, and there are half a dozen women for a hundred men, then I want to weep for the countless women who have never dreamed of higher education, or of entering the professions. And when a woman has finally achieved something in the world and is recognized for her abilities, as a novelist, a great musician, a physician, then I feel a pain almost as great that there are not more like her, that she is an exception, an anomaly by any count."

"Do you think a man would be incapable of suffering for women, as you do?"

"I see no reason why a man could not feel the wrongs of women, as, for example, a European can feel the wrongs of Africans, can feel that his privilege and power and ease of life are intolerable while other human beings live like animals. I have known several Europeans who feel the wrongs of the blacks as their own, who see that their comfortable lives are built on the sufferings of the blacks, and who can't rest until they join hands with their injured brothers. They are a tiny minority, of course; most Europeans accept their privileges as God-given. But even this tiny minority does not feel the wrongs of women in the same way, perhaps because the wrongs of women are different in kind. Their oppression is more diffuse, more subtle."

"Isn't it possible, my Olive, that your grief for women has more to do with your own circumstances than with the oppression of women?"

"Quite possibly I am grieving for my own missed opportunities, my inadequacies, my lack of confidence, my physical cowardice, my social shyness. Quite possibly my grief is simply anger at not having been born male. It's certainly true that I believe secretly that if I had been born male I would not have been cursed by these feelings of inadequacy, unconfidence, physical cowardice. But I am also weeping for my mother, for not making more of her talents. I am weeping for my little sister, who died. I am weeping for my infant daughter, who did not live to see her second dawn. On their account, and my own, I am filled with rage at men, at my father, my brother who lived, the male doctors who could not save my sister or my infant daughter."

"But surely there are many men who do not realize their dreams, who remain unfulfilled, unawakened, throughout their adult lives. Children die in infancy and early childhood whether they are male or female. Surely struggle is the natural condition of our lives, and suffering the norm, for men and women alike."

"Yes, my Havelock. Struggle is our condition, suffering is our fate."

"Then you choose to blame men for conditions over which they have no more control than women. It's a matter of choice. You choose to hate men, and to love women."

"Yes, you're quite right. I choose to love women; or rather, I choose no longer to suppress my love of women. I would deny my body if I could. I can't—I'm lustful, easily roused to passion. As you know. But I can choose the object of my passion. I can love a woman as an equal. I need not abase myself to a man in order to indulge his lust."

"Then do you not play the part of a man yourself?"

"I wouldn't put it that way. These roles are meaningless in love. The part of a man to court, of a woman to be courted or seduced."

"Surely if the woman is young and inexperienced, you play to some degree the role of a seducer."

"To some degree."

"Then isn't there always a danger of exploitation? I don't

suggest that you would abuse your power over a young girl. But isn't there a temptation to exploit the young, and to corrupt them, in any homosexual relationship?"

"Some would say that it's the young who exploit the old, and who corrupt them."

"But in any case you can seldom have a relationship of equals. One is more powerful than the other, one maintains the other, one is fickle while the other is constant. . . ."

"Isn't it the same in a relationship between a man and a woman? I see no difference. Except for the risk of pregnancy, and the hold that gives the man over the woman."

"Or the woman over the man."

"Yes. But I see no reason why sexual relations between men and women should be inherently more loving than relations between women. All the evils that beset relations between men and women—jealousy, fickleness, coldness, brutality, unkindness—can occur in relations between women. But their economic and indeed their physiological roots are absent. They *need* not occur, they need not persist. Women in love are not constrained by their circumstances to love well or ill. They are free to love as their feelings dictate."

"Then why, so often"—he searched for a delicate way of phrasing the question—"does a follower of Sappho—a mature woman—fasten her affections upon a young girl, who is flattered by her interest, responsive to her affection, innocent of sexual experience, and hence, perhaps, unaware of conventional sexual taboos—but who is quite likely to leave her patroness for a young man as soon as someone suitable presents himself?"

Olive shrugged. "The Greeks understood the beauty of youth very well. There's no reason why we should expect love to be a happy experience. We retain our capacity to love, to fall in love, throughout life. But no doubt we cease rapidly to be lovable."

At this point, Hannah, the East London waif, who, Havelock noted, was neither beautiful nor young, appeared silently, and looked to Olive for instructions.

"Dr. Ellis will have a cup of tea," Olive said.

"Mrs. Aveling stopped by to ask, did you want a ticket to the play tonight. She said she'd call in on the way."

"Would you rather I stayed with you, Hannah?"

134

"It'll do you good to get out."

"Well, perhaps I'll go, then."

Hannah slipped out as silently as she had appeared.

"She has eyes for nothing but you," Havelock said.

"The real thing is always so different from what one expects."

Tussy thought she could see the process of aging in Olive's face; the strong lines of cheek and jaw seemed more prominent, the beautiful eyes were shadowed underneath by a network of fine lines, the lines around the mouth had deepened. She loved to watch Olive as she read or sat at her table, writing, but there was something unaccountably sad about her now, a grief etched into her body, for the lost child, her lost youth, her failed marriage.

She was working on a new novel, or rather, an old novel, for it had been started before *Story of an African Farm*, and she had discarded it and returned to it half a dozen times since. Into its pages Olive poured all her knowledge of women, young and old and middle-aged, their dreams and their suffering.

What was wrong with the book? Why was she unable to finish it? The material was too painful, too close to her life; or there had been some fault of conception from the start. The true artist must be able to cut his losses, to move on; it was a sign of weakness to return over and over to the sprawling, flawed work of adolescence.

But there was nothing professional about Olive's writing. She wrote out of her whole heart, or not at all; the inward vision must be clear and all-embracing. The success of *African Farm* was an accident; the subject had the charm of novelty, and the story was intensely poetic, simple, sensuous, and passionate. But her real work was not easily to be understood.

When Tussy arrived, Havelock was seated on the thin wooden chair, his soft, ample bottom edging over the sides. He walked with the two women down Berners Street and through Soho toward Shaftesbury Avenue and the theatre district. It was still early, and they stopped at The Coach and Horses, on Old Compton Street. Havelock ordered Pilsener for himself and Tussy, and soda water for Olive.

"I never see you at the Museum," he said to Tussy.

"I've been working at the People's Palace. My life has changed in the past year. I take the tram to Mile End Road each morning, and between my committee work for the Gasworkers and my English lessons I stay in the East End often until ten or eleven at night. I hardly come back to Bloomsbury except to sleep."

"How admirable! I'm sure your work must be very gratifying."

"Gratifying and frustrating. One doesn't see much tangible progress. It happens, but one doesn't see it."

"Isn't that generally true of political work?"

Olive laughed. "You would say that, Havelock. You're the least political being I know. You have a fine Shakespearean detachment—it really doesn't matter to you who's in, who's out. But Eleanor and I can't afford to be detached—not when there's a chance that we may at last be able to change the lives of thousands."

"Do you really think you have a chance of changing the lives of thousands?"

"There's no question about it," Tussy said. "Two years ago I would have been as skeptical as you are. But something's happened just in this past year. You can sense it in the Sunday meetings at Victoria Park—every week the crowds are larger and angrier, and more disciplined. It's only a matter of time before they break through that invisible line that separates the East End from the rest of London."

"Do you expect them to march on Westminster?"

"Oh, yes, I expect them to march, and to stay until the government capitulates. They've learned a great deal since the dock strike. They know the vote is the least of their weapons; they know the strength in numbers."

"And will you be on the barricades too, Olive?"

"When the time comes. Not just yet. But I'm with Eleanor in spirit."

"May I bring my Edith to meet you, Olive? She is also a socialist, a feminist, an activist—a marvelous speaker. I think you would like her."

"I'm sure I would. But Eleanor will tell you that I see no one. I've become very selfish—I can't afford to meet anyone I might want to love."

"We've all become selfish," Tussy said. "We have no choice if we're to avoid being swept in a hundred different directions.

You yourself, Havelock, put your work before your friends. You told me so."

"Did I? I can't remember. I can't imagine saying anything of the sort to you. You're confusing me with one of your political friends. Writing is an avocation, a pleasurable hobby. How could I possibly put it before friendship?"

Olive sat back in the dark wooden booth and gazed from one to the other of them.

"I'm so glad that we're together now, the three of us," she said. "Even if it's only for half an hour. If ever I am far from either of you, or if I seem distant, you must promise to remember that I loved you both. You were the first person to befriend me, Havelock, when I came to London as a young girl, a manuscript clutched in my hands, knowing no one, without the slightest idea how one met people, or even how people engaged in conversation. I shall never forget your kindness to me. And you, dear Eleanor, were the friend a woman must have if she is to survive in this world dominated by men—a kindred being of her own age and sex, to whom she can open her heart."

"Why do you speak as if we are never to meet again?" said Tussy.

"It's something I feel . . . how can I put it? a conviction that we shall not meet again as we are now, not the three of us, not here."

"I see no reason why Eleanor and I should give in to your mystical notions," Havelock said cheerfully. "I drink to many more meetings of the three of us, exactly as we are now."

"To the three of us," said Tussy. "To friendship. To love."

But she thought Olive was right. It was impossible to go back.

15

Havelock left them at the corner of St. Martin's Lane, and they went on to the Lyceum. The theatre tickets, courtesy of Tussy's friend E. Belfort Bax, the editor of the optimistically named *Time*, were for Miss Elizabeth Robins in Ibsen's *Lady from the Sea*, in William Archer's new translation. Bernard was there, and Oscar Wilde, and William Archer and Ernest Rhys, and Clementina with her sister Constance and brother-in-law Richard, and William Morris with May and Harry Sparling, and the eminent Zionist Israel Zangwill—indeed, all the contributors to the short-lived *Time*, and the ephemeral *To-Day*, and the anarchist *Commonweal*, along with reviewers for *Modern Thought* and the *Fortnightly*, and *Nineteenth Century*, and the *Times* and the *Daily Telegraph*—in short, virtually everyone who was serious about literature and politics, thought and culture. All were there to applaud Miss Robins as the troubled Ellida, and to take pleasure in her radiant beauty of voice and person, and to think seriously, for a few hours, about the problems of identity facing the Modern Woman.

Edward appeared briefly at the first interval, stayed for the second act, then left without speaking to Tussy. Bernard nodded to her, but was soon the center of a crowd of admiring listeners. She and Olive seemed to be protected by a wall of respectful silence. Olive was unconcerned; absorbed by the play, she wanted only to surrender to its power without the ordinary world impinging in any way.

"Does it make you sad to have given up your dream of acting?" she asked Tussy later.

"It was so long ago I can hardly remember if I was serious about it."

"Oh, you were serious enough. I remember, if you don't."

"I started late. The great performing artists seem to be singled out in childhood. By the time one reaches adulthood the critical habit is too marked, the habit of self-criticism, at any rate. And I should have hated to be merely good."

"Why, I should think a good actress would find immense satisfaction in her work."

"Olive dear, you have no idea how miserable an actress's life can be. Unless she's one of the two or three great ones, her services are for sale to the first bidder. She's the victim of insincere flattery, false promises, sexual bribery. Her closest companions are rivals who would sacrifice her at the first chance. She's dependent on a fickle audience, a corrupt manager. . . . She's frightened of failure, uncertain what will become of her when she grows old. . . . Oh, it's not a life to envy. The glamour doesn't last long, I assure you. One can hardly blame a young actress for choosing the easy way out, if a wealthy admirer should make an offer."

"Marriage, do you mean?"

"More likely an arrangement of some sort."

"It seems to me it's a very precarious way out if it depends on the man's interest."

"Oh, yes. In the end she's sure to be abandoned. Why, even our own Alec Nelson has been known to leave one actress . . . for another."

"I don't see how you can make light of it, Tussy."

"Why not? We're on very good terms now, Edward and I. Everything's open and aboveboard. We've agreed to be honest with each other. So there need be no misunderstanding, no recriminations. Don't you think honesty is a good foundation for marriage? or such a marriage as ours?"

"It depends on what's uncovered. You may not like what you see."

"I'm willing to risk it. I'm not easily shocked, Olive, not any more. I'd rather know what there is to know."

"If you're strong enough to bear it."

"Oh, I'm as strong as an ox, I don't seem to need to sleep, or to eat."

"You don't seem strong to me, dear. You look pale, overwrought. You're probably working too hard."

"I can't possibly work too hard. There's far too much work to be done. In any case, I'd rather be working than thinking."

She urged Olive to come back with her and stay the night. Edward was leaving directly for a lecture tour of the Midlands; he would be away for three or four nights at least.

"Not tonight, dear. But I'll sit with you for a while."

Tussy's rooms were hardly changed since she and Edward had moved into them seven years before, books and papers everywhere, framed sepia photographs of Mohr and Jenny on the mantelpiece, Laura's watercolor of Hampstead Heath hung between Edward's anatomical diagrams, Mohme's silver coffee service on a small china cabinet. Tussy cleared the two armchairs of books and poured two glasses of wine. She pointed to a stack of envelopes on the table.

"There is my work for next week. Five hundred envelopes to address for the Brussels Conference, a year's accounts to balance for the Gasworkers, Clementina's notes for Mr. Booth to be typewritten. She's surveyed the whole of Bethnal Green for him, house by house. Between the Jewish charities, Israel Zangwill, and Beatrice Potter, the East End is going to be the best-researched slum in Europe."

"Do you think research into the conditions of the poor is going to change people's lives?"

"If I didn't believe that the poor are ripe for change, and that knowledge of their true condition is going to hasten their revolt, then I'd have no reason to continue working. Why, I'd have no reason to continue living . . . since my work is my life."

"I'm not at all convinced that the great changes will be accomplished by the rising of the masses. I too believe that change is imminent—but I believe it's going to come in ways no one has foreseen. I have a vision of a New Woman leading a spiritual rebirth of all men and women, the final triumph of Nature over the Machine. The New Woman free and generous and loving . . . Nature bountiful and life-affirming, the great teacher,

140

healer, preserver . . . But first I see a time of bitter conflict between man and woman, in which all ties shall be cut, parents rejected by their children, husbands cut down by their wives. I see armies of women smashing all the machines invented by men in this cursed century, the machines that have destroyed the ancient home crafts of women, and forced them into the marketplace, where their labor is bought cheap and their lives are shortened, to satisfy the luxurious whims of their wealthy and corrupted sisters."

"I can't agree with you, Olive. Women will never be free until they master the machines that enslave them, and that enslave men as well. To smash the machines is exhilarating, as our anarchist friends know, but it's never a solution, only an irritant. Those who control the machines also control social and economic power. Of course, the New Woman might choose to use her power differently, but she has to understand her enemies before she can destroy them. She can't call the modern world back to Nature from its dream of scientific progress. She has to reintegrate science with Nature, which is far more difficult."

"But you talk as if men and women are the same. They're not—any more than rich and poor are the same, or black and white, or prey and predator. Their interests are diametrically opposed. They are locked in a conflict unto death."

"It seems to me that the common interests of men and women must always be greater than the conflict that divides them."

"That's why you refuse to leave Edward. You cannot recognize that you're engaged in a life-and-death struggle, your soul is at stake. He's your enemy, Tussy. He wants to destroy you."

"If I thought that— But you're mistaken, Olive, I assure you. He needs me. He depends on me. He wants me to stay—he insists on it."

"You say that women have to master the machine before they can be free. Perhaps so. But first they must free themselves from sexual oppression. Surely the worst slavery is to love when there is no love on the other side."

"So you too think I must leave him."

"I would never tell you what to do."

"But that is what you think."

"You know I've never been one of his partisans."

"But he has no partisans now; they've all abandoned him.

He's been asked to leave the Socialist League, he's been blacked by Radical clubs in a dozen cities. You have no idea how humiliating it is—we have to check beforehand when we're invited anywhere. Anonymous letters are sent, invitations are mysteriously withdrawn, lectures canceled. At the Paris Conference that tool Gilles circularized all the delegates with a list of accusations going back all the way to the King's College row. We're boycotted now by fourth-rank union hacks who wouldn't have dared to show their faces at the ILP a year ago. . . ."

"Surely you're not boycotted—"

"Certainly I'm boycotted. Do you suppose I would go without Edward? It's blackmail—I refuse to give in to it. If I leave Edward, it will be because I've decided it's the best course for both of us. I won't be forced to leave him by our supposed comrades."

"Then, as long as he's under attack, you're not free. It's worse than I thought. There's no way out for you. He's free to behave exactly as he pleases, and you're bound more and more tightly."

"Why do you insist that I'm in some sense his victim? All our arrangements are by mutual consent, housekeeping, the question of children."

"And sexual relations?"

"Certainly. We choose to share a bed; we can choose to sleep separately."

Sexual relations by consent. Here was a curious concept, which Tussy was not particularly anxious to examine too closely.

Yet this most intimate of relations could be considered a paradigm of all human relations, familial, social, economic.

There was the contractual relation, written or unwritten, the agreement to love, honor and obey, the solemn exchange of connubial rights and financial obligations.

Then there was the living relation, susceptible to infinite variation and adaptation, created and renewed from day to day, or corrupted, poisoned. . . .

But what transpired between a man and woman in the privacy of the bedroom had little of consent about it, little of conscious intention. Desire found its own means and ways to satisfy itself; it was prior to thoughts and words and transcended them in the act.

142

If one chose to learn from the sexual relation, its lesson was that the fundamental human relations were born of necessity, were not free associations undertaken for mutual profit or pleasure, but instinctive bondings dictated by the struggle for survival. The weak gave themselves up to the protection of the strong, and the strong used the weak to extend their power and domain.

Indeed, it could be argued that a woman's body was curiously well designed to satisfy a man's lust, her softness a continual temptation to his strength; force was as natural to his mating as persuasion. And as long as men remained physically stronger than women, as long as they had the power to force women sexually, whether or not they used their power, equality in the sexual relation was an impossibility. Especially if the woman chose not to conceive.

More and more Tussy felt it was the child that justified and sanctified the sexual relation. She yearned to conceive, though her rational mind objected: what would she do with a child? how could she manage? and above all, what possible good could come to a child of such a union?

16

Clementina's notes on Rydal Street, for Mr. Booth's Life and Labour of the People, *Volume II. Typed by E. M. A.*

Rydal Street. A wretched-looking place. The women standing about look poverty-stricken, the children ill-cared-for. Some of them are to be seen looking out from beneath the lifted window curtains of front parlors—probably they are locked in awaiting their mother's return from work. Each house has five small rooms and a kitchen, and are let in tenements by the landlord, or to one tenant and sublet. The rents are 7s 6d for the whole, 4s 6d for the half house. Occupants are continually moving, but do not go far. Many of those described as out of work do casual work, or have cokar-nut shy-stands, etc. Most of the wives do charring or some occasional work; some work at a jam factory near.

No.		Rooms	Persons		Occupation
1 & 3	condemned				
5	ground	3	6	Man, wife, and 4 children	Cork cutter. Two children at work. Industrious family.
	upper	3	7	Man, wife, and 5 children	Laborer. Out of work. Sells vegetables in street. Was lately in prison. Wife gets a chance day's work.
7	ground	3	10	Man, wife, and 8 children	Printer. Always out of work; a loafer. Wife chars and supports family with aid of children.

No.		Rooms	Persons		Occupation
9	ground	3	9	Man, wife, and 7 children	Bricklayer. Out of work. Wife makes matchboxes. One of the children at work. Very poor.
	upper	3	9	Man, wife, and 7 children	Pastry cook. Out of work.
11	ground	3	4	Deserted wife and 3 children	Matchbox maker. Hard-working woman. One boy works.
13	ground	3	5	Man, wife, and 3 children	Tin toy maker. Very poor trade.
	upper front	2	7	Man, wife, and 5 children	Dock laborer. Out of work. One child at work. Extremely poor.
	upper back	1	7	Man, wife, and 5 children	Laborer. Out of work 12 months. Great distress.
17	ground	3	9	Man, wife, and 7 children	Foreman dustman. One girl in service, one boy at printer's, one child blind, and one imbecile. Hard-working and teetotalers.
19	ground	3	7	Man, wife, and 5 young children	One or two days' work a week. Wife tailoring when she can get it.
	upper	3	7	Man, wife, and 5 young children	Painter, out of work. Wife washes and occasional acts at theatres.
21	ground	3	10	Man, wife, and 8 children	Barge laborer, good wages when at work. Wife a fearful drunkard, has twice jumped from top window when intoxicated. Eldest boy out of work, rest too young.
	upper	3	8	Man, wife, and 6 children	Potman, 10s a week. Wife washes. Eldest girl in service. Boy at work. Others young. Man given to drink. Wife clean and respectable.
23	ground	3	7	Man, wife, and 5 children	Was in gasworks. Met with an accident and now cannot work. Clean respectable people. Great poverty.
	upper front	2	3	Man, wife and grown son	Father and son sell coke in the street. Drink heavily. The son cannot read. Very poor.

145

No.		Rooms	Persons		Occupation
upper back		1	2	Widow and son	Works in laundry. Son at school. Very poor. There is a daughter who will not live here because mother drinks.

and so on.

These were the facts and figures of poverty, the bare bones, multiplied by hundreds and thousands in this wealthiest of cities, where one and a half million men were out of work, and one million women. What was to be done? The overwhelming reality of poverty made ideology almost irrelevant. Clementina and Shaw, Morris and the Avelings, Fabians, socialists, trade unionists, social democrats, and revolutionaries agreed in principle; they joined together on almost every issue. Their common task: to educate, agitate, and organize; to build toward the confrontation that seemed inevitable.

The organizational affiliations of the Avelings during these years present a puzzling contrast to the careers of their socialist comrades, all of them, regardless of ideology, united in opposing the evil system chronicled in Booth's *Life and Labour of the People*, a street-by-street breakdown of the poorest London boroughs, appearing with monotonous regularity, two volumes a year.

William Morris, for instance, the greatest and most original English socialist, used his own Hammersmith Socialist Society as his propaganda base up until his death in 1896. Although he broke with the Social Democratic Federation to found the Socialist League, he retained a working relationship with his former associates and, subsequently, with the League when it was taken over by the anarchists in 1886.

Shaw left the SDF to join the new Fabian Society, where he became one of the leading publicists, along with the Webbs, for gradualism and legislative reform. Clementina also became a Fabian, and presented carefully researched papers on women's labor, factory conditions, etc., in her pleasant rooms on Bedford Place.

The Avelings, on the other hand seem to have had no settled organizational home; indeed, their rapid shifts of allegiance seem not to have been entirely voluntary. A list of Aveling's associations in 1883, when he joined forces with Tussy, and after, represents merely the top of the iceberg. 1883: Member of Westminster School Board; on executive of National Secular Society; sub-editor of *Progress*. Resigns from National Secular Society, August, 1884. Resigns as editor of *Progress*, August, 1884. Resigns from school board, October, 1884. Joins Social Democratic Federation, 1884. Sub-editor of *To-Day*, July, 1884. Resigns from Social Democratic Federation, December, 1884. Resigns as sub-editor of *To-Day*, December, 1884. Helps to found Socialist League, 30 December 1884. Resigns from Socialist League, 1886. Founds Bloomsbury Socialist Society, unaffiliated, 1886. Helps to found Legal Eight-Hour Day Committee, 1889. Attends founding conference of International Labour Party, 1893, elected to executive. Expelled from International Labour Party, 1894. Resigns from Legal Eight-Hour Day Committee, 1895. Eight-Hour Day Committee dissolved, 1895. Rejoins Social Democratic Federation, 1895.

None of which would be particularly noteworthy were it not that each change of affiliation was accompanied by accusations and counter-accusations having to do, always, with money. It took all the ingenuity of their friends, the General and Morris in particular—the General because his family loyalty came first, Morris because he despised intramural squabbling and regarded money as totally unimportant—to silence the ugly rumors. But certainly a dangerous pattern was established, and cynics might be forgiven for wondering, when the Avelings' names were suddenly dropped from a current labor journal, which would be the next group to find its coffers emptied.

To be part of a mass of 500,000 human beings impelled by a common emotion is a wonderful experience. It seems impossible that governments should still stand, that the rich and powerful should hold on to their wealth and power, that the prisons should remained locked and the factories humming, in the face of such determined, passionate opposition springing from the hearts and minds of the vast majority. The thousand voices raised in song, chanting the cries of liberation, break down the artificial barriers that separate human beings from their fellows in drawing room and parlor, factory and bank, school and university. The titles and signs, the clothes and accent that identify master and servant, rich and poor, educated and uneducated, cease to matter as individuals are caught up in a crowd of thousands surging toward an end that all feel to be just and right. All are brothers and sisters, and their common humanity tells them that to live as human beings they must be free. Gathering in the central squares of the city in their thousands, they are affirming that most basic of all rights, and the powerful, locked in their palaces and churches and marble reception rooms, disregard the muffled cries from without at their peril.

These great communal gestures are valuable not only in themselves but as a reminder of what is possible. For they are often unrepeatable, or seem so. Mass movements seem to feed on opposition, to build to a crest, and when they reach their maximum force, and the opposition quakes and crumbles—or prudently gives a foot or an inch—then the impetus is lost, and exceedingly difficult to regain. Meetings are called, and no one attends; marches are scheduled and a few handfuls turn up; speakers harangue the park benches, and their words, true and persuasive a year earlier, sound like empty rhetoric.

To understand what the late eighties and early nineties meant to Tussy and her dedicated comrades in the East End, Will Thorne, Ben Tillett, Keir Hardie, R. B. Cunninghame Graham, Clementina Black, and of course Aveling, it would be necessary to live through a movement of this kind in both its phases—to be swept along with a vast multitude, to embrace strangers, and to feel oneself transfigured by the love of one's kind; and then, over a period of years, to witness the movement that had once seemed irresistible falter and split, its leadership quarreling, its ends confused, its followers bewildered or apathetic.

The signposts along that route are familiar names in the mythology of the East End, celebrated in cartoon and popular song: Dod Street, Black Monday, Bloody Sunday, the Match Girls' Strike, the Dock Strike, Silvertown. The issues were not very different from those that have marked liberation movements in more recent times: freedom of speech ("Dod Street"), freedom of assembly ("Bloody Sunday"), the right of workers to organize and to negotiate working conditions and pay. Demonstrations were supported by a "united front" of the left, the SDF, the Socialist League, Fabians, Radicals, the trades unions. A police ban—for instance, on the Sunday speechmaking in Dod Street—

was violated, arrests followed, the police ban was defied again, the crowds were larger, the police more menacing; confrontation led to violence or jail sentences or both. And, at a critical point, support for a just cause came from the uncommitted, the press, Members of Parliament, the public. The match girls, led by Annie Besant, won the right to a lunch break; the Gasworkers won the right to an eight-hour shift; the dockers, after five weeks of a strike that effectively paralyzed London, won sixpence an hour, the dockers' 'tanner,' or thirty shillings for a sixty-hour week—sixpence having then the purchasing power of three loaves of bread, or three pints of beer.

But the cause with greatest revolutionary potential was the international movement for a "Legal Eight-Hour Day." In December, 1888, the American Federation of Labor, meeting in Chicago, called for nationwide demonstrations on the first of May in support of the legal eight-hour day. The American call was endorsed by the Second International—the International Socialist Working Men's Congress—meeting in Paris on July 14, 1889, the centenary of the storming of the Bastille. The first great May Day demonstrations, in 1890, drew half a million workers into Hyde Park, 100,000 to the Place de la Concorde, and equivalent numbers to the great central squares of Brussels, Hamburg, New York, Rome. The response in London, indeed, led the General to write to Laura that England, after its long quiescence, "at last was stirring," and that Tussy and Edward, with the help of the Gasworkers, had "done it all."

May Day, 1891, though few persons realized it at the time, was probably the crest of the wave, the high point of solidarity on the left, among scientific and Fabian socialists, old and "new" unionists, anarchists, Possibilists, Boulangerists and Proudhonists, Blanquists and Collectivists, Secularists and the New Christian League, in short, among all political groups committed to fight for the emergent proletariat of three continents.

Tussy's Speech, May Day, 1891, Hyde Park, Platform 10.

Comrades, friends, fellow workers,

We are gathered here today with two great purposes in mind: to demonstrate our solidarity with our brothers and sisters in Europe and America; and to demand our rights as free men and women.

Our demands are reasonable and just, and if the governments of the world were reasonable and just, there would be no need for us to be standing here today in our thousands. (cheers) First, we demand legal regulation of the working day to a maximum of eight hours, with no reduction in pay. Second, legal regulation of night work and holidays and working conditions for women and children. Third, inspection of factories and workshops, along with domestic industries. And fourth, the abolition of standing armies and the arming of the people. (cheers)

A century ago the great liberal bourgeois revolution in France proclaimed the liberty, equality, and fraternity of all citizens. Today we know that personal freedom is a mockery unless it is based on economic justice; liberty, equality, and fraternity can be realized only when all men and women have the right to work and to receive and enjoy the reward of their labor.

But you see how matters stand in this wealthy nation of ours, where the poor work for sixteen hours in mill, factory, and mine, and the idle rich have the reward of their labor and the leisure to enjoy it.

Yes, you see how it is, my friends. You have seen your husbands beg for work, so that they may feed their children; you have seen them turned away day after day, while others, the lucky ones, work sixteen hours a day and still must watch their children sicken and die, for their wages suffice to buy neither adequate food nor warm clothes. You have watched your sweethearts turn from blooming young girls to exhausted old women in five years of childbearing. You have served at the tables of the rich and had the pickings of their leftovers. You have built their great houses and sewn and hemmed their fine linen. You have sold them your sweat and your labor, you have given them your sons and your daughters, and still it is not enough, they must have more, they must have your souls as well.

But let me tell you a secret, my friends. All is not well inside the great mansions and council chambers and palaces. The rich are cowering, yes, they are trembling in their fur capes and fine jewels. For they hear the rumbling of a mighty wind, the slow steady roar of the oppressed and suffering millions rising in righteous anger, to say with one voice: we too are men and women, we too are human. We demand what is our right, no more, no less. We demand the profits of our own labor.

And finally may I appeal to the men here present to support their wives and daughters and sisters in their courageous fight for union recognition and decent working conditions. Let us be allies in our common fight; let us stand together as equals, comrades, friends, men and women thinking and working together in a common cause. Thank you, good friends.

It was difficult to be heard past the very front of the crowd, with the bands blaring and the megaphones from nearby platforms 7 and 11 echoing each phrase a second later. But they applauded and cheered, and the Liberal *Daily News* complimented Mrs. Marx-Aveling on a stirring speech, delivered in quiet, sincere tones which belied its fiery message. The Radical papers, the *Daily Chronicle* (morning) and *Star* (evening) published summaries of all the speeches, platform by platform. And Tussy's speech was reported in full in the *People's Press*, the official organ of the General Railway Workers; the Gasworkers and General Labourers; the Potters; and Coach, Bus, Cab and Van Trades; the Shop Assistants; the Printers and Stationers; Warehousemen; Cutters and Assistants; and the Plain and Fancy Box Makers—otherwise known as the "red" unions.

Who else spoke at the May Day rally, Hyde Park, 1891?
For the Fabians, Platform 9: Bernard Shaw, Sidney Webb, Beatrice Potter, Clementina Black.
For the Socialist League: William Morris, and in one of his rare public appearances, Friedrich Engels.
For the Social Democratic Federation: Harry Hyndman.
For the Gasworkers: Will Thorne, Tom Mann.
For the women's unions: Mrs. Annie Besant
Also Keir Hardie, R. B. Cunninghame Graham, and many others.
In all there were twelve platforms sponsored by the London Trades Council and the Legal Eight-Hour Day and International Labour League, along with four SDF platforms and one anarchist platform. And an impartial observer, listening attentively to the full range of speakers, and observing the enthusiastic response of the crowd, asked to predict the course that English society would take in the next fifty years, might well have concluded that England was at last ripe for revolution. Certainly

it seemed that the great army of the unemployed and underemployed, the underpaid and overworked, angry and militant, were at last united, their organization disciplined, their leadership politically sophisticated. It would simply be a matter of time before they were ready to seize power.

Was the General right when he wrote proudly to Laura that Tussy and Edward had "done it all"? Or perhaps we should ask in what sense it is true that Tussy and Edward did it all, and in what sense untrue. Or perhaps it is impossible at this late date, almost a hundred years after the event, to determine the extent to which Tussy and Edward "did it all." Certainly the reactionary *Daily Telegraph* gave Dr. Aveling full credit for organizing the events of the great day, and described him, "bareheaded and pale," leaping upon the platform to announce, "in thunderous tones," the purpose of the gathering. But what the General meant, probably, was that Tussy and Edward had done all they could to assure that in all committee decisions, the drafting of demands, the inclusion or exclusion of certain issues, such as the franchise, arming of the people, imperialism, the English workers agreed with their international comrades. Where they had to give way, they did.

"We shall oppose you at every turn," Bernard said. "You don't understand the English worker. It's a beast that won't be led."

"I quote my great teacher," Edward said. " 'Force is the midwife of every old society pregnant with a new one.' "

"My teacher as well as yours. But where is your force? You have no allies among the army or the police. You're just like us—all you can do is talk, and distribute a few hundred pamphlets."

"We intend to arm the people."

"You can't be serious. Arm your Irishman or your Frenchman, but your Englishman wants nothing to do with it."

"We shall start the revolution in Ireland, then," Tussy said.

"Good luck to you, my girl. You can drop pamphlets into a Dublin street from a hotel balcony, like Shelley, or send them in a bottle across the Irish Sea. The Irish are in a perpetual state of revolution; one pamphlet more or less isn't going to make much difference."

"What do you imagine England will be like in fifty years?" Tussy asked.

"I foresee a day fifty years from now," Bernard said, "when England will be one vast middle class devoted to self-betterment."

"Certainly," Clementina said, "we can expect great improvement in the material conditions of life. No one will die of starvation."

"Perhaps no one will die of starvation," Tussy said. "But you will still have a nation of rich and poor, of the privileged few and the disinherited many. And, if no one is actually starving, if the poor are decently housed and regularly employed, then the privileged few will congratulate themselves on their innate superiority, and dig in even deeper."

"According to my father," said May Morris, progress "lies in the formation of an independent labor party. If labor is firmly set on a collision course with capital, then all things are possible. But the signs are unmistakable—labor leadership believes it has more to gain eventually by collaboration with the masters than by confrontation. Unless we have an independent labor party, we shall see an amicable splitting of the profits. The only question will be how large a share labor can carve out for itself, and at what price. We're too rich in natural resources to risk a revolution and we have no tradition for it; we prefer buying and selling."

"Certainly we prefer change by consent to change by force," Clementina said. "The franchise is crucial to us. And achievable, if we press on steadily. What we must do is replace every Liberal and Radical Member who will not vote for us with one who will."

"You see, Dr. Aveling," Bernard said, "you're in a minority of two."

"We don't believe in counting heads," Edward said. "England is the only country in which the material conditions for revolution are mature. We don't intend to give up. I don't intend to give up."

17

Laura swept through London briefly in the wake of May Day. She stayed with the General, as usual, but accompanied Tussy on her East End rounds, and pronounced critically on each aspect of her life in turn.

The People's Palace she found worthy but depressing, the workingmen's clubs sweet but ineffectual, Bethnal Green squalid, English food inedible, English beer watery, Englishmen effeminate, Englishwomen lacking in style. And wherever she went she was idolized—the ragged costermongers of Stepney, the poor Jewish tailors of Spitalfields, the dandies of St. James, the intelligent ladies of Hampstead with their scrubbed faces and sensible walking shoes—all adored Madame Lafargue, and admired her indefinable style, her beauty, her masses of rich chestnut hair, her charm and wit.

"How can you live like this, Tussy?" she said, shuddering at the torn upholstery, the crumbs and books indiscriminately scattered on the table. "Surely you can get the landlord to clean the hallways, or at least to repair the plumbing. Everything stinks of cats. I don't know how you stand it."

"The building is scheduled to come down in a few months. You can't expect the landlord to care. We've been looking desperately for a larger flat."

"You could find something charming outside London for half the price you'd have to pay in town. With a garden for the cats."

"We thought of moving to Kent. But it's too far; all our friends are here."

"Your friends will follow you, if they care for you."

"Edward needs to be near the theatre."

"Does he? I should think Edward needs to be somewhat further from the theatre."

"It's his livelihood now, or he thinks it could be."

"Edward will do as he pleases, no doubt. But I see no reason for you to live in such discomfort. You could at least buy yourself some clothes. If I were here for more than a few days I'd take you in hand."

"Why don't you stay, Laura? We haven't had any real time together for years. We could go down to Margate for a day, just the two of us. Do you remember the house we stayed in with Mohme, before she became ill? with the Colonel's widow, and her pug dog that had the same sad wrinkled face and fat bottom . . . ? It would be lovely to have a rest after May Day. You have no idea how hard we worked, Edward and I."

Tussy sat at the table; Laura sat down opposite, holding herself somewhat aloof from the crumbs, and examined her sister carefully.

"You look terrible. I'm afraid you need more than a day at Margate. What's wrong, Tussy? You might as well tell me, since I'm here."

"You're here very seldom. What would be the point?"

"Suit yourself, then. You're a grown woman. But it's obvious that you're not well."

"There's nothing physically wrong with me."

"What is it, then?"

"I don't know, Laura."

"Nonsense, you must know if you have pain, if you're not eating properly, or if you're unable to sleep."

"I've never been a very good sleeper. It's true that I've been sleeping very badly for months now. Edward has had to prescribe laudanum; it seems to be the only medicine that works."

"How often?"

"More often than you would approve."

"Have you seen Donkin?"

"What's the use? I told you, there's nothing physically wrong with me. The truth is, I haven't felt well since Nim died."

"Helen was seventy-two—you couldn't expect her to live forever."

"It brought back the old pain, each day of it, each hour, as if no time had passed, as if nothing had changed. . . . Why can't I get used to it, Laura? When Nim died I felt like a small child that's lost its mother, totally bereft; I wanted to stand and howl. . . . You loved Mama, and Nim, but you don't feel orphaned every day."

"I was trained in a hard school."

"Oh, Laura, I shouldn't speak of my own troubles; they're as nothing, I know. Though I sometimes think it must be better to have had children and lost them than never to have had them at all."

"One survives. The human spirit is an amazing thing . . . how it can take blow after blow, and somehow go on, baffles the imagination. But if I ever came to feel that my life was pointless, of no use to anyone or anything, I should end it, as painlessly as possible."

"Your life could never be pointless. You are loved wherever you go. All you have to do is walk into a room and people feel their lives have been brightened. You've always had that special aura about you."

"Nonsense. The only person to whom my life makes the slightest difference is Paul."

"Ah, you have a real marriage, Laura, in spite of everything you've suffered. You are all in all to each other. It makes up for everything else."

"Why do you stay with him, Tussy?"

"Why do you ask? You know why I stay with him."

Laura rose irritably, and paced back and forth in front of the window.

"I can't understand why you submit. The uncertainty of it, the humiliation . . . no wonder you look ill, unkempt, uncared for. . . ."

"It's all very well for you to come here for a week and criticize me for things over which I have no control. . . ."

"Oh, Tussy, you seek out misery. If you wanted to change your life, you could."

They discussed the problem of Freddy.

"Shouldn't we do more for him?" Tussy asked.

"I can't see what more we can do. He knows that he can always turn to us."

"Edward wants him to live with us."

"That seems most unwise."

"You don't know him as I do, Laura. He's a very simple man, without an ounce of malice or self. He just seems to have bad luck."

"Still, you needn't have him to live with you. And I doubt if he'd want it. Probably he prefers to be with his own people."

"Aren't we his people?"

"No, I hardly think we are."

Laura also had some advice to give about Edward, since Tussy clearly had no intention of leaving him.

"You'll have to do something about his drinking, Tussy. It looks to me as if he's crossed that invisible line—he really seems to need his wee dram first thing in the morning."

"What would you suggest that I do?"

"Talk to him frankly."

"He won't listen to me. He claims he's not drinking. He's rather clever at disguising the effects."

"Ask the General to talk to him."

"I couldn't possibly."

"I'll ask him, then."

"If you do, I'll never forgive you."

"You must realize that if he goes on like this he won't live more than three or four years. He's had kidney disease since you've known him."

There was enough truth in this to cause Tussy to become exquisitely agitated.

"Ah, Laura, help me . . . what am I to do? I can't force him to change. He has to do it himself."

"Impossible."

"Why is it impossible? He's a reasonable human being—he must know he's destroying himself."

"When was that ever sufficient reason to change bad habits? You probably make it possible for him to go on as he does, by tolerating behavior that anyone else would find intolerable."

"Don't you think I find it intolerable?"

"That doesn't seem to matter. Either to you or to him."

Tussy deliberately allowed her rage at Edward to be deflected onto Laura. "You've watched me suffering and haven't said a

157

word. You can see that I'm caught in a vicious circle, no way out, no way at all, you watch me drown and don't lift a hand to help me."

"That's very unfair, Tussy. You say you don't want me to interfere. I've tried not to interfere. I realize that there's very little an outsider can do."

"But you're not an outsider, Laura, you're my sister, my flesh and blood. You're all I have left. Who am I to turn to if not to you?"

"I can't understand you, Tussy. You're most unreasonable. When I offer advice, you scorn it; when I don't offer advice you accuse me of indifference."

"That's because your advice is worse than useless. You only tell me what I already know."

"I see. You want me to tell you that I think Edward is a reformed character, that you have nothing to fear from his drinking or his long unexplained absences. You want me to say that I think you've done exactly what you should have done, and that it's going to work out all right in the end."

"Why not? That would be the sisterly thing to do."

"Would it make it easier for you if I lied?"

"I don't think it's possible for me to live with the truth, not the unvarnished truth. Perhaps there's no need to—you see, we're very busy, Edward and I. We have literally so many committee meetings, so many speeches to give, so many letters to write, quite apart from my typewriting and Edward's teaching, that we hardly have the time to face the truth about each other. And there are times when you would think that Edward is the most considerate of men, the kindest, the best. Why shouldn't that be his true nature, after all?"

"As long as he's considerate and kind to you."

"He is, from time to time. A good part of the time. Enough of the time for me to overlook the rest of it."

It had begun to seem to Tussy that Edward simply drifted into his worst excesses. She realized that his affairs with women were casual and unplanned; they finished as easily as they had begun, and receded immediately into his amorphous, forgotten past. Laura was quite right: alcohol had a good deal to do with his behavior. Heavy drinking made it easy for him to give in to impulse, with no regard to consequences. When he came to her after a drunken night, he was simply coming home, shedding the night's debauch as if it had never happened. It hardly occurred to him that the money borrowed and squandered, the drink consumed, the casual fornication, might impinge on his life with Tussy.

Yet the drinking was not a cause only, was more a symptom, and she doubted that it was the key to reform. Drink loosened the barriers, but in fact he needed to live recklessly, to indulge the dark side of his nature. He worked very hard; he had fought heroically on the Legal Eight-Hour Day Committee, attended every meeting, organized the demonstration virtually single-handed. He drove himself and everyone around him remorselessly, antagonizing many of his less-committed allies in the process; he needed some light relief.

Or was she simply finding excuses for him? Others worked equally hard for causes they believed in—William Morris, Shaw, the General—and their social principles carried over naturally and easily to private life.

It sometimes seemed to her that her life's work had narrowed to one absorbing task: to understand the man whose life encompassed and ruled hers. Though she had studied him for all the days of their intimacy, though she brought her full intelligence, her knowledge of others, her reading, her imagination, to bear on the problem, she seemed to come no closer; she could no more predict his next step than she could that of a stranger whose life crossed hers for an hour.

18

Havelock Ellis had a pedantic streak which made him unhappy with half answers , unresolved puzzles, loose ends. His conversation with Olive several months before had left him in a state of extreme irritability; he felt they had not approached anything like the truth. He returned to the attack armed with new arguments. Olive was the most intelligent woman he knew; if she could not explain what it meant to be female, then the subject was not open to rational discussion.

"It seems to me," he began—for he wanted first of all to clarify his own position—"that the wrongs of women are very different in kind from the wrongs of the blacks. It is by no means clear that, in their relations with men, women are invariably victims and men oppressors. Often their roles are reversed, which can never be true of black native and colonial governor, or factory worker and mill owner. And, although it's quite true that men hold legal, political, and economic power over women, it doesn't follow that they invariably use their power to oppress women. Quite apart from their legal and economic relations, men and women are surely capable of establishing a personal relationship of equals, should they consider it important."

Olive replied, "I too would like to think that a relation of true equality between a man and woman is possible. Certainly if it were possible it would be the most beautiful and satisfying relationship imaginable. But humans don't form relations in accord with theory; they form relations out of need. The weak need the strong; and the strong evidently need the weak. It's true that weakness and strength know no sex, any more than intellect and feeling. But it would be naïve to think that where legal, political, and economic power are all on one side men will not tend to dominate in their relations with women. That is why women must do without men if they are to become strong. They must learn to hate before they can allow themselves to love."

"But that seems to me a very dangerous doctrine, which is bound to injure women more than it can help them. To be forced to hate, to be filled with rage and resentment, is the worst form of oppression. It's a slavery of the mind as well as the body. It's as if the oppressor now has an ally in his victim; he has cunningly established a hold from within. Perhaps that's why so many oppressed people instinctively adapt to their circumstances. It's not because it's the easiest way—sometimes it's easier to struggle—but because their instinct warns them that in struggling they will be wholly lost to the struggle, while if they submit, they can keep a part of themselves free."

"I fail to see how, if you submit to tyranny, you can keep any part of yourself free. It seems to me axiomatic that you can be mentally free only if you are physically free. You must be the master of your own fate."

"My dear Olive, which of us is master of his own fate? We are prisoners of our inheritance, our abilities, our limitations, our situation in life, our obligations to others. Freedom is a matter of degree, a small space one carves out for oneself in the midst of chartered territory. Or perhaps it's an illusion, a myth peculiar to our culture, an ideal we choose to worship as the Greeks worshiped love and beauty.

"And yet I know that my nature craves freedom more than anything else, more than love, more than beauty. What I dread most of all is being enslaved to another, losing my liberty of movement, my freedom of thought. To have to be always in one fixed place, to follow a routine set by others, to perform day after day the same soul-stifling tasks—"

"Yet this is how most of the world lives. Of their own free choice."

"They are bribed to do it, and vanity will not allow them to question the premises of their lives."

"Are you happy now, Olive?" He looked about her drab room,

at the torn curtains, the peeling walls, the patches of damp along the ceiling.

"I feel a sense of possibility. I suppose that's what I mean by freedom—the knowledge that one can change one's life, that all doors have not been shut."

"You haven't told me much about your life in Pietermaritzburg."

"I don't think I can. I've put it away from me. When I can understand it myself, I will try to tell you about it."

"I gather it was a mistake."

"It was something I had to do. You can't experience marriage from the outside. Nobody can tell you what it is. How can you know if it's right for you, or wrong, terribly wrong, until you've lived through it?"

"Shall you go back to your husband, Olive?"

A long silence followed. Havelock thought perhaps she hadn't heard him, but he didn't like to repeat the question.

"It's strange, but I'm certain we have the natural capacity to be reborn. Dead tissue regenerates, sometimes after the passage of months or years; surely love can renew itself. If we are alive to the hidden processes of nature we can become sensitive to our own cycles, the great flowering of sexual passion, its death and rebirth. I am listening to the earth, Havelock, I have my ear pressed to the dark soil—I am listening for my own heartbeat."

Suddenly he knelt at her feet and buried his head in her lap. He shook with sobs. She sat passively until the spasm passed.

"I can't bear what has happened to you," he said, raising his tear-stained face to her calm one. "You're like ice."

She stroked his hair.

"You haven't changed at all," she said.

"I have changed, my Olive, in the most important way of all. If I came to you now you wouldn't be disappointed. But how badly we've arranged our lives! I failed you when you needed me, and you are lost to me now when I could save you, perhaps."

She looked earnestly into his eyes. "Come to me, then. Now. For the first and last time."

"Ah, you don't want me, Olive."

"Yes, I want you. I'm used up, sour, I won't meet your expectations. I have an ugly scar across my belly from the birth, and I've been dry as a withered fruit ever since. But I want to feel you inside me. I want us to have a night together."

She began to unbutton her blouse, and as Havelock sat somewhat bemused at her feet, stripped off her clothes until she stood naked before him.

"Hannah!" she called.

The girl appeared in the doorway.

"Bring me my dressing gown, please."

"Olive!" Havelock protested. "The girl—surely—"

Hannah brought in a man's dressing gown and laid it on the chair. Naked, Olive embraced the girl and kissed her on the lips.

"Thank you, Hannah. When you go out be kind enough to close the door behind you. . . . Are you planning to make love fully clothed, Havelock?"

"Olive—dearest—you've caught me unawares. I'm not prepared . . ."

"You've surely seen a naked woman before. Why, you've seen me naked many times. You've sucked at these nipples." She cupped one breast invitingly.

"Yes, of course. I do wish you'd put on your dressing gown."

"Won't you at least loosen your cravat? No? Not even that?"

She shrugged her shoulders, and put on the dressing gown.

"There you are. Or there we are, I should say. What's the use of talk? I shall never know if you have truly reached manhood. I'm stuck with my poor Hannah."

"I'm sorry, Olive. You put me in an impossible position. You know I'm to be married."

"Yes. When is the happy date?"

"We haven't yet set a date. We're planning to go away together first, for a long weekend."

"To test the marriage, do you mean?"

"I think it's wise."

"I doubt that a weekend will tell you much that you don't already know."

"True, it's a plunge into the unknown, under the best circumstances. But Edith wishes us to do it this way."

"And you honor her wishes."

"Certainly. In this and other things. We're to have separate

163

residences and separate accounts; she has a small private income, and earns money from her journalism and speeches. We shall probably not have children. I would very much like you to meet her. But with your clothes on."

"Why—do you think she would be tempted?"

"She's a lover of beauty and an enthusiast. I see no reason to take chances."

Tussy hadn't seen Bernard since the May Day demonstration, when he had promised to call on her. She sent a note to 88 Fitzroy Square.

Dear Mr. Shaw,

Are you too boycotting us? I know how busy you must be, but on the strength of our former attachment I conjure you to come and see me. May I suggest this Wednesday or Friday evening, around nine? Or if not this week, then next week? I am happy to watch your light from afar, but need a few hours of its brightness closer to home. You will not begrudge your old friend,

E.M.A.

It was probably a mistake to send such a begging letter; what if there were no answer? But she could not believe that Bernard would ignore a cry for help. She needed him to help her see more clearly; she wanted the benefit of a cool, detached intelligence that could throw light on dark corners which struck terror into her soul, and which might in the clear light of day turn out to be harmless shadows, no more offensive than a discarded newspaper.

Her women friends were no use to her; they were too much on her side. But Bernard, who really liked women, who enjoyed their company and conversation, who relished gossip and intrigue and was fascinated by the ins and outs of social and sexual relations, still was wonderfully even-handed in his perceptions. He alone of her friends refused to blame Edward for his lapses. First of all, he refused on principle to be shocked by the conventionally outrageous; second, he professed to see nothing moral or immoral about sexual behavior of any sort. Sex lay outside the realm of morality, which had to do with relations between human beings; men and women were another matter.

An answer came in the afternoon post, two days later.

I am certainly not "boycotting" you, but unfortunately am very busy. This week and the next are out, but try me later in the month.

G.B.S.

She read the note twice, then crumpled it in her fist. Laura had gone back to Paris; Edward was on a lecturing tour in the North. She was alone in the rooms she shared with Edward, with piles of unfinished work on every surface—table, bureau, chair, mantelpiece, bookshelves. She stared at herself in the mirror and saw what Laura had seen: dark circles under her eyes, her skin sallow, unhealthy, her hair frizzy and wild, a deep line etched on either side of her nose, marks of exhaustion or age. She combed her hair and rubbed some rouge into her cheeks, then rubbed it off; the effect was to make her look feverish. She felt feverish, but thought it was from lack of food. When Edward was away she often forgot to take meals, and it struck her that she hadn't had anything to eat or drink but coffee since the morning.

She opened the cupboard above the sink: dry biscuits, a stale piece of Cheddar cheese. She couldn't force herself to eat. Instead she poured a small glass of brandy and drank it in two gulps. She immediately felt better.

She would go to see Olive and sit with her for a while.

But Olive would be working.

If Olive wanted to work, she would leave immediately.

It would do no harm to walk in the direction of Olive's rooms. A walk would do her good, would clear her head. She could decide whether or not to call on Olive when she reached Middlesex Hospital.

It was drizzling but there were as many people as usual on Tottenham Court Road, walking quickly with bent heads. The Italian and Swiss shops on Goodge Street were crowded; students filled every table in the cafés. Her own solitude oppressed her, as if she were a visitor in her own city, cut off from the purposeful, connected lives around her. She observed details of dress and expression in a paralysis of feeling; she could have been invisible.

When she reached Olive's door Hannah let her in and took

her damp cape and bonnet, then sat down in her corner with a pile of darning. A coal fire burned in the grate; Olive was writing at a small table. Tussy sat at the other side of the fire, leaned back, and shut her eyes. It was comforting to sit and dream a few feet from her friend, while Olive worked steadily, undisturbed by her visitor. How few people there were in whose presence one could sit quietly, not talking, not feeling the need to fill up silences.

After a while Olive put aside her papers and turned to Tussy.

"You're not well," she said.

"I feel strangely light-headed. Yet my feet are like lead. I could hardly drag myself over."

"You could have sent for me."

"No, I wanted to go out. I needed to breathe. I felt so strange— I was very frightened. I felt somehow . . . cut off. I think it was Laura's visit—it brought back so much that I've pushed away from me."

"Did I tell you a strange thing that happened to me in Pietermaritzburg? I went by myself to the hills where I had lived when I was sixteen. It was a glorious day, and I felt quite cheerful. I decided to come back, and suddenly I found myself shouting in an amazingly loud voice: 'My youth! my youth! Give me back my youth!' I hadn't known that I could cry in a voice so loud and deep."

"Ah, Olive, how dreadful! And no one to hear . . . Do you know, if I shouted the same words on Tottenham Court Road, I doubt if anyone would notice. People would assume it was just another madwoman, or a drunk, like a hundred others."

"I suppose I was a bit mad. Quite mad, in fact."

"Why do you never tell me about your life in Africa? about your childhood?"

"I can tell you, if you like. I can tell you about the children of the provinces, and the wild ambition that seizes them. Everything they see close at hand, their entire familiar world, stinks of mediocrity. They aspire to greatness, and because they know of greatness only from books, they conceive of it as something that exists elsewhere, in ancient civilizations, in brilliant universities, above all in the great European cities, in London and Paris and Rome. Their yearning after greatness is fueled by a secret conviction of greatness within. The child from the provinces knows that he has something unique to communicate to the world, but these children lack opportunity, their private vision is stifled, and gradually imagination sickens and dies. And so they wait impatiently to escape. In time, they rush to the great city, which cares nothing for their genius and imagination. Their dreams fail, they experience a loneliness, a sense of abandonment, so huge as to be inconceivable—the provinces have nothing to match it."

Hannah had stopped darning to listen, and sat attentive, her small features strained with the effort to understand.

"And then what happens to them?" Tussy said.

"They marry."

"Because they can't tolerate the loneliness?"

"Yes. Otherwise they would die."

"But there must be one or two who survive—whose dreams survive."

"There may be one or two who can create out of their loneliness."

"I have always thought that genius creates out of joy, not out of grief."

"Modern genius has to forgo joy. It is too sophisticated for joy—it knows too much. It is too democratic."

At a signal from Olive, Hannah brought Tussy a cup of tea and a slice of bread and butter. She was able to eat, but as soon as she had finished she realized how dead tired she was.

"You'd better stay the night," Olive said. "If you don't mind having me as a bedfellow. Hannah can take some blankets into her corner."

"Are you quite certain? Suddenly I feel that I could sleep for a day and a night—I'll just lie down as I am."

"Hannah will give you a night dress—you'll be more comfortable."

"Will you come to bed now?"

"I'll work for a few hours."

In the middle of the night she felt the pressure of Olive's soft, compact body next to hers. She turned to her, and they clung together without speaking. Tussy wept, and Olive stroked her cheeks, and kissed her tears, as if she were a child. Then

167

she rocked Tussy to sleep on her shoulder, and the two of them slept.

This was the night Olive referred to in her letter to Dollie, when, she said, she held Tussy in her arms, but did not become her lover.

When Dollie Radford was pregnant with her third child, she bought a four-story brick house on East Heath Road, a stone's throw from the three ponds where Mohr had sailed paper boats for his daughters. Busy as she was, Tussy seldom visited her friends in Hampstead. But one Sunday morning in late June she yielded to Dollie's pressing invitation, and arrived to find her distraught.

"Can you talk to him?" she said. "He's been taking laudanum for his stomach; he's positively wild."

Ernest lay in bed, wrapped in shawls, though the day was mild, and the window open to the sweet grassland beyond, the hedges awash with roses and brambles just coming into bloom. She thought he was asleep, and sat down quietly in Dollie's pretty chintz-covered bedside chair.

"Scum," he said. "They're not fit to wipe your shoes. Kill 'em, I say."

Something uncontrolled in his voice and manner made her uneasy.

"It's too much trouble," she said. "We can leave it safely to others."

"No trouble at all." He patted his pillow significantly. "No trouble if you know what you're doing."

She stared at his pillow as if by willpower she might be able to see what lay under it. Firmness was indicated, and common sense.

"You're one of the least violent persons I know, Ernest dear. Why would you want to injure another human being?"

"It's all very well for you to preach tolerance. You've made your bed. But there are things I won't stand for."

She talked to him as one might talk to a wayward child, soothing his fears, calming his anger, pretending to share his fantasy so that she might disarm it.

"I am beset by enemies," he said. "Even you."

"You know very well that I'm your friend, not your enemy."

168

"You went back to that man."

"I did what I had to do. My relations with Edward in no way interfere with my friendship for you."

He leaned toward her conspiratorially.

"I'll get rid of him for you, Tussy. You'll be free. He'll get what he deserves."

For an insane minute she contemplated his offer.

"You forget that I love him."

"He should be lying in a ditch, eaten by dogs. All of them, whoring, thieving bastards. They don't appreciate us; they think we're simpletons, to be pushed around and kicked and imposed on by any fool in uniform. But you—you, of all women—should know that there's only one way to get rid of your enemies. . . ."

He leaned closer to her and drew his finger expressively across his neck.

"Slit their throats," he whispered, and winked at her. "Then there's no arguing, is there? Then you're finished with broken promises. Then your debts are paid, once and for all. Then you've rid the earth of these swindlers and murderers."

He rummaged under his pillow, keeping his eyes on her, extracted a pistol, and waved it about wildly.

"It's them or us, isn't it? It's a question of who gets there first."

"Put that down, Ernest," Tussy said. "Put it down at once, or you'll hurt someone."

He put it down on the bedside table, shuddering. He held his head in his hands and wept.

"The only one I'm likely to hurt is myself. One of these days I'll put a bullet through my brains."

"You're much too good-natured to be a murderer," Tussy said. "Anyway, it wouldn't solve the problem. New oppressors always leap up to take the place of the old."

Once the immediate danger was past, she was haunted by Ernest's mad offer. Men and women of the most diverse background, regardless of their politics, recognized the legitimacy of the *crime passionel.* It satisfied a universal, primitive sense of justice: the exaction of violent revenge for violence suffered. Why did she refuse to strike back at Edward? Her anger was deflected onto herself, so that she was filled with self-loathing.

If she could hate him, she would regain her self-respect; if he were brought to her dead, and she could rejoice in his death, the world would applaud her.

In the end Ernest took a shot at a magazine editor who had the poor judgment to reject his poems. Dollie took him to University Hospital, where he was put into a closed ward, visitors forbidden. He was released a year later with strict instructions to avoid anxiety, tension, and hard mental or physical labor. He seemed perfectly normal, though changed; he had put on several stone, and was somewhat remote. He seldom smiled, or, indeed, initiated conversation of any kind, and Dollie fell into the habit of talking nonstop, both when she was alone with Ernest and in company, in a continuous stream of anecdote, musing, question, answer, and commentary. It was as if she hoped, by surrounding Ernest with an undifferentiated mass of trivial chitchat, to embed him more securely in the ordinary world, from which he demonstrated an unmistakable tendency to drift away.

And she created out of their narrow Hampstead house a wonderful sanctuary, an oasis of warmth and hospitality, in which Ernest had his "study," with French doors into the rose garden and a reclining chair in which he sat smoking his pipe and dreaming, and the children and dogs raced about upstairs or in the garden, and Dollie presided in the drawing room, with kind friends dropping by, mostly literary and vaguely socialist, and always hungry.

Tussy accused her of abandoning her genuine if small creative gift to become a "hostess."

"It suits me to have friends around, and it suits the children, and it's the best thing imaginable for Ernest."

"How can you possibly get any work done?"

"I've never been very industrious. Even when I had all the time in the world, my 'work,' if you can dignify it by the name, never amounted to much. I shall never be an actress, and I can still write poetry now and then, and an occasional short story. Perhaps this is my real work—making a home for my children and my husband. It's different for you, of course. Your real life will always lie in the larger world. But I'm a domestic being, Tussy—why should I pretend otherwise?"

Tussy tried to imagine settling with Edward into a Hampstead cottage, in the pleasant world of cultivated, comfortably circumstanced neighbors and friends that Dollie found so congenial. If they owned a house with a garden, a proper kitchen and dining room, a study, a guest room, would their union take on a more permanent character? Certainly the four walls of a modest brick villa, the privacy and self-enclosed nature of the living space, made it easier to imagine a loving family life within. Mohr always had a healthy respect for property; and with prices rising and the real value of money decreasing, it was plain that the only secure investment was real estate.

But investment was out of the question without capital, and for the moment, at least, the purchase of a house remained fantasy.

19

Tussy worked with the General in his study every Tuesday morning, then took a sheaf of papers home to return typewritten the following week. In this way volume three of *Capital* came into being, and volume four was begun.

She avoided the Sunday suppers at Regents Park Road; since Nim's death the General had been ruled by Karl and Louise Kautsky, and she hated to see him basking in their false solicitude. Everything she saw reminded her of Nim, and the new regime—cold, bloodless, self-seeking—was the antithesis of everything Nim stood for. Karl Kautsky fell in love with another Louise and left for Austria; his first Louise remained in London, triumphantly in charge. She gradually cut down on the General's pleasures, limited him to one bottle of Pilsener with meals, and a glass of claret after, forbade cigars in the drawing room, sent him to bed early, restricted visitors, and ruled the entire household with an iron thumb. When he fell ill she put him on a diet of gruel; nobody was allowed to see him, not even Tussy or Edward; "Doctor's orders," she lied. The doctor was another young Austrian, Ludwig Freyberger, who was soon installed downstairs; Louise, three months pregnant, became Mrs. Dr. Freyberger, with the General's blessing.

But of course he was ill; she was not lying about that. The General made light of it and kept on cheerfully with his work; but he knew what his symptoms meant. He referred jokingly to the "potato field" on his neck; he had an inoperable cancer of the throat.

He made a special effort to make his position clear not only to Tussy and Edward but to Laura and Paul, who were strategically placed, or so he hoped, to influence the direction of labor politics on the Continent.

The English labor movement, he felt, had matured beyond expectation, largely through the growth of the unskilled unions and the eight-hour movement, in both of which Tussy and Edward had played a small but significant role. It was time to consolidate gains, to concentrate on building a united, independent labor party. This party must have a two-pronged strategy: to strengthen union solidarity and to elect local councillors and Members of Parliament. If a united labor party could gain control of the new Greater London Council—which had fallen into their laps, as it were—it would take a major war to dislodge them.

On the Continent, the German party had made gigantic strides; it had polled one and a half million votes in the 1893 election. On the other hand, the Germans were unquestionably arrogant; in the international movement they tried to play schoolmaster and commander at one and the same time. The French were amateurs in comparison, which was a pity, since they were the only party with a revolutionary tradition. But, as soon as the French left was numerically stronger than the right, it split into two warring factions; party discipline had no meaning for the Latin temperament.

The great danger, still, was nationalism. And, to be honest, the General had moments of pessimism about the prospect for a truly international workers party. The force of European nationalism had yet to be tested, and in the event might well destroy the good work of the twenty-five years since the Commune.

In a somewhat solemn conference with Tussy and Edward— the claret rationed by Louise to two bottles—he gave them what amounted to last instructions.

The May Day demonstrations, they agreed, were spent. Edward was quite right to resign from the Legal Eight-Hour Day Committee and its proxy, the Legal Eight Hours and International Labour League (though his motives, as usual, were impugned by his colleagues), and to move on to the Independent Labour Party, where he now had a seat on the executive. Their best hope at the moment lay in the provinces, as London was split between the SDF and the Fabians, the Socialist League having long since been abandoned to the anarchists. Let them argue among themselves, while Edward built a secure base in the North, where the rank and file, especially in the new unions of the unskilled, were solidly with them.

In the long run, the General believed, the most dramatic developments would take place not in Europe but in the East and West—Russia and America.

He was leaving Tussy a sum of money, he said. It was to be hers, not Edward's.

"I want you not to have to worry about money," he said. "It's the least important of all things, as long as one has enough of it."

As for Edward, "Keep a tight rein on him, Tussy," the General warned her. "He wants close watching. I've done what I can. . . . You and Laura will take back all of Mohr's papers. The German party wants them, of course. We shall have to find the best means of keeping them together. I am naming Sam Moore co-executor with you; you'll have to rely on his judgment, to some extent. You and Laura will have to work out where the papers are to be kept, who is to do the transcribing, and so on. You've both done heroically, in spite of an occasional tiff. But it's a pity you weren't born male. None of Mohr's sons-in-law has a tenth of his daughters' abilities—but there we are."

"I'm sorry you're disappointed in me."

"It's not your fault, Tussy. How well Mohr understood the problem! How well he knew that knowledge unless it is put into action is useless; while action based upon ignorance is catastrophic. But there are very few who are genuinely driven to know, and half at least of those few find that knowledge incapacitates them for action. Which means that those who are left to act, nine times out of ten, are the ignorant, confident rabble, or the fanatics."

"Do you think it's harder for women to take action?"

"So it seems. They have no lack of intelligence, but they suffer from inhibitions which men of comparable intelligence find it easier to throw off. Certainly this has been true of Laura."

"Do you think it's true of me?"

"You work very hard, Tussy, I don't deny it. You never excuse yourself from work that has to be done. But you're very reluctant to assume a position of leadership. You leave that to Edward, whose judgment often leaves much to be desired. I doubt very much that some are born leaders and others followers; it is a matter of experience and confidence. You are more confident than you were; you've gained in confidence as your experience has broadened. But you are still less confident than I should like you to be."

She rose in agitation.

"It's too much," she said. "You ask too much of me."

"I don't mean to upset you, my dear. I'm not asking you to do more."

"You don't understand. I've been completely drained. I'm exhausted—it's a battle to get up each morning. And there's so much to be done—you have no idea how much work I have to turn down, lectures to give, articles to be typewritten. . . . I am continually putting off earnest workers who want only to be enlightened, and to share in the great awakening of the age. I can't be in ten places at once; the day has only so many hours. But the worst part of it—oh, I shouldn't tell you this now, when it's too late—but why shouldn't you know? Even as I am in the middle of a lecture, and I see the eager upturned faces of my comrades before me, suddenly I must stop—I can't go on. I feel that I am feeding them lies. Not that I am deliberately lying to them, but I am withholding the truth. And yet I couldn't tell you what this truth is, or what it might be—it is nothing I could put my finger on. The lie is in me, it is a falsehood in my life, it is the lie I have been living since we started working together, Edward and I. . . ."

The General made no attempt to interrupt her, neither did he argue with her. Perhaps he knew; perhaps he had seen it all before.

"You're overtired, Tussy. You should take a holiday; you need sun, air, warmth."

"No, it suits me to be in this dark, damp, cursed climate. I'd die in the sun. I'd wither up; I'd die of exposure to light and heat."

"You can't expect a sick old man to listen to such nonsense. Be reasonable, Tussy."

175

"I can't bear to let you down so. I can't bear to let Mohr down."

"In the end we have to think of ourselves. No one blames you."

As the General lay dying, a terrible truth was borne about the radical and socialist clubs in London, whispered from Berners Street to Hammersmith, from Woolwich to Paddington. It was not the first time scandal had touched the Marx family; letters from Mohr to the General, four years before Tussy's birth, allude to vicious lies circulated by his enemies, denied categorically, and to all intents and purposes laid to rest. But this time the rumors were allowed to float, because those whom they could harm were all dead. The living, on the other hand, might conceivably benefit from the truth, and in any case had the right to know.

Unfortunately it was Louise who was delegated or who chose to inform Tussy, in a short letter calculated to raise more questions than it answered. The truth was so obvious that Tussy could well have deduced it for herself. Nim's lover half a lifetime ago had been not the General, not a comrade long since vanished, but her own father, Nim's beloved friend and master.

Information long after the event has a curiously unreal character. The mystery remained as mysterious as before; nothing in Tussy's experience qualified her to understand it.

Surely it was untrue, a fabrication of Louise's ingenious malice. If she had set out to destroy Tussy, she could not have hit upon anything closer to the mark.

Tussy had lost her freedom of the house; she was a visitor at Regents Park Road, like any outsider, and came by invitation only. Through the General's last illness she saw him by appointment, as before. But as soon as she had read Louise's letter she rushed to his bedside; she must see him at once.

Louise admitted her without a word and took her upstairs to the darkened bedroom, where the General lay unable to speak, unable to move his head. He was surrounded by the mementoes of his long, fruitful life—dark framed photographs of his German comrades, his books and Mohr's translated into French, Russian, Spanish, Italian, Portuguese. He dozed fitfully and woke almost at once, in pain.

Louise stood like a sentinel by the side of the heavy wooden bedstead. "Ask him," she whispered, arms folded across her chest.

Tussy leaned across the bed; she could smell the thin, sour breath of the old man.

"Is it true?" she said. "Was Mohr Freddy's father?"

He looked at her with the fathomless gaze of the dying, for whom the concerns of the living are remote and perplexing.

"Was he?" she said. "Is it true?"

Louise placed a slate in his hand. He made an immense effort to concentrate. In crude, spidery letters he scrawled the letters: J A. Louise removed the slate and he shut his eyes.

"Come," she said to Tussy.

Trembling uncontrollably, Tussy followed her out of the bedroom. In the dark hallway she wept, and the two women embraced.

"He was a man like any other," Louise said.

"You didn't know him," Tussy sobbed.

"True. But I can imagine. Living like that, in two rooms. What would you expect? Your mother is away for a few weeks visiting her family, the babies cry, nobody can get any sleep. Your father is trying to work, he has maybe a little more schnapps than is good for him, she keeps him company. It gets late, it's cold, there's no money for a fire. It's lonely sleeping alone, you and I know it, eh, Tussy? By the time she knows she's pregnant, it's finished, your mother is back, they must be discreet for her sake. Oh, Tussy, you're such a baby—why are you crying? These things happen all the time—people pick up the pieces and go on living. Men fancy a bit of fun, and the woman is left with a big belly. It's always been the same. If the man's free to marry and willing, so much the better, but if he's already married to someone else, then she's stuck with it. She'll have to manage the best she can; he's not going to be much use to her. Your Nimmy knew which side her bread was buttered on."

"I must go," Tussy said. "I'll powder my face and go home."

"Why don't you stay? He can't last much longer."

"No, I'll go home."

She left the house, pulled her gray cape closer about her shoulders, and hunched against the wind, walked quickly along Re-

gents Park Road, across the railway bridge, up Haverstock Hill
to Maitland Park, and across to Grafton Terrace, where she
stood uncertainly in front of number 9, as if unsure whether
or not to enter. Lights filtered through the narrow bay window
on the first floor. Behind the thick curtains Mohr sat at his
desk surrounded by papers, and Lenchen, her beautiful hair
pulled back in a bright flowered scarf, stood behind him massag-
ing his neck and shoulders. Mohme lay in the upstairs bedroom,
a wet napkin on her aching forehead. The lamp went out upstairs, and Mohme slept, and downstairs Mohr worked until
dawn; Lenchen, dear, faithful Lenchen, sat by his side dozing,
to wake at a moment's notice if he should need the strong coffee
that only she could brew properly.

What was he writing as his pen sped rapidly over the paper
in that crabbed scrawl that only the General and Mohme could
decipher?

*The force that brings men together and puts them in relation with
each other is the selfishness, the gain, and the private interests of each.*

"Are you looking for someone, miss?"

A policeman stood a few feet away, swinging his truncheon,
waiting for an answer.

"No," she said. "No one."

"Shall I get you a cab?"

"No, I don't think so."

"You don't want to loiter here, miss."

"No. Thank you."

Please go, she begged him silently. She had almost understood.
She was within touching distance of the truth.

What force held Nim to the side of that harried, melancholic
genius, with his imperious needs, his coarse humor, his violent
rages?

Private interest, or hope of gain? No—a love pure, strong,
simple, that asked for nothing, that accepted and endured.

In return for which he demanded only one thing of her: that
she give up her child.

Retching violently, Tussy made her way to the corner and
hailed a cab.

Outside her door she heard men talking, Edward's penetrating
tones, and a softer, apologetic voice—Freddy.

She couldn't look at him.

"Why are you here?"

"I told him that Louise wrote to you," Edward said. "He came at once."

"I knew you'd take it hard," Freddy said.

It had nothing to do with her. He was the injured one, injured beyond recompense. He should be tearing up the cobblestones and hurling them through the windows of the house on Regents Park Road.

"I must lie down," she said. "I'm afraid I'm going to be ill."

"I'll leave, then," Freddy said. "I'll call in later in the week."

"No, stay," Edward said. "I insist."

"Can you give me something?" she asked Edward.

"Certainly." He went to the cabinet with the photographs of Mohr and Jenny, and took out a small jar filled with a ruby-colored liquid.

She went into the bedroom, undressed, and lay down. He measured out twenty drops of laudanum and brought it to her.

"Drink it. You'll soon feel better."

"No. But I must sleep."

"It should make you sleep."

"Why don't you send him away?"

"He came all this way to see you. You needn't talk—we'll both sit with you until you fall asleep."

But she was asleep almost at once, or half asleep. Through her sleep, or half sleep, floated two shadowy presences, one on either side of her, brother and lover. One was kind, fussy, protective; the other was demonic, cruel, savage. And, if she clung to the hand of her good brother, her demon lover grasped her more tightly, his grip was iron, she had no way of breaking it. She was cunning enough to know that remonstrance was useless, and she had no strength to fight. She abandoned herself to his grasp, when suddenly he released her, pushing her away. She reached for her brother, but he faded into the far distance, until he was no more than a speck waving to her forlornly. Alone, she sank past immense cliffs, past waterfalls, deep into the cleft earth. Voices called to her from the water and the rocks, but she must descend further, past dark pine forests clothing the hills that rose to either side, and it seemed that falling was her condition, her state of being, and would end only with

179

her death. Until in the surprising shift of dream landscape she found herself lying spread-eagled, floating on a vast sea of mist and soft cloud, and her lover lay beside her, bending over her with a look of infinite concern. He caressed her face tenderly, and she wept tears of gratitude, and slept.

20

She began to sleep sixteen and eighteen hours a day, a thick, drunken sleep from which it seemed impossible to extricate herself. She would force herself to get up and dress, feeling as if layers of net were enveloping her face and arms, impeding her movements, slowing her down to a snail's pace. She went through her day's work like a sleepwalker, took the tram to Stepney, and addressed envelopes for the Gasworkers, went through her English classes at the People's Palace in a trance, her speech thick to her ears, her own puzzlement reflected on the faces of her pupils.

In this state of semi-consciousness she attended the General's funeral, and took the train with the handful of close mourners to Eastbourne, where his ashes were scattered at sea in a brief ceremony. In the same enfeebled state she sat with Edward in the front sitting room at Regents Park Road to hear the will read. Her share of the General's share of Ermen and Engels would probably amount to around seven thousand pounds. Edward pressed her hand; he was most solicitous. Later he put her to bed with a draught of laudanum, and sat by her side until she slept. He was always there now when she needed him, postponing commitments that she felt unable to keep, shielding her from her friends.

Freddy appeared one Sunday when Edward was lecturing in South Place. Shocked by her appearance, he urged her to walk out with him. They walked to Russell Square, Tussy leaning on his arm, walking slowly as if relearning how to move, and they sat on a bench in the thin sunlight.

"I want you to know that it's not going to come up again, Tussy, not as far as I can help it. You know, and I know, but nobody else is going to know."

"They'll make it their business to know, Freddy."

"Then we'll see to it that they don't find out."

"Oh, Freddy, it's so wrong, so very wrong. We should acknowledge you. We must make it up to you. I shall never understand how they could bring themselves to send you away. But we mustn't continue to cover up for them." *The sins of the father shall not be visited on the child,* she thought. It was the first principle of a moral being. . . . "I can't see any reason for us to perpetuate their crime . . . for that's what it is, Freddy. They lied to us, but why should we lie to ourselves?"

"If you can't see their reasons, Tussy, I can't explain them to you. You have to trust me—I know more than you do. You'll do no good by telling the world your father had a bastard by his housekeeper."

She pressed her gloved fingers to her forehead and rubbed her temples.

"I'm so confused, Freddy. Tell me what we should do."

"Why, go on as before. Laura will tell you the same; she's known for as long as I have."

"How long is that?"

"Oh, a good many years now."

"Since Nim died?"

"Longer."

"Did Nim tell you?"

"No, she didn't tell me. We never talked about it, but she knew I knew."

"Why was I never told, Freddy?"

"For the same reason that you're taking it so hard now. You were too close to him, Tussy."

She shivered and clung to Freddy's hand.

"Help me, Freddy. I feel that I'm to blame. That can't be right, can it? It's not a fault to be ignorant. Or perhaps it is—perhaps it's the worst fault of all."

"I don't see how you can be to blame, Tussy. It's not your fault that you didn't know. They meant to protect you."

"He used her—oh, I can't bear to think of it. He used her exactly as men have always used women, to satisfy his animal needs. She was there, always there to be used, whatever he did to her, whatever sacrifices he required of her. She was so patient, so loving. And none of it mattered."

"Oh, Tussy, you expect too much of people. You shouldn't be so unforgiving."

She pulled back from him, shocked.

"Do you think I'm unforgiving?"

"I don't mean to critize you, Tussy. To me you're a beautiful, perfect woman. The best woman I've known. But I think you could be easier on yourself. And I guess I think you could be easier on your father."

She tried to consider whether Freddy might be right, but her mind was too tired to concentrate. They sat in the sun for a while without talking, then Freddy walked her back to Great Russell Street, kissed her on the cheek—a brother's privilege— and watched sadly as she dragged herself upstairs.

All she wanted to do was to sleep. She had a continuing dream that seemed to have its own complex life quite apart from her. She couldn't bear to tear herself away from its heavy sweetness on awaking, couldn't wait to return to its dark embrace at night.

In this dream she was walking through rough moorland, making her way toward the summit of a hill some distance away. She was tired, yet she must go on; a difficult task of undefined nature awaited her. Suddenly in her exhaustion she realized that she was not alone. "You!" she cried, astonished, unwilling to trust herself to joy.

"Why, of course," he said. "You surely didn't think I'd leave you to go on alone."

He took her hand, and she was flooded by relief and happiness. She wanted to tell him how mistaken she had been; she thought he despised her, she was convinced that their friendship was at an end. But she couldn't trust herself to speak. In any case, he understood; he had understood all along. There had never been anyone else for him. The simple truth broke on her; how had she ever doubted it? Her heart expanded, her step was lightened; the oppressive weight under which she had been suffering, her fear, anxiety, torturing self-doubt were entirely gone. It was an error, pure and simple.

Waking, she tasted the sweetness still.

Not Edward. Lissagaray. It had been Lissagaray, she was virtually certain. Faithful Lissa, calumniated, long forgotten.

Should she tell Edward, who snored beside her, his mouth open, a smell of stale whiskey hanging about him?

"I dreamed I was with Lissagaray, in a room somewhere, or out-of-doors," she might say. "It could have been Hampstead Heath, where we often walked on a Sunday—we were working together on some kind of project or book. I could hardly believe it was he. He was so kind, so gentle—he bore no grudge, he forgave me for everything. Isn't that amazing? I do believe he loved me, after all."

No, better not to tell Edward; better to hold on to the fragments, the wisps of dream that lingered in her mind, fading fast. It was twenty years ago; there was no link between the child she had been and the woman she had become.

After a while her dreams turned nightmarish. She fought off sleep but was sucked under against her will. The man who appeared to her as she neared the summit of the hill was not Lissa but Edward. She greeted him and he shrugged and turned away. Frantic, she pleaded with him not to leave, not to abandon her. He turned back, and it wasn't Edward, she had been mistaken; it was Mohr. The face of Edward and the face of Mohr merged, the older man's rugged features superimposed on the younger man's smooth-shaven face, and his eyes were full of pain, and stared at her without recognition.

She woke shrieking, and splashed cold water on her face and neck. How long had she been in this drugged stupor—a week? a month? three months? Long enough—she was finished with it, and vowed to pull herself together. Though she was confused, unsure what had really happened, and what she had dreamed, she knew that there was one task which she must pursue to the end. She must secure for her own needs the money left her by the General.

This money, given to her with no strings attached, must be the instrument of her liberation, as the General had intended it to be. By telling her the truth about Freddy, he had freed her from her childhood. And, by leaving her this large sum, in effect he was freeing her from Edward.

It was Edward's suggestion that she should invest the money

in Russian railway shares. In the City they were promoting Trans-Siberian shares at a guinea each; in twenty-five years the shares would be worth a fortune. But with unexpected firmness Tussy laid claim to her money, and Edward withdrew.

An idea took hold of her, presenting itself with the force of a hallucination. She would use the money to buy a house, with a garden, space for the cats, a study for Edward, a guest room for her nieces and nephews. No longer would she and Edward live in furnished lodgings, with prying landladies, the sounds of shouting and blows or lovemaking from the couple upstairs or across the hall. She would use the General's legacy exactly as he had meant it to be used, to provide security for her future. Edward might come and go as he pleased, but a house would, at last, constitute a true home, a true sanctuary.

She began to follow the housing advertisements in the daily papers. Fashionable sections—Kensington, Bayswater, the pleasant North London suburbs of Hampstead and Highgate—were too expensive, she regretfully decided. But there were new housing estates south of the river, beyond the decayed boroughs of Southwark and Bermondsey, that were virtually countryside—Dulwich, Bromley, Lewisham, Forest Hill. Spacious semi-detached brick villas, with electric lights and gas fires, seemed to be selling for five and six hundred pounds, well within her means.

She made a concentrated effort to look south of the river, presenting herself to Mr. Vance, the enterprising estate agent in Forest Hill, with the earnestness of a buyer who has cash in hand. Together they found a house that seemed distinctly possible in Sydenham, not far from the railway station. The West End was accessible in forty minutes, and the lush hills and green fields of Kent were almost within sniffing distance. She liked the feeling of it as soon as she left the railway station: the neat, prosperous-looking shops clustered near the station and continuing up the hill along Kirkdale; the wide, curving roads planted with sycamores and elms; the solid brick houses, built to accommodate large families; the clean air, unpolluted by factory smoke. The house itself—and these dull facts of brick and mortar take on a compulsive interest when one is looking at houses with a view to purchase—the house was a semi-de-

185

tached villa, twenty years old but in good condition, on two floors, with a front parlor, a back room ideal for a study, a morning room with a scullery opening onto a pleasant walled garden with apple trees, and wild roses climbing the weathered brick walls. Upstairs was a large sunny bedroom, a small closet adjoining it which would do very well for a second study, a guest room, a bathroom with hot and cold water and a separate lavatory, and a small servant's room. The house was easy to run; she could manage with one servant, Mr. Vance thought, or at most two. There were gas fires in each room, and electricity was installed; it would be possible to have a telephone put in.

She liked the comfort and cleanliness of the house, the absence of urban dirt and noise. The name of the street—Jews' Walk—appealed to her, and the street itself, lined with mature elms, curving up past an old church and rectory to a pleasant pub, the Fox and Hounds. From the top of the road one could still sense the outlines of the green fields and open spaces the new houses replaced.

"I shall have to consult my husband," she said.

On the train back to London, she leaned back against the leather upholstery, shut her eyes, and surrendered to the prospect of a home of her own. For twelve years they had lived in two rooms, the bedroom doubling as a study, the sitting room doubling as a dining room. With enough space to shut a door or two, perhaps they might not find it so difficult to work at the same time. Edward would no longer be driven away by the sound of her new typewriting machine as she slowly picked out the keys; she would not find herself stopping to listen to his pen scratching, thinking to herself, *Lies, lies.*

Yes, the sensible thing was to buy a house, far from the scene of their troubles. She would become a property owner, a rate payer, no longer one of the dispossessed. There did not seem to be many of the poor in Sydenham, at least as far as she had seen; but one did not need to live with the poor to work for them, and her first obligation, now, was to herself.

In the end, Edward left the choice of a house to her; he was too busy to make the trip. But he offered to buy the furnishings. It was only right, they both felt, that he should contribute something, and Tussy gladly advanced him the money as an interest-free loan.

From the time she delivered the banker's draft to Mr. Vance, she luxuriated in a new self-confidence, born of pride in possession. The house was hers—tangible, real, proof of her existence, a demonstration of the permanence of her domestic arrangements. She was now a person of means, and whatever reverses she might experience, she need never again suffer from the desolating conviction of nullity that had poisoned her days.

And she found she liked having money, knowing that it was hers to spend. How much of her desperation, of Edward's anger and resentment, had been caused by their mean, penny-pinching existence, the impossibility of ever clearing their account? If she managed her affairs prudently—and she had every intention of doing so—they need never be in debt again.

Indeed, she found that money made a difference—something she had not been prepared to believe. It caused her spirits to expand; it liberated her from fear, anxiety, pain; it gave her strength to go on.

"There's no reason why you shouldn't be comfortable," Dollie said. "You of all people."

"Why me in particular?"

"Because poverty brings out the worst in you. It makes you unhappy and difficult to live with. Why shouldn't your life be a little easier? You work very hard; you tear yourself to pieces for people who have no conception of real sacrifice because they've never had anything to lose. But you have a great deal to lose—your youth, happiness, well-being."

"My youth is gone, Dollie. And I doubt that I shall ever be truly happy. Life doesn't seem to hold that kind of joy for me. But this is the first time I've had that feeling of ease that many people must take for granted. You have no idea how liberating to the spirit it is to be able to send a pretty dress to Mémé, or to buy a pair of sturdy boots for Freddy's boy, without stopping to think whether we shall have to go without dinner for a week to pay for it. To be always borrowing, always begging scraps from one's friends, forever weighing one debt against another to see which can be postponed more easily, or more conveniently forgotten . . . it eats away at the soul, it poisons friendship, trust, love. Or do you think it's very wrong of me to feel pleased at having money?"

"Not at all. Given the present state of society, I can't see any reason deliberately to prefer poverty to riches."

"It's hardly a matter of having riches . . . though it does seem to me like a vast sum. We've talked about investing some of it. Edward is very keen on Trans-Siberian railway shares."

"Ah, Tussy, you'd never live it down. What would your Russian comrades say if you invested in Czarist railway shares?"

"Why, it was our Russian friends who suggested it in the first place. But the General advised against it when Edward first raised the possibility; he was very shrewd about these things. He kept his own fortune entirely in British gilt-edged securities. I do think, though, that we may hire a servant to live with us."

"Of course you must have a servant. You can't take care of a large house on your own, you'd have time for nothing else. You can easily find a young girl . . . though you might be better off with a woman well past her prime."

"Don't joke about it, Dollie—there's no need. Edward can do as he likes. One of the pleasantest things about money is the power it gives you, not only over other people but over yourself. Whatever happens, I'm my own mistress now. I really think Edward has lost his power to hurt me; I'm no longer capable of jealousy."

"Oh, my dear—if that were true!"

"I think it is. I've learned something about Edward, and about myself. What I took to be peculiar to us isn't uncommon at all; it's probably the rule rather than the exception. Edward isn't morally sick or vicious; he's simply a man, with a man's natural instincts. There are a thousand like him for one that's different. It's only our self-love that deludes us into thinking that our brothers or our fathers are . . . peculiarly virtuous. And I think we must learn to love men as they are—weak, self-indulgent—even if we despise them for it at the same time. Perhaps we love them better for despising them a little."

"Oh, Tussy—how can you say that to me?"

"Isn't it true, Dollie? Isn't it true of you and Ernest?"

"No, I swear it's not. I loved Ernest when he was well. I'd give anything for him to be well again. You are actually suggesting that I want him to be ill, as if I gained by his illness in some obscure way. But illness kills love, no matter how one fights against it. You can't love when the need is all on one side. You can be kind, and you can try to do the right thing, the practical thing. But love, real love, is squeezed out of you drop by drop; you look for it and it simply isn't there any more."

"Well, we shall see. I've been so often the one in need that it's rather exhilarating to be the strong one, for a change."

She hired a servant, a young girl named Gertrude Gentry, who was the first to answer the ad she had put in the local newspaper. The girl seemed neat and eager to work. She was third in a Sussex farming family of thirteen, and had come to the city to find work; it was hard going. She was only sixteen. Tussy thought that she and Edward would stand *in loco parentis.*

"You must come to me if you are in trouble," she said. "I should like you to think of me as a friend."

"Yer very kind, mum."

"If you find it hard to manage, or if you're needed at home, you'll let me know."

"I'll do that, indeed."

"And if you need more time off, or if you should wish to take some lessons, we'll try to arrange it for you."

"Oh, I shouldn't think I'd want to take lessons. I like working with me hands."

"Shouldn't you like to learn a skill, child? You could become self-supporting, then, if you learned dressmaking, or fine needlework."

"Oy, I'd never be able to do it—me mum says I'm that clumsy. I like cleaning and cooking and taking charge of little uns, that best of all. And I can do a nice pease pudding and mutton stew."

"Well, if you enjoy cooking, I shall teach you some of my sister's French recipes."

"Yes, mum."

Her solicitor, Mr. Crosse, advised her to make a will. Since Edward's rights over her estate, in the absence of a legal marriage, would be subject to endless litigation, she made him her sole legatee, should she predecease him, for the duration of his life, after which her estate would revert to Jenny's children. Against her solicitor's advice, she arranged for the house on Jews' Walk to be in joint ownership.

Thus did she bind her "husband" ever more tightly to her.

21

Though she pleaded with Olive to make the trip to Sydenham, her friend declined, giving one reason or another—prior commitments, ill-health, reluctance to leave Hannah.

Tussy sensed a deep-rooted disapproval behind Olive's reluctance.

"I'm forty years old," she said. "I can't invent my life from day to day—I don't have the energy. I need to have a home, Olive. I've lost everyone, all my family, except for Laura and Paul, and they're almost as far from me in Le Perreux as if they too were gone. Astonishing as it seems, I'm now the older generation. Jenny's children must come to me. They can't come to me unless I have a place for them."

"Why must we always find reasons for the choices we feel obliged to make? I don't quarrel with your choice, Tussy. It seems to me that you need to make a radical change in your circumstances. I hope the house will answer your needs."

"Do you think it's wrong to tie oneself down to a piece of property?"

"Not really. For myself—and one can only speak for oneself—I know that I could not shore up my life with material things. It wouldn't work; I would come to hate everything I owned. But I can see that, for many people, goods, and especially property, mean comfort and security. They provide familiarity, continuity, a sense of rootedness. They are tangible in a way that merely human relations can never be, and they make human relations seem less important. Ownership gives the illusion that one has some control over one's life, or at least over one's surroundings. And perhaps it's not an illusion; perhaps goods and property make up the identity of some persons. Certainly this was true for Cron. . . . You know, Tussy, I did something very wrong in making him give up the farm he had created out of his own labor. I think that may be why I was forced to leave him, because I had done him such a great wrong. Yet I know perfectly well that my leaving only makes it harder for him. It makes his sacrifice pointless."

"Surely he could have kept the farm if it was so important to him."

"No, he had no choice but to give it up; he saw that I was dying. And then, you see, after the baby, I couldn't bear for him to touch me. How unfair it is!—I know the cruel unfairness of it as well as he does. But my child's death taught me who I am. I can't lie with a man, knowing who I am. Not with a man who loves me, as Cron does, who wants me whole and entire."

"Does Cron know how you feel about . . . marriage?"

"He knows I'm a lover of women. He knows everything, and, I suppose, forgives. He has an extraordinary capacity for forgiveness. And I think in the end I shall probably go back. He wants me back, on any terms I like. I may even take Hannah with me, if she thinks that she can survive away from her grimy back streets. And of course Cron knows he's always free to take a lover. He has a lover now, an older woman whom I knew in Pietermaritzburg, divorced, unhappy, very much in love with him."

Tussy shuddered. "I couldn't live like that."

"But you do live like that, Tussy. You agree to allow Edward his freedom; he allows you yours."

"Don't speak of it. I allow Edward nothing but what he takes. We have no agreement."

"Then why do you stay together? Why do you buy a house that will hold you bound to each other for the rest of your lives?"

"Stop—I beg of you, Olive. I shut my ears to everything you've said. If you love me, don't say another word. I can't bear it."

192

It struck her that in moving to Sydenham she was cutting herself loose from her closest friends. Or perhaps she was only marking physically a break that had occurred long since.

She doubted whether Dollie would make the long trek from Hampstead to Sydenham, tied down as she was by her children, Ernest's illness, her endless chores.

Olive, it was clear, would never come, though Tussy might continue to visit her in Middleton Buildings. In any case, Olive said firmly that she would be leaving for South Africa shortly, to rejoin her husband.

Havelock, married now for a year, had settled into an "arrangement" that, while it caused him exquisite anguish from time to time, also left him free to pursue his arcane research undisturbed by financial, political, or amatory distractions.

"It's of the greatest importance not to be distracted," he had told Olive.

"I'm afraid that in the end I constituted a rather prominent distraction," Olive said. "He was wise to call a halt."

"Some people would call it selfishness," Tussy said.

"I'm sure Havelock would agree. 'It's important to be selfish' is probably what he meant to say. Don't you find it refreshing when someone actually comes out and says it?"

"I think some people feel their own necessities far more acutely than those of others."

"Granted, Havelock is somewhat immature. He doesn't willingly give of himself; he's afraid of being trapped by a woman, by fatherhood, by life. It's a not uncommon fear in a man of limited experience."

"Why, Havelock must be forty, at least. If he's immature, it's part of his character by now."

"Why shouldn't people change after forty? He's only just married, after all."

"Doesn't his marriage represent a distraction?"

"Not at all. In fact, it provides him with material for three more volumes. Poor Edith, you see, is one of us. . . . And of course, since she doesn't wish to have children, her work is very important to her, almost as important as Havelock's is to him. So they have given a good deal of thought to their working arrangements. They have rooms in town, a cottage in Surrey, a studio for Edith in Cornwall, each equipped with two bed-rooms and two desks. Edith brings a succession of young women around, some of whom eventually fall in love with Havelock, which is flattering to him and satisfies his fairly modest sexual needs. It all seems to be working out very well."

Clementina had been appointed Her Majesty's Inspector for Factories in Hackney, the first woman to hold the position. Her life was even more tightly organized than before; she had to receive complaints, appear before official inquiries, present evidence to Parliament. Still, she set aside some hours a week for writing; she had published six novels, all on working-class themes, well researched, simply written, clear in their message.

Clementina had been the only one of her friends to see the inheritance as Tussy's last chance to break with Edward. She came right out and said it, in her usual forthright way.

"Leave him, Tussy. Don't give him any money, don't take him back."

"Impossible. I can't do it."

"Why is it impossible? He has no claim on you whatsoever. Any claim he had he's canceled a hundred times over."

"It's not that simple."

"You're destroying yourself. I refuse to watch you do it, when you have the chance of saving yourself. It's not only you I'm thinking of, it's your work. We need you, Tussy—you're the only one among us who combines theoretical knowledge with a real feeling for the poor."

"I'm so confused, Clem. You see things so clearly—tell me what to do."

"In a way it would be easier if you were married. You could then arrange a formal separation. This way you have only your own strength of mind."

This struck Tussy as a novel idea, worth pursuing.

"It's often a great help to have rights and obligations clearly laid down in black and white," Clementina continued.

"Do you really think that there are rights in human relations?"

"Certainly there are, in the eyes of the law."

"No, there are no rights, only obligations."

"And are these all on one side?"

"If that is how life arranges itself. Edward may deny his obligations to me. I can't imitate him."

"Ah, Tussy, you're lost. I believe you are still in love with him, after all."

"I don't know what the word means. I see only that I can't abandon him now, when everyone has turned against him."

One of those who had turned against him, bitterly, permanently, was May Morris. Edward hinted that May had been in love with him when they first met; he had introduced her to the manager of the Princess Theatre, and encouraged her to send in her first efforts at one-act plays. But the rift, if such it was, had deeper causes.

May's father, William, died just after Tussy moved out to Sydenham, and May began to sort out his papers with the intention of publishing them in full—a task which was to occupy her for the next forty years. And it was clear that in the records of his socialist activities, many of them undertaken jointly with the Avelings, their role came to seem more and more ambiguous, tainted. Somehow Morris had preserved his idealism intact through the ups and downs of socialist fortunes; perhaps he knew that he was quietly effecting a revolution in domestic taste while working for the larger social revolution. In that larger revolution the Avelings were the realists, and in the end the villains, loyal to unstated international interests which often subverted what Morris saw as the immediate task: the liberation of the English working classes. May could not forgive them; she thought they were responsible for the failures which broke her father's heart and destroyed his will to live: the surrender to the anarchists of the Socialist League, doomed to be a mere sect from its inception; the succession of journals subsidized by Morris, largely written and edited by him, with a circulation cut from ten thousand to two thousand to two or three hundred.

Why had the movement which at its height enlisted thousands to march, to protest, died away to a mere trickle? Her father gave the same speeches the year he died as he had given five and ten years earlier, and where a thousand had crowded into a small hall to applaud and to demand action, twenty came to listen, merely out of curiosity, and drifted away when the entertainment palled. May held Edward to blame, with his inflexible priorities, his capacity to alienate all support, his essential indifference. And Tussy, because she refused to dissociate herself from Edward, was equally to blame.

The move to Sydenham marked a turning point, then, a break with the past. Tussy called her house on Jews' Walk "The Den"; it would be her lair, where she might hide from her enemies, nurse her wounds, restore her bruised ego to health, her distracted mind to sanity. She became the Jew of Jews' Walk.

"Face the facts, Tussy." The General's kindly practical advice echoed in her ears.

Well, why not? For the first time in her life she was financially secure, a property owner. Her work had practical demarcations now; her first duty was to her father's lifework. She must preserve his private papers, gather together the unpublished material of permanent importance, and prepare a biography. Her private worries must remain manageable; she had before her the example of others who had lived with unpleasant facts, faced them, carried on.

She had a stream of guests: Freddy and his boy every Sunday; delegations from Berlin, Paris, and Brussels who paid their respects to the grave in Highgate, and stayed on for the International Trades Union Conference. Johnny, Jenny's oldest boy, visited for a month, and had to be entertained, educated, pushed toward some sort of future.

But Edward appeared once when she was alone, took a long, hard look at her, and said: "Why so gloomy? Life can't be worth living if you go about with such a tragic face."

"Perhaps life isn't worth living, to me."

"Come, come, Tussy, you're doing very well these days, better than you and I have any right to expect."

"I haven't the faintest idea what you mean."

"I mean, my dear, that you should be grateful for good things, and not sulk about matters over which you have no control."

"What good things have I to be grateful for?"

"Why, your new prosperity."

"The prosperity of a widow. I am in mourning, Edward. I feel with the ancient Egyptians that to lose a husband is to lose one's reason for living."

"Why, I appear as regularly as any husband of fourteen years' standing."

"Yes, you appear regularly . . . to collect your weekly allowance."

"That's cruel, Tussy—am I not to live? You know perfectly well that I'm going through a slack period. As soon as work comes in I shall repay every penny."

"I don't expect you to repay me. I don't want you to repay me. Oh, Edward, we should marry, after all. Then we would know exactly where we stand. You're a free man now; we could marry tomorrow."

"It's out of the question."

"Why is it out of the question? Oh, my dear, let us say we are man and wife now, when we are beset by enemies. Whom do we have but each other?"

She threw herself at his feet and clung to his knees.

"Now, Edward," she cried. "Now, or soon, before it's too late. If you knew what a strange sense I have of events closing in—every fiber of my body tells me to act now, to act to save us both." She brought his limp hand to her lips and kissed it passionately. He sat passive under her attack.

"Oh, love me, dear, hold me as you did when we were young and had no thought for anything but each other."

He looked earnestly at her pale, haggard face, admiration vying with a certain distaste.

"Listen to me, Eleanor. Listen carefully to what I'm about to say to you. If there were one woman in the world whom I could love in the way you describe, whole-heartedly and for life, with no thought of anything else, or anyone else—then it would be you."

She sat back, exhausted. "I really think we should marry, Edward."

"I don't think you heard a word of what I said."

"I heard you. It still seems to me that the most sensible course, for both of us, is to marry. There's no reason why we can't, at the same time, come to some practical arrangement with regard to money."

He rose impatiently and paced back and forth.

"There's no point in being honest with you; you refuse to listen. I told you, it's out of the question. It's too late, too late by far."

"I find my situation intolerable."

He looked at her coldly. "Then you are perfectly free to take measures to end it."

She needed time to think. Some hours later, when Edward was mellowed by several brandies, she returned to the attack.

"I wonder whether you would mind much if I were to disappear from your life."

"I would take it in my stride."

"Tell me the truth, Edward, would you have no regrets? no tears?"

"I long ago decided that life is too short to waste time regretting events over which one has no control. You're the one who is suffering; you're the one who must decide whether or not to cut your suffering short. You're a free agent."

"Oh, entirely free . . . This cursed freedom of mine, that I would sell my soul to be rid of. That is why I would like us to marry, so that I shall no longer have the name of freedom without the thing. Yes, I want us to marry even if such love as there is between us is all on one side."

"Why must you keep harping on the one string? As if marriage was something either of us needed. Look at the marriages of your friends—is there a real marriage among the lot? Your precious Olive goes mooning about the London slums while her husband sits waiting like an idiot halfway across the world. May Morris has thrown young Harry out of that happy nest and sent him to Paris for his wounds, where he announces to all the world that Mr. Shaw—our own dear philanderer—is the guilty one. I understand that Dr. Ellis's wife is a prominent Sapphist. Mr. Shaw's position on marriage, poor Harry notwithstanding, is well known; if he marries his Irish millionairess, you can be sure it will be purely for the seven hundred a year that she means to settle on him."

"They all marry, in the end. For better or worse. They have enough feeling for one another to solemnize their union."

"I'm amazed at you, Tussy—suddenly to long for a piece of paper with an official stamp on it. It's positively childish."

"Let me be childish, then. I want the piece of paper."

"For the hundredth time, it's out of the question. I warn you, you're making me quite ill. I can feel an attack coming on."

He was not a well man. He suffered from an abscess in his side; it healed, then opened, healed more slowly, reopened. Each time it opened, the chances of a total cure receded; it was a condition he had to live with, disagreeable, painful. His old kidney complaint flared up. Urination was difficult, sex risky. The liberal doses of brandy did nothing to help, but he couldn't get through the day, and especially, the night, without brandy and laudanum; he couldn't tolerate the pain.

Tussy knew how physical illness eats away at the soul; it was unwise to push him when he was irritable. She remembered Mohr suffering unbearably from carbuncles, unable to sit, groaning, shouting at Mohme when she begged him to stop working.

Edward did not groan or shout when he was ill; he withdrew into a morose sullenness. Or he became melodramatic. He enjoyed frightening her with the thought of his death, for which she would be in some obscure way responsible. If he didn't say it, it was plain that he thought it: it's your fault that I'm ill. If it weren't for you I'd be strong and vigorous. It's you who have made me old, ill, impotent.

He submitted grudgingly to her nursing. She insisted that he sleep in her bed, while she slept in her little study across the hall. Not that she slept more than an hour or two. She lay awake listening for his querulous call; for hours, it seemed, she heard his bed creaking as he turned restlessly in his sleep, until from her open window there was a short, tentative burst of bird song, then a full chorus of trilling and shrilling, followed by that dreary lightening of the sky that signaled a new day.

In the morning she wanted him to stay in bed. He insisted that he was getting up and going into town.

"You'll do nothing of the sort. You'll stay here and I shall call our good neighbor Dr. Shackleton to have a look at you."

"I'm very sorry, my dear, but I have a prior engagement."

"No engagement could justify the risk."

"Oh, but I'm a man of my word—you forget."

She watched in silence as he slowly shaved, and examined his face in the glass.

"Hmm . . . I don't like these pouches under the eyes. Signs of age and dissipation. We could both do with some rouge and powder, eh, Tussy?"

"I warn you, Edward, if you go now, I take no responsibility for what happens to you."

"Oh, you'll come round soon enough, I dare say."

"You're very sure of me."

"If you mean that I expect you to be here when—if—I return, and to take me back in spite of—or because of—my multifarious sins, why, I suppose I am as sure of you . . . as one can be of a woman."

"Oh God, it would be better for one or the other of us to be dead—"

"Well, at this rate it's very likely to be me. So I wouldn't worry about it too much if I were you; your consols are perfectly safe."

22

A slight, stooped figure waited at the side door of the Royalty Theatre in Dean Street, his gray cape closed against the fine drizzle, his hat pulled down low over his eyes. Two or three persons leaving the theatre late nodded to him. "Evening, Dr. Aveling."

A young woman appeared, took his arm, and he hailed a hansom cab.

"Where are we going, then?"

"Why, I'm taking you to a private room at the Savoy, my dear. Oysters and champagne seem in order."

"Oh, Edward, I was awful tonight. Wasn't I awful?"

"Nonsense—you were your usual delicious self."

"I forgot my lines in the second act. It was the most horrible sensation. I just stood there, and no words came out. I had no idea why I was standing on the stage, in front of all those people, dressed in someone else's clothes."

"It happens to all of us, my dear, the most hardened professionals. One panics—then the panic miraculously passes, and the play-acting begins. Until the play-acting becomes habitual, and then, of course, there's nothing in the world to match it."

"Do you think so? I wonder—I'm ever so much happier sitting here with you."

She didn't like oysters. But she loved the red velvet curtains and the gilt mirrors and crystal chandeliers and the deferential waiter, and she adored the champagne, which made her merry and silly and amorous.

"D'you know what I keep thinking about?" she whispered, and giggled.

Aveling speared an oyster, opened his mouth to take it in, and allowed it to slither down his throat, in the approved manner. He washed it down with a glass of champagne.

"What do you keep thinking about, my pretty one?"

She leaned closer to him, so he could breathe in her perfume, and whispered in his ear.

He smiled, pleased. "So do most women," he said. "But they won't admit it."

"Would you think it was my first time?"

"Quite honestly, no."

"It was the first time I felt like that. On fire."

"Ah, you suit me, my dear. We get on well together, there's no denying it."

He patted her thigh and took another oyster.

"I can't see how you can eat those," she said.

"It's very simple. You take the flesh of the oyster in your mouth; you mustn't make the mistake of chewing it, or of swallowing it too soon. You allow it to remain in your mouth, you savor it, and then it makes its slippery way down your throat. There's nothing quite like it. Try one—you have to educate your palate."

She took one gingerly and put it in her mouth.

"Don't expect too much at first," he said. "It's an acquired taste. Have some more champagne."

She sipped daintily from her glass, then leaned closer to him and whispered once again in his ear.

"Naughty girl. Thee wants to be smacked for that. I'm of two minds whether to give you a little something I picked up the other day. . . . "

He took from his vest pocket a thin box wrapped in silver paper.

"Oooo—is it for me? I adore presents."

"Yes, it's for you, you goose . . . on one condition."

"What condition? I don't know about conditions."

"Why, that you do exactly as I say, at all times . . . "

She delicately unwrapped the box and opened the jewel case inside. "I've never seen anything so beautiful! Is it real?"

"Would you know the difference? Of course it's real, a real

emerald to match thy green eyes, a real gold chain."

He fastened the clasp, and kissed her bare shoulder.

She sat back demurely. "You haven't told me what I must do."

"Why, exactly what you are doing. Remain young and beautiful and pleasure-loving, with a voice like an angel. . . . How old are you, my dear?"

"Guess."

"Hmm . . . Twenty-one, and two months."

"However did you know?"

"A practiced eye, my dear . . . Dost mind my gray hairs, little one?"

"Oh, I don't like young men. One, two, three, and they're finished, like that. They have no idea of how to treat a woman. You make me feel like a lady."

"Why, we're nothing if not respectable."

He had taken a suite of rooms at Savage's in the Waterloo Road, and it was there that they made love, at night after the theatre, in the morning before her lessons began, in mid-afternoon when her lessons finished; whenever she could steal an hour he was free, waiting for her.

In bed—and a fine bed it was, with a carved rosewood frame, bouncing springs, the finest linens—she was a ready pupil, preserving in her nakedness a shy, virginal innocence that set his blood racing.

He waited for the infatuation to pall. But this was unlike all the others. He, the sensualist, the worldly sybarite, who knew that all women were the same, could not let a day pass without seeing his Eva, without touching her fine hair, kissing the tender nape of her neck. When she looked to him for approval after singing "Love's Old Sweet Song" in her thin, true soprano, he melted; he could not live without her.

He began to stay away from the house on Jews' Walk for days at a time, and when he made an appearance it was with such obvious reluctance, he was so ill-tempered, so ready to pick a quarrel, that Tussy must surely suspect something. Out of charity, if nothing else—for she was in the end a realist about sexual as about social and economic relations—she must surely release him.

Eva met him one day in despair. "My father has forbidden me to see you. He is very angry at me. He threatened to shoot you if you come to the house. He says everyone knows you are a married man."

"Oh, my dear, I've explained it to you a dozen times. The woman who goes by the name of Mrs. Aveling is not my wife. My wife died five years ago; I am quite free. Your father must consider me as eligible as any suitor."

"He's very stubborn once he's made up his mind."

"Then we must go away together. . . . I have a tour of working-men's clubs in the North in a month; you must come with me. We shall perform together—Alec Nelson and Eva Frye in an entertainment of song and recitation, 'Love's Old Sweet Song,' the 'Ode to the West Wind,' *The Tables Turned*—an excellent part for you, my dear, in Mary Pinch, innocence maligned by society but triumphant in the end."

"Won't Mrs. Aveling be there?"

"Oh no, she's far too busy. She's the official translator for the International Trades Union Conference; she's off to Brussels one week, Paris the next, or else she's entertaining the German delegates with sturgeon and the best schnapps in London. She never goes with me now; they have all but forgotten her existence. I shall take Mrs. Nelson instead."

And thus a plan was born, a secret marriage, performed on June 27th in the Chelsea Town Hall, between Alec Nelson, widower, and Eva Frye, spinster. Rooms were taken for Mr. and Mrs. Nelson in Southampton Buildings, Holborn, and were occupied thenceforth by the pretty Mrs . Nelson, joined as often as he could manage it by her stoop-shouldered, graying, but distinguished husband. And love of a sort blossomed in those neat rooms with their new mauve wallpaper and chintz-covered chairs. As Alec was embraced by his eager bride, it was plain that she sang for him alone, all her life centered upon his rare appearances and the long nights of lovemaking, in which she proved, with a sweet inventiveness matching his own, that she suited him, as he had said, better than anyone in the world. With Eva he was young again, virile and manly; he was her shield against the world. She thought he was the most interesting man she had ever met, the most knowledgeable, and the kindest.

She didn't ask him about Mrs. Aveling, whom she had only seen at a distance, never spoken to. She had marked her sad, haggard face, and shuddered to think that her Alec was bound to such a joyless companion. She trusted him to break it off; she took his word that the marriage which had never been a marriage in deed was no longer a marriage in fact. Had she known that her Alec, to free himself for her, would have to inflict a mortal wound on another woman, she would have been sorry indeed. She had no wish to hurt anyone; she wanted only to be happy.

Olive had left London—not for South Africa, but for a hegira across the length and breadth of Europe, a desperate search for a place where she could breathe and work. Tussy carried on a running dialogue with her starting innumerable letters, then tearing them up.

Why should it seem so hard to me? she asked. Am I wrong in feeling it to be terrible, the worst thing that could happen to me? Isn't it the way of the world? Why should I feel that I am stripped of all resources, "naked to mine enemies"? I really don't think I shall be able to bear it.

And in her imagination, Olive answered, stern, just, remote. *You are suffering because a great wrong has been done to you.*

There was nothing specific for her to fasten on to. Edward appeared from time to time, or if he didn't appear himself, bills appeared for mysterious purchases, running accounts at wine shops, restaurants, tailors. He was very busy; he had a tour of clubs in the North to organize; he was on the executive of the ILP; political meetings made it advisable for him to stay in town several nights in the week. For every absence there was some explanation; yet she had a sense that matters were building to a crisis, as if her heart were anxiously registering signals that her intellect rejected as contemptible, beneath notice.

Perhaps it was her Jewishness that separated her most radically from her English friends. For, they unquestionably belonged to a particular place, group, country. She belonged nowhere. What was primary, for her, was the experience of separation, and the overpowering sense of isolation that followed. Her first childhood affections—the close, indissoluble tie to mother and father—were all that came between her and the abyss. Her adult ties were pale reflections of the primary tie; they never had as much reality for her as the passionate attachment to her mother and father. But the separation, the terrible loneliness of adulthood, she experienced with the full, unassuageable grief of childhood.

Why did she hold on to Edward? Not because she loved him as a husband, for he was no longer a husband to her. Not because she valued him as a human being, for she knew him to be selfish, cruel, and dishonest. She held to him because abandonment held such terrors for her that she could not conceive of deliberately abandoning another human being.

No matter how carefully we prepare for the worst, it always strikes with a difference.

He came right out with it one evening, on one of his increasingly rare visits.

"I need a thousand pounds," he said.

"You can't be in earnest."

"I have never been more in earnest."

"I haven't got it to give you."

"How much can you borrow?"

"I certainly cannot borrow a thousand pounds."

"How unfortunate . . . I must tell you that the alternative is unpleasant."

"We've been through this before. It's tiresome, Edward. I refuse to fritter away the General's legacy. He meant it to be my security; I can't use it to bail you out time and again."

"Do you refuse to help me?"

"You don't permit me to help you."

"Very well. Remember, it's your choice. I shall no longer trouble you. Now or ever." He began to pack up his things.

She watched in silence, only half convinced that he was leaving.

"Where are you going?"

"It's no concern of yours."

"How childish you are!"

"Very well, I shall no longer be childish. Why shouldn't we face the truth? We're finished, you and I, why pretend otherwise?"

206

He continued to pack, his face set and angry.

"Would that we were finished. . . . Oh, Edward, if we had the courage to end it once and for all! I've thought of it a hundred times, with such longing. . . . You can have no idea how I long to finish it."

"Yes, you'll talk about finishing it. But it's quite a different matter to do it. No, I refuse to leave it to you. I shall do the gentlemanly thing in going."

She felt a hot rush of blood to her head, a pounding in her temples.

"You're not going anywhere."

"What is to stop me?"

"I say you shall not go."

"You cannot prevent me."

"Oh God . . . if I were dead—"

"I thought we agreed that God has nothing to do with it."

"You shall not have a penny from me."

He turned to her quite coolly.

"Here's an interesting possibility for you. Dr. Aveling, in debt to the tune of a thousand pounds—more, perhaps, but we won't quibble about a few pounds more or less—Dr. Aveling, I say, vanishes. Mrs. Aveling, a woman of honor, no doubt to clear her own good name, assumes full responsibility for her late husband's debts—he, poor man, dead or vanished, sunk without trace."

"It wouldn't do on the stage of the Royalty."

"Perhaps not. But it may do very well for you and me. I'm willing to chance it."

She sent for Freddy by special messenger.

"I want him back," she said. "I've written to him."

"He won't come back, Tussy. Surely you can see that."

"He can't refuse, in all conscience. Not when he realizes all that's at stake. I'm ruined, Freddy, he means to take everything I have."

"I've thought about it very carefully, Tussy. You'll not like what I'm going to say to you. You'll have to let him go."

"Oh, you have no idea what he's like, what he's capable of doing. I can't let him go—it would mean total disgrace for me, for you, for all of us. I haven't told you what he proposes to

207

do. He's mad; he's like an animal at bay, totally reckless. *He must have money*—and he doesn't care what or whom he destroys in the process. Why, he's perfectly capable of going to the *Daily Telegraph* with the wildest stories about Mohr—about all of us. I can't let him go, Freddy, it's out of the question. You must find him, and make him see that he can't do it."

"Oh, Tussy, it's no use. Suppose I find him, and he refuses to come back. For that's what'll happen, I promise you. You've got to take the risk. Let him go. He's no good to you now. If there's money to pay then it will have to be found, that's all there is to it."

"You don't know how bad it is, Freddy. You can have no idea. . . . I'm afraid he's taken the subscriptions for the next Congress. He told me he needs a thousand pounds; that's how much we had. If that's what it is, don't you see, I shall never be able to face them. . . ."

"If worse comes to worst, he'll be brought to account, and declared bankrupt."

"No, Freddy, if there's an accounting to be made, it's I who will be declared bankrupt. By law my property is his. The house is in our joint names; it will all go at once, there's no way of preventing it. So you see, we must find him. He has to tell me exactly where I stand. Perhaps I can raise the money somehow; I still have some resources."

"Perhaps he's counting on that."

"I imagine he is. But he has other ideas as well. He seems to think that he can disappear into the great maw of London unseen, and leave me alone to deal with his debts. . . . Oh God, Freddy, who would think it could come to this? Tell me you'll find him—I really don't think I can go on if you refuse."

"I'll do what I can for you, Tussy, you know that."

"Oh, Freddy, I've tried so hard to understand him. So often it's seemed to me that he's not really responsible for his actions; he's simply done things on impulse, carelessly, because the fancy took him. At other times I see a terrible consistency in everything he's done, his teaching, his speeches, his work for the movement. He believes in 'cracking eggs to make an omelet'—how often have I heard him say that, as if it's an unanswerable argument, justifying all evils. . . . Do you know, in some dreadful way I can see that he is like Mohr? Not that he has Mohr's genius, or his devotion to those he loved. But Mohr too was incapable of feeling remorse; once something was done, it was done, and it was only sentimentalists and women who wished it undone."

"Tell me what I can do for you."

"Go to the Princess Theatre, ask for Mr. Wilson Barrett. Tell him you must see Edward immediately. Tell him I'm ill, dying, anything you like. And bring him back with you—tell him I have the money for him. Tell him I mean to let him go. And I will, Freddy, I promise—I will let him go as soon as we are clear of this horror."

23

The seeds had been planted long since. It is probably safe to assume that anyone who actually succeeds in a suicide attempt has brooded over it long before, has explored various methods and chosen the one most appropriate to his or her circumstances. Indeed, the hours of thought that precede the act, stretching as far back as despair, are devoted not to the consideration of *should I* or *shouldn't I,* but to the careful, fastidious planning of the *how* and *where.*

Tussy had an insistent vision of herself calmly walking upstairs to her bedroom, shutting the door, undressing, draping her clothes neatly over the chair by the window. She would change to a loose white gown, unpin her hair, and carefully brush it out. And this was as far as her imagination took her: she sat before her dressing table, brushing out her thick black hair, a draught waiting on her night table. A draught of what? Scientific opinion leaned to potassium cyanide, which was quick and certain. She would procure it from Mr. Dale, the chemist on Kirkdale. Edward would procure it for her. Sufficient potassium cyanide to put away a dog suffering from illness or age, incurable.

On the night table, then, a draught of potassium cyanide. She would brush out her hair, sitting at her dressing table, studying for the last time her own pale image, a face never beautiful, marked now by lines of suffering, but strong in character, determined, not lacking in courage. She would write a short note, little more than a signature, testifying that what she was about to do she did knowingly.

She could not think of anyone she would injure by her death, anyone whose life would be thereby diminished.

Life is messier than fiction or fantasy; the best-laid plans, etc. etc. Illness intervened, and Edward admitted to himself that his departure had been premature. He must be operated on; Tussy must pay. He returned to her, unrepentant, the crisis temporarily shelved. Illness has its own necessities, chief among these, money.

He was close to death. Infidelity seemed a trivial aberration, fraud forgivable. What mattered, in the end? In her unutterable loneliness, pacing the hospital corridor as she waited for word after the operation, Tussy felt the question no longer had any meaning for her. The naked human being, in need—child, husband, father, flesh of one's flesh—had the primary claim. Everything else paled beside it. Only love mattered, and love came down to a single imperative: to be there when needed.

Yet in odd moments she clung to her vision of herself mounting the stairs, changing into her loose white gown, brushing out her hair, the saving draught by her bedside.

A cutting from the *Chelsea Gazette,* six months old: two lines announcing the wedding of the daughter of W. Frye, Professor of Music, 2 Joubert Mansions, to one Alec Nelson, "writer."

She faced him with it when he came downstairs, still weak from the operation.

"Who sent you this?"

"Is it true?"

"Yes. It's true."

She sat down heavily. "I don't understand."

"Really, I'm too ill to go into a long explanation. How much do they want?"

"I have no way of knowing. I assume this was simply to inform me of the fact."

"No doubt you'll be told in due course."

"I have nothing left. Ede Bernstein had to lend me money to pay the doctor."

"You have the house."

"Oh my God." She stared at the newspaper clipping, as if staring at it might elicit a meaning that would neutralize the fact, or make it comprehensible.

"Who is the girl?"

"I refuse to go into it. It was probably a mistake, but there it is. It's your own fault, entirely; you made it impossible for me to leave. When I left, you forced me to return; you bribed me to stay. I had no alternative."

She rose in agitation and paced back and forth, a nervous pacing that he found particularly irritating.

"I bribed you, you say? You blackmailed me . . . oh, for how many years have you blackmailed me! I, who would have given you the clothes from my own back! I bribed you, you say— it's a cruel, vicious lie! Oh, you are low, Edward. And I've sunk with you, to the bottom, and lower. We're a pair now, you and I, the lowest of the low, fit to be blackmailed, to be dragged through the gutter, the bankruptcy courts. Better for you to have died, when you lay so close to death and I prayed that you might live, so that I too might live. . . ."

He shrugged. "It hardly matters now. We pay for our sins."

She turned on him in a white rage. "I pay for your sins, you mean."

"You choose to pay for my sins. It's the privilege of a wife."

"You shall pay too this time, Edward. We shall be evenly quit before we're done."

"Whatever you say. I'm at your service."

She sat with her head in her hands, shaking violently. *It seemed to her that fiery spheres were exploding in the air like fulminating balls when they strike . . . Alors sa situation, telle qu'un abîme, se représenta. . .*

"I want you to write out a prescription for prussic acid."

"Very well. No sooner said than done."

She rang for Gertie. "Will you take this to Mr. Dale, Gertie? Thank you."

"I've known for a long time that it would end like this," she said. "For the longest time I've had a dream of going to sleep. . . . I've longed for sleep as if for a lover. I'm very glad that we both see it. All ways are closed, all ways but one. It simplifies. I could almost be content."

Edward rose stiffly.

"Where are you going?"

"I have a few matters I must take care of in town."

"You can't be serious."

"Oh, but I'm quite serious."

"But we've decided, at last—"

"We haven't decided anything. You've decided."

"You agreed."

"I agreed to nothing. I did as you asked. But I agreed to nothing. And I will not stay to witness your folly."

"You can't leave me now. I refuse to allow you to leave me."

"Oh, how tiresome you are. Why should you expect me to take you seriously? If you've threatened once, you've threatened a hundred times to end it all. But it's never ended, is it? It just goes on, the same tedious refrain over and over. I'm sick of it, of you, of the whole miserable business."

He put on his cape and hat.

"You can't go, Edward. It's out of the question. You're not well enough to go."

"I shall do as I please."

"I say you shall not."

"You're a destroyer of men, Tussy, you, your friend Olive, Mrs. Sparling, Miss Black, the lot of you, destroyers of men. If you can't whip them live you'd just as soon have 'em dead. But I'll not die to satisfy your Hebrew sense of justice. It's a private matter; I refuse to be rushed. I'm going into town, I tell you."

Gertie stood in the hallway, watching the battle with widened eyes. She held a small package wrapped in brown paper.

"Mr. Dale, he asked for you to sign the book," she said.

Tussy took the book to the writing desk in the back room, signed it, and returned it to Gertie.

"I'm going upstairs to rest," she said. "I don't want to be disturbed."

"Yes 'm. I'll just take the book back to Mr. Dale."

"Hold on a minute, Gertie, and I'll walk down to the station with you. I'm still a bit shaky. It's fifteen past the hour; I should be able to catch the ten-thirty into town."

Tussy left the room, slamming the door shut behind her. She stood in the back room for a minute, listening for the sound

213

of the front door. The brown package lay on the writing desk. She unwrapped it carefully; inside were two labeled vials. She had not much time; Gertie would be back soon. Her mind was emptied of all thought; it was concentrated entirely on the task at hand. She filled a tumbler with water, and carried it upstairs, the vial of poison in her other hand. She set them both on her bedside table. Then she changed into a white nightgown. She sat down at her dressing table and brushed out her hair. The face in the mirror was barely recognizable as her own, haggard, wild-eyed, ugly with suffering.

A note—she must write a short note. She took pen and paper from the drawer, and thought for a moment.

"Love," she wrote, and paused. "Now as in the beginning." She signed her name. She folded the note, sealed it in an envelope, and wrote Edward's name on the front.

Next to the note she placed her will, signed and sealed, which left to her husband, Edward Bibbins Aveling, her worldly goods and property, the remains of her legacy from the General, and her interest in her father's papers.

Then she swallowed the poison, lay down in bed, and in a matter of minutes, choked to death.

EPILOGUE

In the end, plans for an investigation were dropped. Aveling lived for only four more months; at his funeral there were no tributes from the Bloomsbury Socialist Society, the ILP, the SDF, or any of the other organizations for which he had worked so assiduously. A young woman, veiled in black, collapsed sobbing as the coffin was removed for cremation. Of the seven thousand pounds the General had left Tussy three years before, Aveling was able to pass on to his young widow only eight hundred and fifty pounds.

Dollie wrote her novel, which she called, after much thought, *One Way of Love: An Idyll.* It was published in the fall of 1898 by T. Fisher Unwin, who had also published some volumes of poems by Dollie and Ernest. The heroine of *One Way of Love* was beautiful, gifted, and immensely sympathetic; abandoned by her unprincipled lover, she drowned herself by walking into the Serpentine, like Shelley's first wife.

Shaw, true to his instincts for comedy, used Aveling for the character of Louis Dubedat in *The Doctor's Dilemma,* first performed in 1906. Dubedat is a charming rascal, cheerfully indifferent to notions of 'mine' and 'thine' who faces death with courage and equanimity. Mrs. Dubedat is beautiful and loyal, and not unlike Dollie's heroine, in fact. But whether Shaw intended any resemblance between his appealing heroine and Eleanor Marx is debatable.

Olive dragged out a miserable, asthma-ridden existence for another fifteen years, driving herself over the face of Europe, from spa to city to village to town, seeking in vain for a measure of health. Her husband devoted the years after her death to writing her biography and editing her papers and letters, which he published in discreetly censored versions. Her unfinished masterpiece, *From Man to Man*, was published in 1926, to universally respectful notices.

May Morris was divorced from Sparling in 1898 and resumed her maiden name. She gave up playwriting, published one book on embroidery and another on housekeeping, and supervised the publication in eighteen thick volumes of her father's complete works, along with a two-volume *Life*, to which Shaw—now over seventy—contributed a delightful preface.

Havelock Ellis lived until 1939, having established an international reputation as a prophet of sexual liberation.

Shaw lived until 1950—long enough to know whether, in fact, he had "got it right."